Praise for *Dreams of My F*

"Deeply, densely symbolic, even allegoric
—Tatyana Tolstaya, *The New York Review of Books*

"Every once in a while, if you're lucky, you come across a book
so special you want to immerse yourself in its world. . . .
Dreams of My Russian Summers is an extraordinarily beautiful and
moving book."
—Heller McAlpin, *Newsday*

"A richly textured novel . . . stunningly perfect prose."
—Alice Joyce, *Booklist*

"A deeply felt, lyrically told tale."
—Lisa Rohrbach, *Library Journal*

"Dazzling . . . overflowing with stunning images . . . vivid and
gorgeously written . . . lush, dreamy, haunting, sensual, and evocative."
—Lev Raphael, *Detroit Free Press*

"Absolutely magical . . . the closing pages of the book are, quite simply,
beautiful."
—Cyril Jones-Kellert, *The San Diego Union-Tribune*

"A mesmerizing celebration of the influence of memory and longing in
shaping our imaginations and lives. . . . A Russian novelist of substantial
power and originality . . . reflective, sensuous, frank . . . a superb
exploration of the sustaining power of memory, and one of
the most distinctive novels of the season."
—*Kirkus Reviews* (starred review)

"Haunting . . . this latest installment in the great European tradition [is]
also one of the toughest and, ultimately, one of the most hopeful."
—*Publishers Weekly* (boxed review)

"*Dreams of My Russian Summers* sent me back to *Dr. Zhivago,* and I don't
think the association is too outrageous. . . . This is a powerful novel
[filled with] passion but objectivity."
—Barbara Wright, *The Times Literary Supplement* (London)

"A haunting autobiographical novel . . . beautiful . . . mesmerizing."
—*The World & I*

Regina   828-295-9859

Sam & Reg after 9
    Mr   Laney's

house
Gave to in '88 -

Yadkin Valley

DREAMS OF MY RUSSIAN SUMMERS

Andreï Makine

TRANSLATED FROM THE FRENCH BY

Geoffrey Strachan

SCRIBNER PAPERBACK FICTION
Published by Simon & Schuster

SCRIBNER PAPERBACK FICTION
Simon & Schuster Inc.
Rockefeller Center
1230 Avenue of the Americas
New York, NY 10020

Originally published in French under the title *Le testament français*

First Scribner Paperback Fiction edition 1998
Published by arrangement with Arcade Publishing, Inc., New York
SCRIBNER PAPERBACK FICTION and design are trademarks of
Simon & Schuster Inc.

Designed by API
Manufactured in the United States of America

5 7 9 10 8 6 4

Library of Congress Cataloging-in-Publication Data
Makine, Andreï, date.
[Testament français. English]
Dreams of my Russian summers / Andreï Makine ; translated from the French by
Geoffrey Strachan.
p. cm.
1. Grandmothers—Russia—Fiction. 2. Grandparent and child—
Russia—Fiction. 3. Boys—Russia—Fiction. 4. Russia—Fiction. I. Title.
PQ2673.A38416T4713   1998
843'.914—dc21   98-16347
CIP

ISBN 0-684-85268-3

For Marianne Véron and Herbert Lottman

For Laura and Thierry de Montalembert

For Jean-Christophe

. . . it was with a childish pleasure and a profound emotion that, being unable to mention the names of so many others who must have acted similarly and thanks to whom France has survived, I gave the real names here. . . .

—Marcel Proust, *Le Temps retrouvé*

Does the Siberian ask heaven for olive trees, or the Provençal for cranberries?

—Joseph de Maistre, *Les Soirées de St. Petersbourg*

I questioned the Russian about his method of work and was astonished that he did not make his translations himself, for he spoke a very pure French, with just a hint of hesitation, on account of the subtlety of his thought.

He confessed to me that the Académie and its dictionary froze him.

—Alphonse Daudet, *Trente ans de Paris*

Translator's Note

Andreï Makine was born and brought up in Russia but wrote *Dreams of My Russian Summers* in French, living in France. In this novel the lives of the characters move back and forth between two countries and two languages. Makine uses a number of Russian words that evoke features of Russian life, and I have generally left these as English transliterations of Russian, for example: *izba* (a traditional wooden house built of logs); *shapka* (a fur hat or cap, often with ear-flaps); *babushka* (a grandmother); *taiga* (the virgin pine forest that spreads across Siberia, south of the tundra); *kasha* (the staple dish of cooked grain or groats); *kulak* (a peasant farmer, working for his own profit); *kolkhoznik* (a member of a collective farm).

But I have also left in French a few phrases where the foreign or evocative sound for Russian ears seems to me as important as the meaning, for example: *"petite pomme"* ("little apple"); *Belle Epoque* (the era in France before the First World War); *"cher confrère"* ("dear colleague"); an echo of Flaubert's remark, *"Madame Bovary c'est moi"* (*"Madame Bovary* is me"); the opening couplet from La Fontaine's fable of the wolf and the lamb, *"La raison du plus fort est toujours la meilleure/Nous l'allons montrer tout à l'heure . . ."* ("The strongest always stand to win/The argument, as shown herein . . ."), which features in an elocution lesson; and the elusive French *"je ne sais quoi"* (an indefinable something).

1

1

WHILE STILL A CHILD, I guessed that this very singular smile represented a strange little victory for each of the women: yes, a fleeting
revenge for disappointed hopes, for the coarseness of men, for the
rareness of beautiful and true things in this world. Had I known how
to say it at the time I would have called this way of smiling "femininity." . . . But my language was too concrete in those days. I contented myself with studying the women's faces in our photograph
albums and identifying this glow of beauty in some of them.

For these women knew that in order to be beautiful, what they
must do several seconds before the flash blinded them was to articulate the following mysterious syllables in French, of which few
understood the meaning: *"pe-tite-pomme."* . . . As if by magic, the
mouth, instead of being extended in counterfeit bliss, or contracting
into an anxious grin, would form a gracious round. The whole face
was thus transfigured. The eyebrows arched slightly, the oval of the
cheeks was elongated. You said *"petite pomme,"* and the shadow of a
distant and dreamy sweetness veiled your gaze, refined your features,
and caused the soft light of bygone days to hover over the snapshot.

This photographic spell had won the confidence of the most di-
verse women: for example, a relative from Moscow in the only color
photo in our albums. Married to a diplomat, she spoke through
clenched teeth and sighed with boredom before even hearing you out.
But in the photo I could immediately identify the *"petite pomme"* effect.

I observed its aura on the face of a dull provincial woman, some
anonymous aunt, whose name only came up when the conversation

3

turned to the women left without husbands after the male slaughter of the last war. Even Glasha, the peasant of the family, in the rare photos that we still possessed of her, displayed the miraculous smile. Finally there was a whole swarm of young girl cousins, puffing out their lips while trying to hold on to this elusive French magic during several interminable seconds of posing. As they murmured their *"pe-tite pomme,"* they still believed that the life that lay ahead would be woven uniquely from such moments of grace. . . .

Throughout this parade of expressions and faces there recurred here and there that of a woman with fine, regular features and large gray eyes. Young at first, in the earliest of the albums, her smile was suffused with the secret charm of the *"petite pomme."* Then, with age, in the more recent albums, closer to our time, this expression became muted and overlaid with a veil of melancholy and simplicity.

It was this woman, this Frenchwoman, lost in the snowy immensity of Russia, who had taught the others the words that bestowed beauty. My maternal grandmother . . . She was born in France at the beginning of the century in the family of Norbert and Albertine Lemonnier. The mystery of the *"petite pomme"* was probably the first of the legends that enchanted our childhood. And these were also among the first words we heard in that language that my mother used, jokingly, to call "your grandmaternal tongue."

One day I came upon a photo I should not have seen. . . . I was spending my holidays with my grandmother in the town at the edge of the Russian steppe where she had been stranded after the war. A warm, slow summer dusk was drawing in and flooding the rooms with a mauve glow. This somewhat unearthly light fell upon the photos that I was examining before an open window, the oldest snapshots in our albums. The pictures spanned the historic watershed of the 1917 revolution; brought to life the era of the tsars; and, moreover, pierced the iron curtain, which was then almost impenetrable, transporting me at one moment to the precinct of a gothic cathedral and the next into the pathways of a garden where the precise geometry of the plants left me perplexed. I was plunging into our family prehistory.

Then suddenly this photo!

I saw it when, out of pure curiosity, I opened a large envelope that had been slipped between the last page and the cover. It was that inevitable batch of snapshots that have not been judged worthy to appear on the rough cardboard of the pages, landscapes that can no longer be identified, faces that evoke neither affection nor memories. One of those batches you always tell yourself you must sort through one day, to decide the fate of all these souls in torment. . . .

It was in the midst of these unknown people and forgotten landscapes that I saw her, a young woman whose attire jarred oddly with the elegance of the people who appeared in the other photos. She was wearing a big dirty gray padded jacket and a man's *shapka* with the earflaps pulled down. As she posed, she was clasping to her breast a baby muffled up in a wool blanket.

"How did she slip in," I wondered in amazement, "among all these men in tails and women in evening dress?" And all around her in other snapshots there were these majestic avenues, these colonnades, these Mediterranean vistas. Her presence was anachronistic, out of place, inexplicable. She seemed like an intruder in this family past, with a style of dress nowadays adopted only by the women who cleared snowdrifts from the roads in winter. . . .

I had not heard my grandmother coming in. She placed her hand on my shoulder. I gave a start, then, showing her the photo, "Who is that woman I asked her."

A brief flash of panic appeared in my grandmother's unfailingly calm eyes. In an almost nonchalant voice she asked me, "Which woman?"

We both fell silent, pricking up our ears. A bizarre rustling filled the room. My grandmother turned and cried out, it seemed to me, joyfully, "A death's-head! Look, a death's-head!"

I saw a large brown insect, a crepuscular hawkmoth, quivering as it tried to plunge into the illusory depths of the mirror. I rushed toward it, my hand outstretched, already feeling the tickling of its wings under my palm. It was then I noticed the unusual shape of this moth. I approached it and could not suppress a cry: "But there are two of them! They're Siamese twins."

And indeed the two moths did seem to be attached to one another. And their bodies were animated with feverish trembling. To my surprise this double hawkmoth paid me no attention and did not try to escape. Before catching it I had time to observe the white marks on its back, the famous death's head.

We did not speak again about the woman in the padded jacket. . . . I watched the flight of the liberated hawkmoth — in the sky it divided into two moths, and I understood, as a child of ten can understand, why they had been joined. Now my grandmother's disarray seemed to make sense.

The capture of the coupling hawkmoths brought to my mind two very old memories, the most mysterious of my childhood. The first, going back to when I was eight, was summed up in the words of an old song that my grandmother sometimes murmured rather than sang, sitting on her balcony, her head bowed over a garment on which she was darning the collar or reinforcing the buttons. It was the very last words of her song that plunged me into enchantment:

> . . . We'd sleep together there
> Till the world comes to an end.

This slumber of the two lovers, of such long duration, was beyond my childish comprehension. I already knew that people who died (like that old woman next door whose disappearance in winter had been so well explained to me) went to sleep forever. Like the lovers in the song? Love and death had now formed a strange alloy in my young head. And the melancholy beauty of the melody could only increase this unease. Love, death, beauty . . . And the evening sky, the wind, the smell of the steppe that, thanks to the song, I perceived as if my life had just begun at that moment.

The second memory was so distant it could not be dated. There was not even a very precise "me" in its nebulousness. Just the intense sensation of light, the aromatic scent of plants, and silvery lines crossing the blue density of the air, which many years later I would identify as gossamer threads. Elusive and confused, this vision would nevertheless be dear to me, for I would succeed in persuading myself that it was a memory from before birth. Yes, an echo sent to me by my French ancestry. For in one of my grandmother's stories I was to rediscover all the elements of this memory: the autumn sun of a journey she made to Provence, the scent of the fields of lavender, and even those gossamers floating in the perfumed air. I would never dare to speak to her of my childish prescience. It was in the course of the following summer that my sister and I one day saw our grandmother weep . . . for the first time in our lives.

In our eyes she was a kind of just and benevolent deity, always true to form and perfectly serene. Her own life story, which had long since become a myth, placed her beyond the griefs of ordinary mortals. In fact we did not see any tears. Just an unhappy contraction of her lips, little tremors running across her cheeks, and a rapid batting of her eyelashes. . . .

We were sitting on the carpet, which was littered with bits of crumpled paper, and were absorbed in a fascinating game: taking out little pebbles that were wrapped in white "sweet papers" and comparing them — now a glitter of quartz, now a pebble, smooth and pleasant to the touch. On each paper were written names that we had, in our ignorance, taken for enigmatic mineralogical labels: Fécamp, La Rochelle, Bayonne. . . . In one of the wrappers we even discovered a rough and ferrous fragment, which bore traces of rust. We thought we were reading the name of this strange metal: "Verdun." . . . A number of pieces from this collection had been thus stripped bare. When our grandmother came in, the game had just begun to take a livelier course. We were quarreling over the most beautiful stones and testing their hardness by striking them one against another, sometimes breaking them. Those we found ugly — like the "Verdun," for example — were thrown out of the window into a bed of dahlias. Several wrappers had been torn. . . .

Our grandmother froze above this battlefield scattered with white blisters. We looked up. It was then that her gray eyes seemed to be on the brink of tears — just enough to make it unbearable for us if she broke down.

No, she was not an impassive goddess, our grandmother. She

too, it seemed, could suffer unease, or sudden distress. We had always thought she moved in such a measured way through the peaceful sequence of days, yet she too sometimes hovered on the brink of tears!

From that summer onward my grandmother's life revealed new and unexpected facets to me. And above all, much more personal ones.

Previously her past had been summed up by a few talismans, a number of family relics, like the silk fan, which reminded me of a fine maple leaf, or the famous little "Pont-Neuf bag." Our legend maintained that it had been found on the bridge in question by Charlotte Lemonnier, aged four at the time. Running ahead of her mother, the little girl had stopped suddenly and exclaimed, "A bag!" And more than half a century later, the muted echo of her ringing cry could still be heard in a town lost amid the endlessness of Russia, under the sun of the steppes. It was in this pigskin bag, with enamel plaques on the fastening, that my grandmother kept her collection of stones from days gone by.

This old handbag marked one of my grandmother's earliest memories, and for us, the genesis of the legendary world of her memory: Paris, the Pont-Neuf. . . . An astonishing galaxy waiting to be born, which began to sketch its still hazy outlines before our fascinated gaze.

There was, besides, among these relics of the past (I remember the voluptuousness with which we caressed the smooth, gilded edges of those pink volumes, *Memoirs of a Poodle, Gribouille and His Sister* . . .), an even older testimony. The photo, already taken in Siberia; Albertine, Norbert, and — in front of them, on one of those artificial pieces of furniture that photographers always use, a kind of very tall pedestal table — Charlotte, a child of two, wearing a lace-trimmed bonnet and a doll's dress. This photo on thick cardboard, with the name of the photographer and replicas of the medals he had been awarded, intrigued us very much: "What does she have in common, this ravishing woman with her pure, fine face, framed in silky curls, with that old man, whose beard is divided into two rigid plaits that look like the tusks of a walrus?"

We already knew that this old man, our great-grandfather, was twenty-six years older than Albertine. "It's as if he'd married his own daughter!" my sister said to me indignantly. Their marriage seemed to us ambiguous and unhealthy. All our textbooks at school were full of stories that told of marriages between girls without dowries and rich old men, miserly and hungry for youth, to such an extent that any other kind of conjugal alliance seemed to us impossible in bourgeois society. We strove to discover some malign viciousness in Norbert's features, a grimace of ill-concealed satisfaction. But his face remained simple and frank, like those of the intrepid explorers in the illustrations to our Jules Verne books. After all, this old man with a long white beard was only forty-eight at the time. . . .

As for Albertine, supposed victim of bourgeois morality, she was soon to be standing on the slippery brink of an open grave into which the first spadefuls of earth were already flying. She would struggle so violently against the hands that restrained her and would utter such heartrending cries that even the funeral party of Russians, in that cemetery in a distant Siberian town, would be stunned by them. Accustomed as they were to tragic outbursts at funerals in their native land, to torrential tears and pitiful lamentations, these people would be stricken in the face of the tortured beauty of this young Frenchwoman. She would flail above the grave, crying out in her resonant language, "Throw me in as well! Throw me in!"

For a long time this terrible lament echoed in our childish ears.

"Perhaps it was because she . . . she loved him," my sister, who was older than me, said to me one day. And she blushed.

But more than that unusual union between Norbert and Albertine, it was Charlotte, in this photo from the turn of the century, who aroused my curiosity. Especially her little bare toes. By a simple irony of chance, or through some involuntary coquetry, she had curled them back tightly against the soles of her feet. This trifling detail conferred a special significance on what was overall a very ordinary photo. Not knowing how to formulate my thought, I contented myself with repeating in a dreamy voice, "This little girl who finds herself, heaven knows why, on this comical pedestal table, on that summer's day that has gone forever, July 22, 1905, right in the depths of Siberia. Yes, this tiny French girl, who was that day celebrating her second birthday, this child, who is looking at the photographer and by an unconscious caprice curling up her incredibly small toes, in this way allows me to enter into that day, to taste its climate, its time, its color. . . ."

And the mystery of this childish presence seemed to me so breathtaking that I would close my eyes.

This child was . . . our grandmother. Yes, it was her, this woman whom we saw that evening, crouching down and silently gathering up the fragments of stone scattered over the carpet. Dumbfounded and sheepish, my sister and I stood with our backs to the wall, not daring to murmur a word of excuse nor to help our grandmother retrieve the scattered talismans. We guessed that in her lowered eyes tears were forming. . . .

On the evening of our sacrilegious game we no longer saw an old-fashioned good fairy before us, a storyteller with her Bluebeard or her Sleeping Beauty, but a woman hurt and vulnerable despite all her strength of spirit. For her it was that agonizing moment when suddenly the adult betrays herself, allows her weakness to appear, feels like a naked emperor under the penetrating gaze of the child. Now she is like a tightrope walker who has made a false move and who, off balance for several seconds, is sustained only by the gaze of the spectator, who is in turn embarrassed at having this unexpected power. . . .

She closed the "Pont-Neuf bag," took it into her room, then called us to the table. After a moment's silence she began to speak in French in a calm and steady voice, while pouring tea for us with her familiar gesture: "Among the stones you threw away there was one I should really like to get back. . . ."

And still in this neutral tone and still in French, even though at mealtimes (because of friends or neighbors who often dropped in unexpectedly) we generally spoke in Russian, she told us about the parade of the Grande Armée and the story of the little brown pebble known as "Verdun." We scarcely grasped the sense of her tale — it was her tone that held us in thrall. Our grandmother was addressing us like adults! All we saw was a handsome officer with a mustache emerging from the column of the victory parade, approaching a young woman squeezed in the midst of an enthusiastic crowd, and offering her a little fragment of brown metal. . . .

After supper, armed with a flashlight, I vainly combed through the bed of dahlias in front of our apartment block: the "Verdun" was not there. I found it the following morning on the pavement, a little metallic pebble surrounded by several cigarette stubs, broken bottles, and streaks of sand. Under my gaze it seemed to stand out from these banal surroundings like a meteorite fallen from an unknown galaxy, which had almost disappeared amidst the gravel on a path. . . .

Thus we guessed at our grandmother's hidden tears and sensed the existence in her heart of that distant French lover who had preceded our grandfather, Fyodor. Yes, a dashing officer from the Grande Armée, the man who had slipped that rough splinter, the "Verdun," into Charlotte's palm. This discovery made us uneasy. We felt bound to our grandmother by a secret to which possibly no one else in the family had access. Beyond the dates and anecdotes of family legend we could now hear life welling up, in all its sorrowful beauty.

That evening we joined our grandmother on the little balcony of her apartment. Covered in flowers, it seemed suspended above the hot haze of the steppes. A copper sun nudged the horizon, remained undecided for a moment, then plunged rapidly. The first stars trembled in the sky. Powerful, penetrating scents rose to us with the evening breeze.

We were silent. While the daylight lasted, our grandmother darned a blouse spread out on her knees. Then, when the air was impregnated with ultramarine shadow, she raised her head, abandoning her task, her gaze lost in the hazy distance of the plain. Not daring to break her silence, we cast furtive glances at her from time to time: was she going to share a new and even more secret confidence with us? or would she fetch her lamp with the turquoise shade, as if nothing had happened, and read us a few pages of Daudet or Jules Verne, who often kept us company on our long summer evenings? Without admitting it to ourselves, we were lying in wait for her first word, her intonation. Our suspense — the spectator's fascination with the tightrope walker — was a mixture of rather cruel curiosity and a vague unease. We felt as if we were seeking to trap this woman who faced us alone.

However, she seemed not even to notice our tense presence. Her hands remained motionless in her lap; her gaze was lost in the transparency of the sky. The trace of a smile illuminated her lips. . . .

Little by little we abandoned ourselves to this silence. Leaning over the handrail, we stared wide-eyed, trying to see as much sky as possible. The balcony reeled slightly, giving way under our feet, and began to float. The horizon drew closer, as if we were hurtling toward it across the night breeze.

It was above the line of the horizon that we discerned a pale reflection — it was like the sparkle of little waves on the surface of a river. Incredulous, we peered into the darkness that surged over our flying balcony. Yes, far away on the steppe there shone an expanse of water, rising, spreading the bitter cold of the great rains. The sheet seemed to be lightening steadily, with a dull, wintry glow.

Now we saw emerging from this fantastic tide the black masses of apartment blocks, the spires of cathedrals, the posts of street lamps — a city! Gigantic, harmonious despite the waters that flooded its avenues, a ghost city was emerging before our eyes. . . .

Suddenly we realized that someone had been talking to us for quite a while. Our grandmother was talking to us!

"At that time I must have been almost your age; it was the winter of 1910. The Seine had turned into a real sea. The people of Paris traveled round by boat. The streets were like rivers; the squares, like great lakes. And what astonished me most was the silence. . . ."

On our balcony we heard the sleepy silence of flooded Paris. The lapping of a few waves when a boat went by, a muffled voice at the end of a drowned avenue.

The France of our grandmother, like a misty Atlantis, was emerging from the waves.

2

*E*VEN THE PRESIDENT WAS REDUCED to cold meals by it."

This was the very first remark to ring out through the capital of our France-Atlantis. . . . We imagined a venerable old man — combining in his appearance the noble bearing of our great-grandfather Norbert and the pharaonic solemnity of a Stalin — an old man with a silvery beard, sitting at a table gloomily lit by a candle.

This news report came from a man of about forty with a lively eye and a resolute expression, who appeared in photos in our grandmother's oldest albums. Coming alongside the wall of an apartment block in a boat and putting up a ladder, he was climbing toward one of the first-floor windows. This was Vincent, Charlotte's uncle and a reporter for the *Excelsior.* Since the start of the flood he had been working his way up and down the streets of the capital in this fashion, seeking out the key news item of the day. The president's cold meals was one such. And it was from Vincent's boat that the mind-boggling photo was taken that we were contemplating. It was on a yellowed press cutting: three men in a precarious little craft crossing a vast expanse of water flanked by apartment blocks. A caption explained: "Messieurs the deputies, on their way to a session of the Assemblée Nationale." . . .

Vincent stepped over the windowsill and sprang into the arms of his sister, Albertine, and of Charlotte, who were taking refuge with him during their stay in Paris. . . . Atlantis, silent until now, was filling up with sounds, emotions, words. Each evening our grandmother's stories uncovered some new fragment of this universe engulfed by time.

And then there was the hidden treasure. The suitcase filled with old papers, the massive bulk of which, when we had ventured under the big bed in Charlotte's room, alarmed us. We tugged on the catches, we lifted the lid. What a mass of paper! Adult life, in all its tedium and all its disturbing seriousness, stopped our breath with its smell of dust and things shut away . . . How could we have guessed that it was in the midst of these old newspapers, these letters with inconceivable dates, that our grandmother would find us the photo of the three deputies in their boat? . . .

It was Vincent who had passed on to Charlotte the taste for such journalistic sketches and urged her to collect them by cutting these brief chronicles of the day out of the newspapers. After a time, he must have thought, they would be seen in quite a different light, like silver coins colored by the patina of centuries.

During one of those summer evenings filled with the scented breeze of the steppes, a remark from a passerby under our balcony jolted us out of our reverie.

"No, I promise you. They said it on the radio. He went out into space."

And another voice, dubious, answered, receding into the distance, "Do you take me for a fool or what? 'He went out . . .' But up there there's nowhere you *can* go out. It's like bailing out of a plane without a parachute. . . ."

This exchange brought us back to reality. All about us there stretched the huge empire that took a particular pride in the exploration of the unfathomable sky above our head. The empire with its redoubtable army; with its atomic icebreakers disemboweling the North Pole; with its factories that would soon be producing more steel than all the countries of the world put together; with its cornfields that rippled from the Black Sea to the Pacific . . . with this endless steppe. And on our balcony a Frenchwoman was talking about a boat crossing a great flooded city and drawing alongside the wall of an apartment block. . . . We shook ourselves, trying to understand where we were. Here? Back there? The whispering of the waves in our ears fell silent.

It was by no means the first time we had noticed this duality in our lives. To live alongside our grandmother was already to feel you were elsewhere. She would cross the courtyard without ever going to take her place on the babushkas' bench, that institution without which a Russian courtyard is unthinkable. This did not stop her greeting them very cordially, inquiring after the health of one she had not seen for several days, and doing them little kindnesses, for example, showing them how to remove the slightly acid taste from salted milky mushrooms. But in addressing her friendly remarks to them, she remained standing. And the old gossips of the courtyard accepted this difference. Everyone understood that Charlotte was not entirely a Russian babushka.

This did not mean that she lived cut off from the world or that she clung to any social prejudice. Early in the morning we were often roused from our childish sleep by a sonorous cry that rang out in the midst of the courtyard: "Come and get your milk!" Through our dreams we recognized the voice and, above all, the inimitable intonation of Avdotia, the milkwoman, arriving from the neighboring village. The housewives came down with their cans toward two enormous aluminum containers that this vigorous peasant woman, some fifty years of age, dragged from one house to another. One day, awakened by her shout, I did not go back to sleep. . . . I heard our door close softly and muffled voices passing through into the dining room. A moment later one of them whispered with blissful abandon, "Oh, it's so cozy here, Shura! I feel as if I'm lying on a cloud." Intrigued by these words, I peeped behind the curtain that separated off our bedroom.

Avdotia was stretched out on the floor, her arms and legs flung out, her eyes half closed. From her bare, dust-covered feet right up to her hair spread out upon the ground, her whole body lolled in deep repose. An absentminded smile colored her half-open lips. "It's so cozy here, Shura!" she repeated softly, calling my grandmother by that diminutive that people generally used in place of her unusual Christian name.

I sensed the exhaustion of this great female body slumped in the middle of the dining room. I understood that Avdotia could only allow herself such a lack of constraint in my grandmother's apartment. For she was confident of not being snubbed or disapproved of. . . . She would finish her grueling round, bent under the weight of the enormous churns. And when all the milk was gone she would go up to "Shura's," her legs numb, her arms heavy. The floor, uncarpeted and always clean and bare, still had a pleasant morning coolness. Avdotia would come in, greet my grandmother, take off her bulky shoes, and go and stretch out on the bare floor. "Shura" brought her a glass of water and sat beside her on a little stool. And they would chat softly until Avdotia had the courage to continue on her way. . . .

That day I heard some of what my grandmother was saying to the milkwoman as she sprawled in blissful oblivion. The two of them were talking about the work in the fields, the buckwheat harvest. . . . And I was amazed to hear Charlotte talking about this farm life with complete authority. But above all the Russian she spoke, very pure, very refined, did not jar at all with Avdotia's rich, rough, and vivid way of talking. Their conversation also touched on the war, an inevitable topic: the milkwoman's husband had been killed at the front. Harvest, buckwheat, Stalingrad . . . And that evening she would be talking to us about Paris in flood, or reading us some pages from Hector Malot! I sensed a distant past, obscure — a Russian past, this time — awakening from the depths of her life long ago.

Avdotia got up, embraced my grandmother, and continued on her way, which led her across endless fields, beneath the sun of the steppes, on a farm wagon submerged in the ocean of tall plants and flowers. . . . This time, as she was leaving the room, I saw her great peasant's fingers touch, with tentative hesitation, the delicate statuette on the chest in our hall: a nymph with a rippling body entwined with sinuous stems, that figurine from the turn of the century, one of the rare fragments from bygone days that had been miraculously preserved. . . .

Bizarre as it may seem, it was thanks to the local drunkard, Gavrilych, that we were able to gain insight into the meaning of that unusual "strange elsewhere" that our grandmother carried within her. He was a man whose very teetering silhouette, looming up from behind the poplar trees in the courtyard, inspired apprehension. A man who defied the militiamen when he held up the traffic in the main street with his capricious zigzag progress; a man who fulminated against the authorities; and whose thunderous oaths rattled windowpanes and swept the row of babushkas from their bench. Yet this same Gavrilych, when he met my grandmother, would stop, attempt to inhale the vodka fumes on his breath, and articulate with an accentuated respect, "Good day, Sharlota Norbertovna!"

Yes, he was the only person in the courtyard who called her by her French Christian name, albeit slightly Russified. What is more, he had got hold of Charlotte's father's name — no one knew any longer when, or how — and formed the exotic patronymic "Norbertovna," on his lips the pinnacle of courtesy and eagerness to please. His cloudy eyes lit up, his giant's body recovered a relative equilibrium, his head sketched a series of somewhat uncoordinated nods, and he forced his alcohol-soaked tongue to perform this act of verbal acrobatics: "Are you well, Sharlota Norbertovna?"

My grandmother returned his greeting and even exchanged some thoughtful remarks with Gavrilych. On these occasions the courtyard had a very singular appearance: the babushkas, driven away by the tempestuous appearance onstage of the drunkard, took refuge on the steps of the great wooden house that faced our apartment block; the children hid behind the trees; at the windows one could see half-curious, half-frightened faces. And down in the arena our grandmother held conversation with a tamed Gavrilych. Nor was he by any means a fool. He had long since understood that his role went beyond drunkenness and scandal. He felt that he was in some way indispensable to the psychic well-being of the courtyard. Gavrilych had become a character, a type, a curiosity — the spokesman for that unpredictable and capricious fate so dear to Russian hearts. And suddenly there was this Frenchwoman with the calm gaze of her gray eyes, elegant despite the simplicity of her dress, slim, and so different from the women of her generation, the babushkas, whom he had just driven from their perch.

One day, wanting to say something other than a simple "Good morning" to Charlotte, he gave a little cough into his great fist and rumbled, "So that's it, Sharlota Norbertovna, you're all alone here in our steppes. . . ."

It was thanks to this clumsy remark that I found it possible to picture (as up until then I had never done) my grandmother without us, in winter, alone in her room.

In Moscow or Leningrad everything would have turned out otherwise. The motley humanity of the big city would have eclipsed what was different about Charlotte. But she had found herself in this little Saranza, ideal for living out endless days, each like the last. Her past life remained intensely present to her, as if lived only yesterday.

She was Saranza: transfixed at the edge of the steppes in profound astonishment before the boundlessness that opened at its gates. Winding, dusty streets that constantly climbed up hillsides; wooden fences beneath the greenery of gardens. Sun, sleepy vistas. And passersby who, appearing at the end of a street, seemed to be perpetually approaching without ever drawing level with you.

My grandmother's building was situated at the edge of the town in the "Western Glade" district: a coincidence (West Europe–France) that amused us greatly. According to the plan of an ambitious governor, this three-story apartment block, built in the second decade of the century, was intended to inaugurate a whole avenue bearing the imprint of the modern style. Yes, the building was a faint replica of the fashion of the turn of the century. It was as if all the sinuosities, twists, and curves of that architecture had flowed in a stream from its European source and, diluted and partly effaced, had reached the depths of Russia. And in the icy wind of the steppes this flow had become frozen into an apartment block with strange oval bull's-eye windows and ornamental rose stems around the doorways. . . . The enlightened governor's scheme had foundered. The October Revolution put a stop to all these decadent tendencies of bourgeois art. And this building — a narrow segment of the dreamed-of avenue —

had remained the only one of its kind. Indeed, after many repairs, it retained only a shadow of its original style. It was in particular the official campaign of struggle against "architectual excesses," which we had witnessed as young children, that had dealt it the death blow. All of it seemed "excessive": workmen had torn off the rose stems, condemned the bull's-eye windows. . . . And, as there are always individuals who want to make a show of their zeal (it is thanks to them that campaigns really succeed), the downstairs neighbor had excelled himself in detaching the most flagrant architectural superfluity from the wall: the faces of two pretty bacchantes, who had exchanged melancholy smiles on each side of our grandmother's balcony. To achieve this, he must have performed feats of great daring, standing up on his own windowsill with a long steel tool in his hand. The two faces, one after the other, had come unstuck from the wall and had fallen to the ground. One of them had shattered into a thousand fragments on the asphalt; the other, following a different trajectory, had hurtled into the dense vegetation of the dahlias, which had broken its fall. We had recovered it at dusk and carried it home. Henceforward, during our long summer evenings on the balcony this stone face, with its faded smile and its tender eyes, would gaze at us from among the pots of flowers and seem to listen to Charlotte's stories.

On the other side of the courtyard, overhung with the foliage of lime and poplar trees, stood a large two-story wooden house, quite black with age, with little dark, suspicious windows. It was this and its fellows that the governor had wanted to replace with the graceful lightness of the modern style. In this structure, two centuries old, lived the most picturesque of the babushkas, straight out of fairy tales with their thick shawls, their deathly pale faces, their bony, almost blue hands resting on their knees. When we had occasion to enter this dark dwelling, the bitter, heavy, but not totally unpleasant smell that hung in the cluttered corridors always caught in my throat. It was that of the old life, dark and very primitive in the way it welcomed death, birth, love, and grief. A kind of oppressive climate, but filled with a strange vitality, and in any case the only one that would have suited the inhabitants of this enormous *izba*. The breath of Russia . . .

Inside it we were astonished by the number and the asymmetry of the doors that opened onto rooms plunged in smoky shadow. I sensed, almost physically, the carnal density of the lives that intermingled here.

Gavrilych lived in the cellar, which three families shared with him. The narrow window of his room was located at ground level, and when spring came, it was obstructed by wild plants. The babushkas, sitting on their bench a few yards away, would cast anxious glances at it from time to time — it was not uncommon to see the broad face of the "scandalizer" between the stems at the open window. His head looked as if it were rising out of the earth. But at these moments of contemplation Gavrilych always remained calm. He would tip his face backwards, as if he wanted to glimpse the sky and the brilliance of the sunset in the branches of the poplar trees. . . . One day, making our way right up to the loft of this great black *izba,* underneath its roof, warmed by the sun, we pushed open the heavy shutter of a skylight. On the horizon a terrifying fire was setting the steppe ablaze: the smoke was soon going to eclipse the sun. . . .

When it came down to it, the revolution had achieved only one innovation in that quiet corner of Saranza. The church, which was situated at one end of the courtyard, had had its cupola removed. They had also taken out the iconostasis and installed in its place a great square of white silk — the screen made up of curtains commandeered from one of the bourgeois apartments in the "decadent" block. The Barricade cinema was ready to welcome its first audience. . . .

Yes, our grandmother was a woman who could happily converse with Gavrilych, a woman who was opposed to all the campaigns and who had one day referred to our cinema, with a wink, as "that decapitated church." Then we had caught a glimpse of the soaring silhouette of a gilded onion and a cross, rising up above the squat edifice, whose past was unknown to us.

Far more than her clothes or her physique, it was these little touches that revealed to us that she was different. As for the French language, we basically regarded it as our family dialect. After all, every family has its little verbal whims, its tics of language, and its nick-names that never cross the threshold of the house — its private slang.

The image of our grandmother was woven from these anodyne peculiarities — eccentricities in the eyes of some people, excesses to others. That was up to the day when we discovered that a little pebble covered in rust could cause tears to glisten on her eyelashes and that French, our domestic patois, could — through the magic of its sounds — snatch from the dark and tumultuous waters a fantastical city that was slowly returning to life.

And from being a lady with obscure, non-Russian origins, Charlotte was transformed that evening into a messenger from an Atlantis, engulfed by time.

3

*N*EUILLY-SUR-SEINE WAS COMPOSED of a dozen log cabins. Real *izbas,* with roofs covered in slender laths, silvered by the rigors of winter, with windows set in prettily carved wooden frames and hedges with washing hung out to dry on them. Young women carried full pails on yokes that spilled a few drops on the dust of the main street. Men loaded heavy sacks of corn onto a wagon. A slow herd streamed idly toward the cowshed. We heard the heavy sound of their bells and the hoarse crowing of a cock. The agreeable smell of a wood fire — the smell of supper almost ready — hung in the air.

For our grandmother had indeed said to us one day, when speaking of her birthplace, "Oh! At that time Neuilly was just a village. . . ."

She had said it in French, but we only knew Russian villages. And a village in Russia is inevitably a ring of *izbas;* indeed the very word in Russian, *derevnya,* comes from *derevo* — a tree, wood. The confusion persisted, despite the clarifications that Charlotte's stories would later bring. At the name "Neuilly" we had immediate visions of the village with its wooden houses, its herd, and its cockerel. And when, the following summer, Charlotte spoke to us for the first time about a certain Marcel Proust — "By the way, we used to see him playing tennis at Neuilly, on the boulevard Bineau" — we pictured the dandy with big languorous eyes (she had shown us his photo) there among the *izbas!*

Beneath the fragile patina of our French words Russian reality often showed through. The president of the Republic was bound to have something Stalinesque about him in the portrait sketched by our imagination. Neuilly was peopled with kolkhozniks. And the slow emergence of Paris from the waters evoked a very Russian emotion — that of fleeting relief after one more historic cataclysm; the joy of having finished a war, of having survived murderous repressions. We wandered along its streets, which were still wet, covered with sand and mud. The inhabitants were piling furniture and clothes outside their doors to let them dry — as Russians do, after a winter they had been beginning to think would never end.

And then, when Paris was resplendent once more in the fresh spring air, whose scent we guessed intuitively, there was a fairy-tale train, drawn by a garlanded engine slowing down and coming to a halt at the gates of the city, before the pavilion at Ranelagh station.

A young man wearing a simple military tunic stepped down from the railway carriage, walking on the purple cloth spread at his feet. He was accompanied by a woman, also very young, in a white dress with a feather boa. An older man, in formal attire, with a magnificent mustache and a fine blue ribbon on his breast, emerged from an impressive gathering grouped under the portico of the pavilion and advanced toward the couple. The gentle breeze caressed the orchids and the amaranths that decorated the pillars and stirred the feather on the young woman's white velvet hat. The two men shook hands.

The master of Atlantis resurgent, President Félix Faure, was welcoming the tsar of all the Russias, Nicholas II, and his wife.

It was the imperial couple, escorted by the elite of the Republic, who were our guides through Paris. . . . Several years later we learned the true chronology of this glorious visit. Nicholas and Alexandra had not come in the spring of 1910, after the flood, but in October 1896, that is to say well before the rebirth of our French Atlantis. But this real sequence hardly mattered. For us only the chronology of our grandmother's long stories counted: one day, in their legendary time, Paris arose from the waters; the sun shone, and at once we heard the still distant cry of the imperial train. This sequence of events seemed just as legitimate to us as the appearance of Proust among the peasants of Neuilly.

Charlotte's narrow balcony hovered in the aromatic breeze of the plain, at the outer limit of a sleeping town, cut off from the world by the eternal silence of the steppes. Each evening resembled an alchemist's legendary vessel, in which an astonishing transmutation of the past took place. To us the elements of this magic were no less mysterious than the components of the philosophers' stone. Charlotte unfolded an old newspaper, brought it close to her lamp with its turquoise shade, and proclaimed for us the menu for the banquet given in honor of the Russian sovereigns when they arrived at Cherbourg:

> *Soup*
> *Bisque of shrimps*
> *Cassolettes Pompadour*
> *Loire trout braised in Sauternes*
> *Fillet of salt lamb with cèpes*
> *Vine quails à la Lucullus*
> *Poulardes du Mans Cambacérès*
> *Sorbets in Muscat de Lunel*
> *Punch à la romaine*
> *Roast bartavels and ortolans, garnished with truffles*
> *Pâté de foie gras of Nancy*
> *Salad*
> *Asparagus spears with sauce mousseline*
> *Ice cream "Success"*
> *Dessert*

How could we decipher these cabbalistic formulae? "Bartavels and ortolans!" "Vine quails à la Lucullus"! Our grandmother, understandingly, tried to find equivalents, citing the very rudimentary produce that was still to be found in Saranza's shops. Enthralled, we savored these imaginary dishes, enhanced by the misty chill of the ocean (Cherbourg!), but already it was time to set off again in pursuit of the tsar.

Like him, entering the Elysée Palace, we were startled by the spectacle of all the black suits that fell motionless at his approach — just think, more than two hundred senators and three hundred deputies! (Who, according to our own chronology, had only a few days previously been traveling to their session by boat. . . .) Our grandmother's voice, which was always calm and a little dreamy, became tinged at that moment with a slight dramatic tremor: "You see, two worlds found themselves face to face. (Look at this photo. It's a pity the newspaper has been folded for so long. . . .) Yes, the tsar, an absolute monarch, and the representatives of the French people! The representatives of democracy . . ."

The profound import of the confrontation was lost on us. But we could now make out, among five hundred pairs of eyes focused on the tsar, those who, without outward hostility, held back from the general enthusiasm. And who felt free to do so just because of this mysterious "democracy." This casual attitude filled us with consternation. We inspected the ranks of the black suits to discover potential troublemakers. The president should have identified them and expelled them by pushing them off the steps of Elysée!

The following evening our grandmother's lamp was lit on the balcony once more. In her hands we saw some newspaper pages she had just extracted from the Siberian suitcase. She spoke. The balcony slowly detached itself from the wall and hovered, plunging into the scented shadows of the steppe.

. . . Nicholas was seated at the table of honor, which was trimmed with magnificent garlands of medeola. At one moment he was listening now to some gracious remark from Madame Faure, seated on his right, at the next to the velvety baritone of the president, speaking to the empress. The reflections from the glasses and the glittering array of silver dazzled the guests. . . . At the dessert the president stood up, raised his glass, and declared, "The presence of Your Majesty among us, acclaimed by a whole people, has sealed the bonds that unite our two countries in harmonious endeavor and in a mutual confidence in their destinies. The union between a powerful empire and an industrious republic . . . Fortified by a proven fidelity . . . As a spokesman for the whole nation, offer to Your Majesty . . . For the greatness of his reign . . . For the happiness of Her Majesty, the Empress . . . I raise my glass in honor of His Majesty, the Emperor Nicholas, and Her Majesty, the Empress Alexandra Fyodorovna."

The band of the Republican Guard struck up the Russian national anthem. . . . And the grand gala at the Opéra that evening was an apotheosis.

Preceded by two torchbearers, the imperial couple ascended the staircase. They seemed to be moving past a living cascade: the white curves of the women's shoulders; the blossoming flowers on their corsages; the perfumed brilliance of the hairstyles; the glittering of jewels on bare flesh; all this against a background of uniforms and tails. The mighty cry "Long live the Emperor!" almost raised the majestic ceiling to the sky with its echoes, mingling it with the sky. . . . When at the end of the performance the orchestra launched into the "Marseillaise," the tsar turned to the president and gave him his hand.

My grandmother switched off the lamp, and we spent several minutes in the dark, the time it took to let all the midges fly away that had been courting a luminous death beneath the shade. Little by little our eyes began to see again. The stars reformed their constellations. The Milky Way became phosphorescent. And in a corner of our balcony, among the intermingled stems of sweet peas, the fallen bacchante gave us her stone smile.

Charlotte paused in the doorway and sighed gently. "You know, it was a military march, in fact, nothing more, the 'Marseillaise.' A bit like the songs of the Russian revolution. At such times blood doesn't frighten anyone. . . ."

She went back into the room, and it was from there that we heard these lines emerging, which she recited softly, like a strange litany from the past:

> Over us the bloodstained banner
> Of tyranny holds sway. . . .
> And drench our fields with their tainted blood. . . .

We waited for the echo of these words to melt into the darkness, and then with one voice we exclaimed to one another, "And Nicholas? The tsar? Did he know what the song was about?"

*   *   *

France-Atlantis was revealing itself as a whole gamut of sounds, colors, and smells. As we followed our guides, we were discovering the different elements that made up this mysterious French essence.

The Elysée Palace appeared in the glitter of chandeliers and the shimmering of mirrors. The Opéra dazzled us with the nakedness of women's shoulders and made us drunk with the perfume exhaled by the magnificent hairstyles. For us Notre-Dame was a sensation of cold stone under a stormy sky. Yes, we could almost touch the rough, porous walls — a gigantic rock, shaped over the centuries, it seemed to us, by ingenious erosion. . . .

These perceptible facets outlined the still-uncertain contours of the French universe. This emerging continent was filling up with things and people. The empress knelt on a mysterious prie-dieu that did not suggest any known reality. "It's a kind of chair with its legs cut off," explained Charlotte, and the image of this mutilated piece of furniture left us dumbfounded. Like Nicholas, we repressed the desire to touch the purple cloak with its tarnished golds, which Napoleon had worn on the day of his coronation. We craved the sacrilegious contact. This universe in gestation still lacked substance. In the Sainte-Chapelle it was the rough grain of an old parchment that aroused the same desire — Charlotte taught us that these long handwritten letters had been penned a millennium ago by a French queen, a Russian woman furthermore, Anna Yaroslavna, wife of Henri I.

But what was most exciting was that Atlantis was being built before our very eyes. Nicholas grasped a golden trowel and spread mortar on a great block of granite — the first stone of the Pont Alexandre-III. . . . And he held out the trowel to Félix Faure — "Your turn, *Monsieur le Président!*" — and the racing wind, which was whiffing up white horses on the waters of the Seine, carried away the words forcefully uttered by the minister of trade as he battled against the flapping of the flags: "Sire! It was France's wish to dedicate one of the great monuments of her capital to the memory of your august father. In the name of the government of the Republic I ask Your Imperial Majesty to graciously consecrate this homage by joining the President of the Republic in cementing the first stone of the Pont

Alexandre-III, which will link Paris to the Exhibition of 1900 —
and thus to extend to our inauguration of this great enterprise of civilization and peace the lofty approbation of Your Majesty and the
gracious patronage of the Empress."

The president barely had time to give two symbolic taps to the
granite block before an incredible incident occurred. A fellow who
belonged neither to the imperial entourage nor to the party of
French dignitaries rose up before the imperial couple, addressed the
tsar with the familiar *tu,* and with an extraordinary urbane dexterity,
kissed the tsarina's hand! Petrified by such cavalier behavior, we held
our breath. . . .

Little by little it became evident what was happening. The
words of the intruder, overcoming the distance in time and gaps in
our French, were clarified. Feverishly we caught their echo:

> Illustrious Emperor, Alexander's heir,
> France welcomes thee, on this occasion fair.
> In tongue of gods she bids me greetings bring;
> Poets alone may thus address a King.

We uttered a "phew" of relief. The insolent braggart was none
other than a poet, whose name Charlotte told us was José Maria de
Heredia!

> And you, Madame, who on this happy day
> Alone a peerless loveliness display,
> Let me, through you, bestow an accolade
> On grace divine, of which your own is made!

The cadence of the verses intoxicated us. To our ears the resonance of the rhymes celebrated extraordinary marriages between
words that were far apart: "stream-dream," "gold-untold." . . . We
sensed that only such verbal artifices could express the exotic nature
of our French Atlantis:

> Behold the city! Fervent acclamation
> From flag-decked Paris soars in celebration,

Where both in palace and in humble street
The three brave colors of our two lands meet . . .

'Neath golden poplars, all along her banks
The Seine conveys a joyful people's thanks.
Affection follows where our eyes may see:
France greets her guests with all her energy!

Great works of peace are put in hand today:
This mighty arch will rise to lead the way
From this age into that which onward lies,
Linking two peoples and two centuries.

From this historic shore e'er each departs
May French hearts find response in both your hearts.
Before this bridge, sire, dream, and meditate,
Which to thy father France doth consecrate.

Like him, be strong: but merciful thy word;
Keep in its sheath thy battle-glorious sword;
Warrior at peace, bring peace to thine own land.
Tsar, let the spinning world turn in thy hand.

And like thy sire, keep earth in balance still:
Thy powerful arm sustain thy tireless will;
This honor is thy greatest legacy:
To win the love of a people that is free.

"To win the love of a people that is free": this line, which had
initially passed almost unnoticed in the melodious flow of the verses,
struck home. The French, a free people . . . Now we understood
why the poet had dared to offer advice to the master of the most
powerful empire on earth. And why to be loved by these free citizens
was such an honor. On that evening, in the overheated air of the
nocturnal steppes, this freedom seemed to us like a harsh and chilly
gust from the wind that had made waves on the Seine, and it filled
our lungs with a breeze that was heady and a little mad. . . .

Later we would learn to put the ponderous bombast of this
declamation into perspective. But at the time, despite its focus on the
particular occasion, what we could already detect in his verses was a

French *je ne sais quoi,* which for the moment went without a name. French wit? French politeness? We could not yet say.

Meanwhile the poet turned toward the Seine and held out his hand, gesturing toward the dome of the Hôtel des Invalides on the opposite bank. His rhymed address was coming to a very painful point in the Franco-Russian past: Napoleon, Moscow in flames, the disastrous Berezina crossing. . . . Anxiously, biting our lips, we awaited his voice at this passage so fraught with risk. The tsar's face went blank. Alexandra lowered her eyes. Would it not have been better to pass over it in silence, to pretend nothing had happened and go straight from Peter the Great to the current *entente cordiale?*

But Heredia seemed to set his sights even higher:

> That distant shining dome against the sky
> Still shelters heroes from a time gone by,
> When French and Russians, jousting without rage,
> Mingling their blood, foresaw a future age.

Bewildered, we kept asking ourselves this question: Why do we detest the Germans as much as we do — still recall the Teutonic aggression of seven centuries ago at the time of Alexander Nevski, as well as that of the last war? Why can we never forget the ravages of the Polish and Swedish invaders, ancient history from three and a half centuries ago? Not to mention the Tartars. . . . So why hasn't the memory of the terrible catastrophe of 1812 tarnished the reputation of the French in Russian minds? Is it precisely because of the verbal elegance of that "jousting without rage"?

But the French *je ne sais quoi* was revealed, above all, as the presence of a woman. Alexandra was there, drawing unobtrusive attention to herself, hailed in every speech in a much less pompous but considerably more elegant manner than her husband. And even within the walls of the Académie Française, where the smell of old furniture and fat, dusty volumes stifled us, this *je ne sais quoi* allowed her to preserve her femininity. Yes, even among these old men, whom we imagined to be peevish, pedantic, and a little deaf, on account of the hairs in their ears. One of them, the director, rose and with a glum expression declared the session open. Then he fell silent, as if to gather up his thoughts, which, we were sure, would quickly make all his listeners aware of the hardness of their wooden seats. The smell of dust grew thicker. Suddenly the old man lifted his head; a sly twinkle came into his eye, and he spoke: "Sire, Madame! Almost two hundred years ago Peter the Great arrived one day unexpectedly at the place where the members of the Académie were gathered and joined in their deliberations. . . . Your Majesty does even more today: you have added one honor to another by not coming alone." (He turned to the empress.) "Your presence, Madame, will bring to our solemn proceedings something quite unaccustomed. . . . Charm."

Nicholas and Alexandra exchanged rapid glances. And the orator, as if he had sensed that it was time to turn to the main topic, amplified the vibrations in his voice as he asked himself in a highly rhetorical manner: "May I be permitted to say it? Your show of interest addresses not only the Académie but our national language itself. . . . Which for you is not a foreign language. In this we sense a particular desire to enter into more intimate communication with French taste and the French spirit. . . ."

"Our language"! Over the top of the pages that our grandmother was reading out to us, my sister and I looked at one another, struck by the same insight. ". . . Which for you is not a foreign language." So that was it, the key to our Atlantis! Language, that mysterious substance, invisible and omnipresent, whose sonorous essence reached into every corner of the universe we were in the process of exploring. This language that shaped men, molded objects, rippled in verse, bellowed in streets invaded by crowds, caused a young tsarina who had come from the other end of the world to smile. . . . But above all throbbed within us, like a magical graft implanted in our hearts, already bringing forth leaves and flowers, bearing within it the fruit of a whole civilization. Yes, this implant, the French language.

And it was thanks to this twig blossoming within us that we gained access that evening to the box prepared to welcome the imperial couple at the Comédie Française. We unfolded the program: *Un Caprice* by Alfred de Musset; fragments from *Le Cid*; the third act of

Les Femmes savantes. At that time we had not read any of those. It was a slight change of timbre in Charlotte's voice that enabled us to grasp the importance of these names for the inhabitants of Atlantis.

The curtain rose. The whole company was onstage in ceremonial roles. The leading player stepped forward, bowed, and spoke of a country that we did not immediately recognize:

> Like a vast world, there is a country fair,
> Whose far horizons never terminate,
> Whose soul is rich and rare,
> Great in the past, in future yet more great.
>
> Blond with her corn, white with the white of snow,
> Leaders and men, her sons walk firm and sure.
> Let fate smile on her so
> She harvests gold on virgin earth and pure.

For the first time in my life I was looking at my country from the outside, from a distance, as if I were no longer a part of it. Transported to a great European capital, I looked back to contemplate the immensity of the cornfields and the snow-covered plains by moonlight. I was seeing Russia in French! I was somewhere else. Outside my Russian life. To be thus torn asunder was so painful and at the same time so thrilling that I had to close my eyes. I was afraid of not being able to return to myself, of being stranded in that Parisian evening. Screwing up my eyes, I inhaled deeply. The warm wind of the nocturnal steppe suffused my being once more.

That day I decided to steal her magic from her. I wanted to be one step ahead of Charlotte, to make my way into the festive city before her, join the tsar's entourage without waiting for the hypnotic halo of the turquoise lampshade.

The day was dull, gray — a sad and colorless summer's day, one of those that, amazingly, stay in the memory. The breeze, which smelled of wet earth, billowed out the white net curtains on the open window. The fabric came to life, acquired density, then fell back again, letting someone invisible enter the room.

Happy in my solitude, I put my plan into execution. I pulled out the Siberian suitcase onto the rug near the bed. The catches emitted that light clicking that we awaited each evening. I threw back the great lid and bent over those old papers like a pirate over the treasure in a chest. . . .

At the top I recognized certain photos; I saw the tsar and tsarina again in front of the Panthéon, then on the banks of the Seine. No, what I was looking for was located farther down, in that compact mass blackened with printer's type. Like an archaeologist, I lifted up one layer after another. Nicholas and Alexandra appeared in places unknown to me. One more layer, and I lost sight of them. Then I saw long battleships on a slack sea, airplanes with ridiculous short wings, soldiers in trenches. In my attempt to locate a trace of the imperial couple, I was now digging at random, mixing up all the cuttings. For a moment the tsar came into view on horseback, an icon in his hands, in front of a row of kneeling foot soldiers. . . . His face seemed aged, somber. But I wanted him to be young again, accompanied by the beautiful Alexandra, cheered by the crowds, celebrated in fervent verses.

It was right at the bottom of the suitcase that I came upon a clue at last. The headline in large letters — "Glory to Russia!" — left no room for doubt. I smoothed out the paper on my knees, as Charlotte used to do, and began softly to mouth the lines:

> Great God, there is good news to tell!
> With joyful hearts we greet the day,
> To see collapse the citadel,
> Where slaves once groaned their lives away!
> To see a people's pride reborn,
> The torch of justice raised on high!
> To celebrate this happy morn,
> Friends, let your flags and banners fly!

It was only when I reached the chorus that I paused, seized by a doubt: "Glory to Russia"? But what had become of that land, "blond with her corn, white with the white of snow"? That "country fair" whose soul was "rich and rare"? And what were these slaves doing here, groaning their lives away? And who was the tyrant whose downfall was being celebrated?

In confusion, I went on to recite the chorus:

> All hail, Russia, all hail to you!
> People and soldiers together stand!
> All hail to you, all hail to you,
> Who now redeem your Fatherland!
> All hail the Duma's newfound power,
> Its sovereign voice will soon have spoken,
> For happiness now comes the hour,
> With all your chains forever broken.

Suddenly some headlines caught my eye, poised above the lines of verse:

NICHOLAS II ABDICATES: RUSSIA'S 1789. RUSSIA FINDS FREEDOM. KERENSKY — THE RUSSIAN DANTON. PETER AND PAUL FORTRESS — RUSSIA'S BASTILLE — TAKEN BY STORM. COLLAPSE OF AUTOCRACY . . .

Most of these words meant nothing to me. But I grasped the essential. Nicholas was no longer the tsar, and the news of his downfall had inspired an ecstatic explosion of joy among the people who, only yesterday, were cheering him and wishing him a long and prosperous reign. Indeed I had a very clear memory of Heredia's voice, which still echoed round our balcony:

> It was thy father forged a bond that tied
> Russia to France, in brotherly hope allied.
> Hear now great Tsar, how France and Russia bless
> Thine own name, with thy patron's name, no less!

Such a reversal seemed to me inconceivable. I could not credit so base a betrayal. Especially on the part of a president of the Republic!

The front door banged. Hastily I gathered up all the papers, closed the suitcase, and pushed it under the bed.

At dusk, because of the rain, Charlotte lit her lamp indoors. We took our places beside her exactly as we used to in our evenings on the balcony. I listened to her story: Nicholas and Alexandra were in their box at the theater, applauding *Le Cid*. . . . I observed their faces with a disillusioned sadness. I was the one who had glimpsed the future. This knowledge weighed heavily on my child's heart.

"Where is the truth?" I wondered, as I followed the narrative distractedly. (The imperial pair stand up, the audience turn to give them an ovation.) "These same spectators will soon be cursing them. And nothing will remain of these few fairy-tale days! Nothing . . ."

The ending, which I was condemned to know in advance, suddenly seemed to me so absurd and so unjust, especially at the height of the celebration, amid all the bright lights of the Comédie Française, that I burst into tears, pushed aside my little stool, and fled to the kitchen. I had never wept so uncontrollably. Furiously I shrugged off my sister's hands when she tried to comfort me. . . . (I so resented her, she who still knew nothing!) Through my tears I cried out despairingly: "It's all a cheat! They're traitors! That liar with his mustaches . . . Some president! It's all lies. . . ."

I do not know if Charlotte had guessed the reason for my distress (doubtless she had noticed the disarray caused by my rummaging in the Siberian suitcase: perhaps she had even come across the fateful page). In any event, touched by this unexpected outburst of weeping, she came and sat on my bed, listened to my fitful sighs for a moment, and then, finding my palm in the darkness, slipped a little rough pebble into it. I closed my fist round it. Just from the feel of it, without opening my eyes, I recognized the "Verdun" pebble. From now on it was mine.

4

At the end of the holidays we left our grandmother's. Now Atlantis was blotted out by the mists of autumn and the first snowstorms — by our Russian life.

For the city we went home to had nothing in common with silent Saranza. This city stretched along both banks of the Volga and, with its million and a half inhabitants, its arms factories, its broad avenues with large apartment blocks in the Stalinist style, it was the incarnation of the power of the empire. A gigantic hydroelectric station downstream, a subway under construction, and an enormous river port proclaimed, for all to see, the very image of our fellow countryman — one who triumphed over the forces of nature, lived in the name of a radiant future, strove mightily for it, and cared little for the ridiculous relics of the past. Furthermore our city, because of its factories, was out of bounds to foreigners. . . . Yes, it was a city where one could feel the pulse of the empire very strongly.

Once we had returned, this rhythm began to set the tempo for our own gestures and thoughts. We were drawn into the snowy breathing of our fatherland.

The French implant grafted in our hearts did not stop either my sister or myself from leading an existence similar to that of our comrades: Russian became our regular language once more, school shaped us in the mold of exemplary Soviet youngsters, paramilitary exercises accustomed us to the smell of powder; to the crack of practice grenades; to the idea of the western enemy we should one day have to fight.

The evenings on our grandmother's balcony were no more, it seemed to us, than a childish dream. And when during our history lessons the teacher spoke of "Nicholas II, known to the people as Nicholas the Bloody," we made no connection between this mythical executioner and the young monarch who had applauded *Le Cid* in Paris. Not at all; they were two different men.

One day, however, more or less by chance, this juxtaposition took place in my head: without being asked, I began to talk about Nicholas and Alexandra and their visit to Paris. My intervention was so unexpected and the biographical details so abundant that the teacher seemed taken aback. Snorts of amazement spread around the classroom: the rest of the class did not know whether to regard my speech as an act of provocation or as a simple fit of delirium. But already the teacher was regaining control of the situation; he rapped out, "It was the tsar who was responsible for the terrible catastrophe at Khodynka Field — thousands of people trampled to death. It was he who gave the order to open fire on the peaceful demonstration of January 9, 1905 — hundreds of victims. It was his regime that was guilty of the massacres on the River Lena — a hundred and two people killed! It was by no means a coincidence that Lenin picked his name. He even used his own pseudonym to excoriate the crimes of tsarism!"

But what affected me most was not the vehement tone of this diatribe. It was a disconcerting question that formulated itself in my head during the break, while the other pupils were assailing me with their mockery. ("Oh, look! He's wearing a crown, this tsar!" yelled one of them, pulling my hair.) The question was apparently quite simple: "Yes, I know he was a bloody tyrant; it says that in our history book. But if so, what is to be done about that brisk wind, smelling of the sea, that blew over the Seine? about the music of those verses that were carried away by that wind? about the scraping of the golden trowel on the granite? What is to be done about that day long ago? For I feel its atmosphere so strongly."

No, for me it was not a question of rehabilitating Nicholas II. I believed my history book and my teacher. But that far-off day; that wind, that sunny air? I was confused in these disordered reflections, part thoughts, part images. As I pushed away my laughing comrades, who were snatching at me and deafening me with their taunts, I suddenly felt terribly jealous of them: "How fortunate not to carry within oneself that day of great wind, that past so palpable and apparently so useless. Yes, to have only one view of life. Not to see as I see. . . ."

This last thought seemed to me so strange that I stopped repelling my tormentors' attacks and turned toward the window, beyond which lay the snow-covered city. So I saw things differently! Was it an advantage? Or a handicap, a blemish? Perhaps this double vision could be explained by my two languages; thus, when I pronounced the Russian word "ЦАРЬ" a cruel tyrant rose up before me; while the word "tsar" in French was redolent of lights, of sounds, of wind, of glittering chandeliers, of the radiance of women's bare shoulders, of mingled perfumes, of the inimitable air of our Atlantis. I understood that this second view of things would have to be hidden, for it could only provoke mockery from others.

This secret meaning of words was subsequently revealed once more in a situation just as tragicomic as that of our history lesson.

I had joined an interminable queue that wound round outside the premises of a food shop, crossed the threshold, and then extended inside it. It was all, no doubt, for some foodstuff rare in winter — oranges, or perhaps simply apples, I no longer recall. I had already passed the most important psychological milestone of this wait, entering the door of the shop, outside which dozens of people were still squelching about in muddy snow. It was at that moment that my sister came to join me: as two people, we were entitled to a double quantity of the rationed goods.

We did not understand what suddenly provoked the anger of the crowd. The people standing behind us must have thought that my sister was trying to worm her way in without queuing — an unforgivable crime! Angry shouts erupted: the long snake contracted, threatening faces surrounded us. We both tried to explain that we were brother and sister. But the crowd never admits a mistake. Those who had not yet crossed the threshold — the shrillest — uttered indignant yells, without knowing exactly against whom. And as all mass actions exaggerate absurdly the impact of their efforts, it was me whom they now pushed out. The serpent quivered, the shoulders stiffened. One heave, and I found myself outside the queue, beside my sister, facing the serried row of hate-filled faces. I tried to return to my place, but the elbows formed a wall of shields. Distraught, with quivering lips, I met my sister's eyes. Unconsciously I sensed that we were particularly vulnerable, she and I. Two years older than me, she was not quite fifteen and did not have the presence of a young woman, while having lost the advantage of being a child, which might have touched this hard-boiled crowd. It was the same for me: at the age of twelve and a half I could not throw my weight about like young lads of fourteen or fifteen, strong in their irresponsible teenage aggression.

We slipped along the queue, hoping at least to be admitted some yards farther back from my lost place. But as we went past them the bodies closed ranks, and soon we found ourselves outside in the melted snow once more. Despite the cry of a saleswoman — "You there, beyond the door: you can give up waiting: there won't be enough for everyone!" — the people still came flocking.

We remained at the end of the queue, hypnotized by the anonymous power of the crowd. I was afraid to look up, or even to move. My hands, thrust into my pockets, were trembling. And when I suddenly heard my sister's voice, a few words tinged with a smiling melancholy, it was as if they came from another planet. "Do you remember? 'Roast bartavels and ortolans, garnished with truffles'?"

She laughed softly.

And as for me, as I looked at her pale face with the winter sky reflected in her eyes, I felt my lungs fill with an entirely new air — that of Cherbourg — with the smell of salt mist, of wet pebbles on the beach, and the echoing cries of seagulls over the endless ocean. For a moment I was struck blind. The queue was moving forward, slowly pushing me on toward the door. I allowed this to happen without letting go of the moment of illumination expanding within me.

Bartavels and ortolans . . . I smiled and gave my sister a discreet wink. It was not that we felt superior to the people squeezed together in the queue. We were like them, we may well have lived more modestly than many of them. We all belonged to the same class: that of people squelching about in trampled snow in the middle of a great industrial city, outside the doors of a shop, hoping to fill their bags with two kilos of oranges.

And yet when I heard the magic words, learned from the banquet in Cherbourg, I felt different from them. Not because of my erudition (at the time I had no idea what these famous bartavels and ortolans looked like). It was simply that the moment held within me — with its misty lights and its marine smells — had put all that surrounded us into perspective: the city and its very Stalinist squareness, the anxious waiting, and the obtuse violence of the crowd. Instead of anger toward the people who had pushed me out I now felt a surprising compassion toward them: for by slightly screwing up their eyes, they could not gain access to that day with its fresh scents of seaweed, its cries of gulls, its veiled sun. . . . I was seized by a terrible desire to tell everybody about it. But how to tell it? I would need to invent a language that did not yet exist. For the moment I only knew the first two words: bartavels and ortolans. . . .

5

After the death of my great-grandfather Norbert, the white immensity of Siberia had slowly closed in on Albertine. True, she returned to Paris two or three times more, taking Charlotte with her. But the planet of the snows never relinquished its hold on the souls who had fallen under the spell of its uncharted spaces and its slumbering time.

Furthermore, the visits to Paris were marked by a bitterness that my grandmother's stories did not manage to conceal. Some family quarrel, the reasons for which we were not given to know. Or perhaps a very European coldness in the relationships between close family members, inconceivable to us Russians, with our exuberant collectivism. Or quite simply the understandable attitude of unpretentious people toward one of four sisters, the adventuress of the family who, far from returning with a fair dream of gold, each time brought back the anguish of a barbarous country and a broken life.

In any event, the fact that Albertine preferred to live at her brother's apartment and not in the family home in Neuilly did not go unnoticed, even by us.

Each time she returned to Russia, she felt more and more fated for Siberia — it was inevitable, a part of her own destiny. It was not only Norbert's grave that bound her to this land of ice, but also that somber Russian life experience, whose intoxicating poison she felt entering her veins.

From being a respectable doctor's wife, known in the entire town, Albertine had become transformed into a most strange widow — a Frenchwoman who seemed to find it hard to make up her mind to return to her country. Worse still, each time she came back again!

She was still too young and too beautiful to avoid the malicious gossip of Boyarsk society. Too unusual to be accepted as she was. And soon too poor.

Charlotte noticed that after each trip to Paris, they settled into smaller and smaller apartments. At the school where she had been admitted, thanks to a former patient of her father's, she quickly became "that Lemonnier." One day her teacher made her come to the blackboard — but not to test her. . . . When Charlotte stood before her, the lady looked at the little girl's feet and, with a disdainful smile, asked, "What do you have on your feet, Mademoiselle Lemonnier?"

The thirty pupils rose from their seats, craning their necks and staring. On the well-polished parquet floor they saw two woolen coverings, two "shoes" that Charlotte had concocted herself. Crushed by all these stares, Charlotte lowered her head and involuntarily screwed up her toes inside the socks, as if she wanted to make her feet disappear. . . .

At that time they lived in an old *izba* on the outskirts of the town. Charlotte was no longer surprised to see her mother almost always stretched out upon a high peasant bed behind a curtain. When Albertine got up, the black shadows of dreams seethed in her eyes, even though they were open. She no longer even tried to smile at her daughter. She dipped a copper ladle into a bucket, drank deeply, and went out. Charlotte already knew that they had been surviving for a long time thanks to the glitter of a few jewels in the case with the mother-of-pearl inlaid work. . . .

She liked the *izba,* far from the fashionable districts of Boyarsk. Their poverty was less visible in these narrow, winding streets, buried under the snow. And it was so good, on returning from school, to climb up the old wooden steps that crunched under your feet; to pass through a dim entrance hall with walls made of great logs, which were covered in a thick coat of hoarfrost; and to push at the heavy door, which yielded with a brief, very lifelike groan. And there, in the room, one could remain for a moment without lighting the lamp, watching the little low window becoming suffused with the violet dusk, listening to snowy gusts of wind tinkling against the window-pane. Leaning back against the broad, hot flank of the big stove, Charlotte felt the heat slowly penetrating beneath her coat. She held her frozen hands to the warm stone — the stove seemed to her to be the enormous heart of this old *izba*. And beneath the soles of her felt boots the last lumps of ice were melting.

One day a splinter of ice broke beneath her feet unusually loudly. Charlotte was surprised — she had already been home a good half hour, all the snow on her coat and her *shapka* had long since melted and dried out. But this icicle . . . She bent down to pick it up. It was a splinter of glass! A very fine one, from a broken medical vial. . . .

It was thus that the terrible word *morphine* entered her life. It explained the silence behind the curtain, the seething shadows in her mother's eyes, a Siberia absurd and inevitable as fate.

Albertine no longer had anything to hide from her daughter. From now on it was Charlotte who would be seen going into the pharmacy and murmuring timidly, "It's for Madame Lemonnier's medicine. . . ."

She always returned home alone, crossing the vast wastelands that separated their cluster of houses from the last streets of the town, with its shops and lighting. Often a snowstorm would descend on these dead spaces. Tired of struggling against a wind laden with ice crystals, deafened by its whistling, one evening Charlotte stopped in the midst of this desert of snow, turning her back on the squalls, her gaze lost in the giddy flight of the snowflakes. She had an intense awareness of her own life, the warmth of her thin body concentrated into a minuscule "I." She felt the tickling of a drop that crept under the earflap of her *shapka,* and the beating of her heart, and next to her heart — the fragile presence of the vials she had just bought. "It's me," a muffled voice suddenly rang out inside her, "I, who am here in these snow squalls at the end of the world, in this Siberia, I, Charlotte Lemonnier; I, who have nothing in common with this barbarous place, not with this sky, nor with this frozen earth. Nor with these people. Here I am, all alone, taking morphine to my mother. . . ." It seemed as if her mind were reeling before tipping over into an abyss, where all this absurdity, suddenly perceived, would become natural. She shook herself. No, this Siberian desert must end somewhere, and at that place there was a city, with broad avenues lined with chestnut trees, lighted cafés, her uncle's apartment, and all those books that began with such dear words utterly beloved simply for the way their letters looked. There was France. . . .

The city with chestnut-lined avenues was transformed into a fine spangle of gold that glittered in her eyes, but nobody noticed. Charlotte could even glimpse its brilliance in the reflection of a beautiful brooch on the dress of a young lady with a capricious and haughty smile: she was sitting in a fine armchair in the middle of a large room with elegant furniture and silk cushions at the windows. "*La raison du plus fort est toujours meilleure*," recited the young woman in a pinched voice.

"*. . . est toujours la meilleure*," Charlotte corrected discreetly and, with lowered eyes, added, "It would be more correct to pronounce it '*meilleure*' and not '*meillaire.*' '*Meill-eu-eure.*'"

She rounded her lips and made the sound last until it was lost in a velvety "r." The young orator, with a sullen expression, resumed her declamation. This was the daughter of the governor of Boyarsk. Charlotte gave her French lessons every Wednesday. She had initially hoped that she might become the friend of this very well groomed adolescent, hardly older than herself. Now, no longer hoping for anything, she endeavored simply to give a good lesson. Her pupil's swift, scornful glances did not find their mark anymore. Charlotte listened to her, intervening from time to time, but her gaze was lost in the glitter of the beautiful amber brooch. Only the governor's daughter was allowed to wear an open-collared dress at school, with this adornment at its center. Conscientiously, Charlotte pointed out all the mistakes of pronunciation or grammar. And from the gilded depths of the amber arose a city with beautiful autumn foliage. She knew that for a whole hour she would have to bear the little grimaces of this great, plump, beautifully dressed child, and then, in the corner of the kitchen, receive from the hands of a maid her parcel, the leftovers from a meal; then she must wait in the street for a good opportunity to find herself alone with the pharmacist and murmur, "Madame Lemonnier's medicine, please. . . ." The little puff of warm air stolen at the pharmacy would quickly be driven from under her coat by the icy blast of the wastelands.

When Albertine appeared at the top of the steps the cabdriver raised his eyebrows and got up from his seat. He was not expecting this. The *izba,* with its sagging roof covered in moss; the worm-eaten flight of steps invaded by nettles. And especially not in this village, with its street buried under gray sand. . . .

The door opened, and in its twisted frame there appeared a woman. She wore a long, extremely elegantly cut dress, such as the cabdriver had only seen on the fine ladies coming out of the theater in the evening right at the center of Boyarsk. Her hair was gathered up in a chignon; it was crowned with a large hat. The springlike wind fluttered the veil that was thrown back on the broad, gracefully turned-up brim.

"We are going to the station!" she cried, further astonishing the taxi driver still more with the vibrant and very foreign resonance of her voice.

"To the station," repeated the little girl, who had just now hailed him in the street. She, on the other hand, spoke very good Russian, with a slight Siberian accent. . . .

Charlotte knew that Albertine's emergence at the top of the steps had been preceded by a long and painful battle, interrupted by several relapses — like the struggle of that man, battling in a black hole in the midst of the ice, which Charlotte had seen one day in spring, as she crossed the bridge. He clung to a long branch that was being pushed toward him and crawled up the slippery slope of the riverbank, sprawled flat on his stomach on the icy surface, progressing centimeter by centimeter, already stretching out his red hand, as he touched those of his rescuers. Suddenly, incomprehensibly, his body shuddered, started to slip, and fell back once more into the black water. The current dragged him a little farther. Everything had to begin again. . . . Yes, like that man.

But on that luminous and verdant summer's afternoon their actions were lightness itself. "What about the big suitcase?" cried Charlotte, when they were installed on the seats.

"We'll leave it. It only has old papers in it, and all those newspapers of your uncle's. . . . We'll come back one day to collect it."

They crossed the bridge, passing beside the governor's house. The Siberian town seemed to unfold like a strange past, where it was possible to forgive with a smile. . . .

Once they were settled in Paris again, it was with just such a lack of bitterness that they would look back on Boyarsk. And when that summer Albertine resolved to return to Russia (in order, as her family understood, to put a definitive end to the Siberian period of her life), Charlotte even showed a little jealousy toward her mother: she too would have liked to spend a couple of weeks in that town, now perceived as being inhabited by people from their past, where the houses, their *izba* among them, were turning into monuments to days gone by. A town where nothing could hurt her anymore.

"*Maman,* don't forget to look and see if there is still a nest of mice there. Beside the stove, remember?" she called to her mother as she stood at the lowered window of the railway carriage.

It was July 1914. Charlotte was eleven.

Her own life did not experience any interruption. It was simply that, as time went by, her last words ("Don't forget the mice!") seemed to her more and more stupid and childish. She ought to have kept silent and scrutinized the face at the carriage window, feasted her eyes on its features. Months, years, passed, and that last remark still carried the same resonance of a foolish happiness. Now the only time in Charlotte's life was waiting time.

That time ("in wartime," the newspapers wrote) was like a gray afternoon, a Sunday in the deserted streets of a provincial town: suddenly a gust of wind appears at the corner of a house, raising a whirlwind of dust; a shutter swings silently; a man melts easily into this colorless air, disappears without reason.

Thus it was that Charlotte's uncle disappeared — "fallen on the field of honor," "dead for France," according to the newspaper's formula. And this form of words made his absence all the more disconcerting — like the pencil sharpener on his desk, with a pencil inserted in the hole and several fine parings undisturbed since his departure. Thus it was that the house at Neuilly gradually emptied — women and men would bend down to kiss Charlotte and, with a very serious air, tell her to be a good girl.

That strange time had its capricious moments. All of a sudden, with the jerky rapidity of films, one of her aunts dressed herself in white and summoned her relatives, who gathered about her with all the speed of the cinema of that period. Then they headed off at a spanking pace to the church, where the aunt appeared beside a man with a mustache and sleek, oily hair. And almost at once — as Charlotte remembered it, they did not even have time to leave the church — the young bride was robed in black and unable to raise her eyes, which were weighed down with tears. The change was so rapid it seemed as if she had already been alone as she left the church, and dressed in full mourning, hiding her reddened eyes from the sun. The two days merged into one, colored by a radiant sky and enlivened by the church bells and the summer breeze, which seemed to accelerate the coming and going of the guests even more. And what the warm breeze pressed against the face of the young woman was a white bridal veil one moment and a widow's black veil the next.

Later this eerie time resumed its regular pace and was punctuated with sleepless nights and a long procession of mutilated bodies. The passing hours now echoed with the resonance of the big classrooms in the school at Neuilly, converted into a hospital. Her first knowledge of a man's body was the sight of male flesh, torn and bloody. . . . And the nocturnal sky of those years would be forever overhung with the pallid monstrosity of two German zeppelins among the luminous stalagmites of the searchlights.

Finally there came a day, on July 14, 1919, when countless columns of soldiers came marching through Neuilly, heading for the capital. Spick and span, with brave looks and well-polished army boots: war was resuming the guise of a parade. Was he among them, that warrior who was to slip a little brown pebble into Charlotte's hand, that shell splinter covered in rust? Were they lovers? Engaged?

This encounter did not alter Charlotte's decision, made several years earlier. At the first opportunity that came along, a miraculous opportunity, she left for Russia. There was still no communication with that country ravaged by civil war. It was 1921. A Red Cross mission was preparing to travel to the Volga region, where famine had claimed hundreds of thousands of victims. Charlotte was taken on as a nurse. Her application had been quickly accepted: volunteers for the expedition were rare. But above all, she spoke Russian.

Once over there she believed that she had come to know hell. In the distance it looked like peaceful Russian villages — *izbas,* wells, hedges — swathed in the mists of the great river. Close to, it froze into shots taken by the mission photographer in those somber days: a group of male and female peasants in lambskin greatcoats, transfixed before a heap of human carcasses, dismembered bodies, unrecognizable fragments of flesh. Then this naked child in the snow with long, tangled hair, an old man's piercing stare, and the body of an insect. Finally, on an icy road — that head, alone, with open eyes, glassy. Worst of all, these pictures did not remain fixed. The photographer folded up his tripod, and the peasants left, stopping outside the frame of the photo — that terrifying photo of the cannibals — and resumed the daily round of their lives with all its disconcerting simplicity. Yes, they continued living! A woman bent over the child and recognized him as her son. And she did not know what to do with this old-man-insect, she who for weeks had fed on human flesh. Then what could be heard arising from her throat was the howl of a wolf. No photo could capture that cry. . . . A peasant looked into the eyes of the head thrown down onto the road and sighed. Then he leaned over and with a clumsy hand thrust it into a great homespun sack. "I'll bury it," he muttered. "After all, we're not Tartars. . . ."

And you had to go into the *izbas* of this tranquil hell to discover that the old woman watching the street through the window was the mummified corpse of a girl who had died several weeks previously, seated at that window in the vain hope of rescue.

Once back in Moscow Charlotte left the mission. Walking out of the hotel, she plunged into the motley throng on the square and disappeared. At Sukharevka market, where barter was king, she exchanged a silver five-franc piece (the trader marked the coin with his molar, then made it ring on the blade of an ax) for two loaves of bread, which would provide for the first days of her journey. She was already dressed like a Russian, and at the station, in the violent and disorderly assault on the carriages, nobody paid any attention to this young woman hitching up her knapsack and fighting her way into the frenetic heavings of the human chaos.

She set off and she saw everything. She braved the country's endlessness, its fleeting space in which days and years are swallowed up. She went forward nonetheless, squelching through this stagnant time. By train, by farm cart, on foot . . .

She saw everything. Horses in harness, a whole herd of them, galloping riderless across a plain, stopping for a moment, then taking fright and resuming their mad race, both happy and fearful at their new-won liberty. One of these fugitives caught everyone's eye. A saber, deeply embedded in the saddle, stood erect upon its back. As the horse galloped, the long blade jammed into the thick leather swayed pliantly, glittering in the sinking sun. People kept their eyes fixed on the scarlet flashes, which gradually faded in the mist of the fields. They knew that this saber, its hilt filled with lead, must have cut a body in two — from shoulder to stomach — before becoming stuck in the leather. And the two halves had slipped off into the trampled grass, one each side.

She also saw dead horses being hauled out of wells. And new wells being dug in the thick, heavy earth. The timbers of the cage that the peasants lowered to the bottom of the pit smelled of fresh wood.

She saw a group of villagers, under the direction of a man in a black leather jacket, pulling on a thick rope wound round the cupola of a church, round the cross. The repeated cracking sounds seemed to fire their enthusiasm. And in another village, very early in the morning, she saw an old woman kneeling before the dome of a church cast down among the tombs of an unfenced cemetery, open to the fragile resonance of the fields.

She went through deserted villages where the orchards were glutted with overripe fruit, falling into the grass or withering on the bough. She stayed in a town where, one day at the market, a salesman mutilated a child who had tried to steal an apple from him. All the men she encountered seemed either to be rushing toward an unknown goal, mobbing trains, getting crushed on landing stages, or else waiting, one never knew for whom, before the closed doors of shops, at gates guarded by soldiers, and sometimes quite simply by the roadside.

The space she confronted knew no happy medium: incredible throngs of people would suddenly give way to a complete wilderness where the immensity of the sky and the depth of the forests made the presence of man unthinkable. Then without transition this emptiness would run into a ferocious jostling of peasants, slithering about on the muddy bank of a river, swollen by the autumn rains. That was something else Charlotte saw. Angry peasants with long poles pushing away a barge, from which arose an unceasing lament. On board could be seen silhouettes holding out their emaciated hands toward the shore. They were victims of typhus, abandoned, who had been drifting on their floating cemetery for several days. At each attempt to go ashore the bank dwellers mobilized to prevent them from doing so. The barge continued its funerary voyage; the people were dying from hunger now as well. Soon they would no longer have the strength to attempt a landing, and the last survivors, woken one day by the powerful and rhythmic sound of the waves, would behold the indifferent horizon of the Caspian Sea. . . .

At the edge of a wood, one glittering frosty morning, she saw shadows hanging from the trees, saw the emaciated rictuses of hanged men nobody had any thought of burying. And very high up, in the sunlit blue of the sky, a flock of migratory birds was slowly melting away, accentuating the silence with the echo of their noisy cries.

*   *   *

The heavy and syncopated breathing of this Russian world no longer terrified her. She had learned so much since she began her journey. She knew that in a railway carriage or on a farm wagon it was practical to carry a bag stuffed with straw, with a few pebbles right at the bottom. This was what the bandits would snatch in their nocturnal raids. She knew that the best place on the roof of a railway carriage was the one near the ventilation hole: it was to this opening that ropes were attached, which enabled you to get down and climb up again quickly. And when by good fortune she found a place in a crowded corridor, she would not be surprised to see a frightened child being passed from hand to hand toward the exit by the people piled on the ground floor. The ones crouched near the door would open it and hold the child above the footboard while it did its business. This passing down the line seemed rather to amuse them: they smiled, touched by this little creature wordlessly allowing itself to be handled in this way, moved by its very natural urge in this inhuman universe. . . . No surprise either when whispering was heard above the clatter of the rails in the night: they were communicating the death of a passenger, lost deep among this confusion of lives.

Only once in the course of this long journey, punctuated by suffering, blood, illness, mud, did she believe she had caught a glimpse of a modicum of serenity and wisdom. She had already reached the far side of the Urals. On the way out of a village half consumed by a fire she saw several men sitting on a bank scattered with dead leaves. Their pale faces, turned toward the mild late autumn sun, radiated a blissful calm. The peasant who was driving the cart jerked his head and explained softly, "Poor people, there are a dozen of them wandering round here now. Their asylum was burnt down. Oh, yes, madmen, you know."

Nothing could surprise her anymore, nothing.

Often, squeezed into the airless darkness of a railway carriage, she had a dream — brief, luminous, and completely improbable. For example, those enormous camels in falling snow, turning their disdainful heads toward a church as four soldiers emerged from the door, dragging behind them a priest who was admonishing them in a broken voice. The camels with snow-covered humps, the church, the gleeful crowd. . . . As she slept, Charlotte recalled that time was when such humped silhouettes would be inseparable from palm trees in the desert, oases. . . .

Then she emerged from her torpor: and it was not a dream! She was actually standing there in the midst of a noisy market in an unknown town. The heavy snow clung to her eyelashes. Passersby came up and felt the little silver medallion she was hoping to exchange for bread. The camels towered over the swarming traders, like strange *drakkar* ships mounted on stilts. And under the amused stares of the crowd the soldiers were pushing the priest along in a sledge stuffed with straw.

After that spurious dream the evening stroll she took was so ordinary, so real. She crossed a street with paving stones that shone by the misty light of a street lamp, pushed open the door of a baker's shop. Its warm, well-lit interior seemed familiar to her, right down to the color of the varnished wood of the counter and the arrangement of the cakes and chocolates in the window. The shopkeeper smiled kindly at her, as she would to a regular customer, and offered her a loaf. In the street Charlotte stopped, overcome with perplexity. She should have bought much more bread! Two, three, no, four loaves! She should have noted the name of the street where this excellent bakery was located. She approached the corner house and looked up. But the letters had an odd, hazy look: they merged into one another, twinkled. "Oh, how stupid I am!" she suddenly thought. "This is the street where my uncle lives. . . ."

She woke with a start. The train, stopped in open countryside, was filled with a confused hubbub: a gang had killed the driver and was currently working its way through the train, confiscating everything it could lay its hands on. Charlotte took off her shawl and covered her head, knotting the corners under her chin as old peasant women do. Then, still smiling at the memory of her dream, she placed on her lap a bag stuffed with old rags wrapped round a stone. . . .

And if she was spared during those two months of her journey, it was because the immense continent she was crossing was sated with blood. Death, for several years at least, was losing its attraction, becoming too banal and no longer worth the effort.

Charlotte walked through Boyarsk, the Siberian town of her childhood, without wondering if this was still a dream or reality. She felt too weak to think about it.

On the governor's house, above the entrance, hung a red flag. Two soldiers armed with guns were stamping their feet in the snow on either side of the door. . . . Some of the windows in the theater had been broken and blocked, for want of anything better, with pieces of scenery as reinforcement. Here one could see foliage covered with white blossom, probably from *The Cherry Orchard,* there the facade of a dacha. And above the gateway two workmen were engaged in stretching a long strip of red calico. "Everyone to the People's Meeting of the Atheists' Society!" Charlotte read, slowing her pace a little. One of the workmen took out a nail he was holding between clenched teeth and drove it in with force beside the exclamation mark.

"There you are, you see; all finished before nightfall, thank God!" he called to his comrade.

Charlotte smiled and continued on her way. No, she was not dreaming.

A soldier, posted near the bridge, barred her way and asked her to show him her papers. Charlotte obliged him. He took them and, probably being unable to read, decided to withhold them from her. He seemed, moreover, quite surprised himself by his own decision. "You can recover them from the Revolutionary Council after the necessary verifications," he announced, visibly repeating somebody else's words. Charlotte did not have the strength to argue.

Here at Boyarsk, winter had taken hold some time ago. But that day the air was mild, the ice under the bridge covered with large damp patches. First sign of thaw. And great lazy snowflakes fluttered down in the white silence of the wastelands she had crossed so many times in her childhood.

With its two narrow windows, the *izba* seemed to observe her from afar. Yes, the house was watching her approach, its wrinkled facade lit up with an imperceptible little grimace, with a bitter joy of reunion.

Charlotte hoped for little from this visit. For a long time she had prepared herself to receive the news that would leave no hope: death, madness, disappearance. Or a pure and simple absence, inexplicable, natural, surprising no one. She forbade herself to hope and hoped all the same.

In the last days her exhaustion had been such that she thought only of the warmth of the great stove, against whose flank she would lean her back as she collapsed on the floor.

From the *izba* steps she caught sight of an old woman underneath a stunted apple tree, her head muffled in a black shawl. Bent over, the woman was pulling at a thick branch buried in the snow. Charlotte called to her, but the old peasant woman did not turn round. Her voice was too weak and was quickly dissipated in the heavy air of the thaw. She felt incapable of uttering another sound.

With a thrust of her shoulder she pushed the door. In the dark, cold hall she saw a whole store of wood — planks from boxes, floorboards, and even, in a little black-and-white heap, the keys of a piano. Charlotte remembered that it was above all the pianos in the apartments of the rich that provoked the anger of the people. She had seen one, smashed with blows of an ax, frozen into the ice floes on a river. . . .

On entering the room, her first gesture was to touch the stones of the stove. They were warm. Charlotte felt a pleasantly giddy sensation. She was already about to let herself slip down beside the stove when she noticed an open book on the table made of broad timbers, browned with the years. A little ancient volume with rough paper. Leaning on a bench, she bent over the open pages. Strangely the letters began to dance, to melt — as they had done during that night on the train when she dreamed of the Parisian street where her uncle lived. This time the cause was not a dream, but tears. It was a French book.

The old woman in the black shawl came in and seemed not to be surprised to see this slim young woman rising from her bench.

The dry branches she carried under her arm trailed long filaments of snow on the floor. Her withered face resembled that of one of the old peasant women of that Siberian country. Her lips, covered in a fine network of wrinkles, trembled. And it was from this mouth, from the desiccated breast of this unrecognizable being, that the voice of Albertine rang out, a voice of which not a single note had altered.

"All these years I only dreaded one thing: that you might come back here!"

These were the very first words that Albertine addressed to her daughter. And Charlotte understood: what they had lived through since their good-byes on the station platform eight years before, a whole host of actions, faces, words, sufferings, privations, hopes, anxieties, cries, tears — all that buzz of life resounded against a single echo, which refused to die. This meeting, so desired, so feared.

"I wanted to ask someone to write to you and say I was dead. But there was the war, then the revolution. Then war again. And then . . ."

"I wouldn't have believed the letter. . . ."

"Yes, I told myself that you wouldn't have believed it in any case. . . ."

She threw down the branches near the stove and approached Charlotte. When she had looked at her through the lowered window of the railway carriage in Paris, her daughter was eleven. Now, soon she would be twenty.

"Do you hear?" whispered Albertine, her face lighting up, and she turned toward the stove. "The mice, you remember? They're still there. . . ."

Later, squatting in front of the fire that was coming to life behind the little cast iron door, Albertine murmured, as if to herself, without looking at Charlotte, who was stretched out on the bench and appeared to be asleep: "That's how it is in this country. You can come in easily but you never get out. . . ."

Hot water seemed like a whole new, unknown substance. Charlotte held out her hands toward the trickle that her mother poured slowly onto her shoulders and her back from a copper scoop. In the darkness of that room, which was lit only by the flame of a burning wood shaving, the warm drops looked like pine resin and tickled Charlotte's body deliciously as she rubbed herself with a lump of blue clay. Of soap they retained only a vague memory.

"You've become very thin," Albertine said softly, and her voice broke off.

Charlotte laughed gently. As she lifted her head of wet hair, she saw tears of the same amber color shining in her mother's lackluster eyes. During the days that followed Charlotte tried to find out how they could leave Siberia (superstitiously she dared not say, return to France). She went to the former house of the governor. The soldiers at the entrance smiled at her: a good sign? The secretary of the new ruler of Boyarsk made her wait in a little room — the same, thought Charlotte, where once she used to wait for the parcel of leftovers from lunch. . . .

The ruler received her seated behind his heavy desk: as she came in his brows were furrowed, and he continued to draw energetic lines with a red pencil on the pages of a brochure. A whole stack of identical little pamphlets was piled on his table.

"Good day, citizen!" he said finally, holding out his hand to her.

They spoke. And with stunned incredulity Charlotte became aware that all the official's remarks seemed like a strange, deformed echo of the questions she put to him. She spoke of the French Aid Committee and heard, in echo, a brief speech about the imperialist designs of the West under the cover of bourgeois philanthropy. She referred to their desire to return to Moscow, and then . . . the echo interrupted her: foreign interventionist forces and internal class enemies were engaged in undermining reconstruction in the young Soviet republic. . . .

After a quarter of an hour of such exchanges Charlotte longed to shout, "I want to leave! That's all!" But the absurd logic of this conversation would not loosen its grip.

"A train to Moscow . . ."

"The sabotage of bourgeois specialists on the railways. . . ."

"The poor state of health of my mother . . ."

"The horrible economic and cultural inheritance of tsarism . . ."

Finally, exhausted, she whispered weakly, "Listen, please return my papers to me. . . ."

The administrator's voice seemed to hit an obstacle. A rapid spasm crossed his face. He left his office without saying anything. Profiting from his absence, Charlotte glanced at the pile of brochures. The title plunged her into extreme perplexity: "Eradicating Sexual Laxity in Party Cells (recommendations)." So it was the recommendations that the administrator had been underlining in red pencil.

"We haven't found your papers," he said, coming in.

Charlotte pressed him. What happened then was as unbelievable as it was logical. The leader vomited forth such a torrent of oaths that even after two months spent on crowded trains, she was shattered by it. He continued to shout at her while she already had her hand on the door handle. Then, suddenly bringing his face close to hers, he hissed, "I could arrest you and shoot you right there in the courtyard behind the shithouse! D'you understand, filthy spy!"

On her return, walking through the snow-covered fields, Charlotte told herself that a new language was in the process of being born in this country. A language that she did not know, and that was why the dialogue in the former governor's office had seemed to her incredible. But everything had its meaning: even the revolutionary eloquence that suddenly slid into gutter language; even his "citizen-spy"; and even the pamphlet regulating the sexual lives of party members. Yes, a new order of things was being established. Everything in this world, albeit so familiar, was going to acquire a new name; they were going to apply a different label to each object, to each being.

"And what about this lazy snow," she thought, "the thaw with its sleepy flakes in the mauve evening sky?" She recalled that as a child she was always happy to find the snow again when she came out into the street after her lesson with the governor's daughter. "Like to-day . . ." she said to herself, taking a deep breath.

A few days later life became frozen. One clear night polar cold descended from the sky. The world was transformed into a crystal of ice, within which were encrusted the trees bristling with rime; the still, white columns above the chimneys; the silvery line of the taiga stretching to the horizon; and the sun surrounded by a halo of moiré. The human voice no longer carried; its vapor froze on the lips.

Now they thought only of survival from day to day, by keeping a tiny zone of warmth around their bodies.

It was above all the *izba* that saved them. Everything in it had been conceived to resist endless winters, bottomless nights. Even the wood of the great logs was imbued with the harsh experience of several generations of Siberians. Albertine had sensed the secret breathing of this ancient dwelling, had learned to live closely in tune with the slow warmth of the great stove that occupied half the room, with its very vital silence. And Charlotte, observing her mother's daily actions, often said to herself with a smile, "But she's a true Siberian!" From the first day she had noticed the bundles of dried plants in the hall. These reminded her of the bouquets that Russians use at the baths to beat themselves with. It was when the last slice of bread was eaten that she discovered the true function of those sheaves. Albertine soaked one in hot water, and that evening they drank what they were later, jokingly, to call "Siberian soup" — a mixture of stems, grains, and roots. "I am beginning to know the plants of the taiga by heart," said Albertine, pouring this soup into their plates. "Indeed I wonder why the people here make so little use of them. . . ."

What saved them was also the presence of the child, the little tzigane whom they found one day, half frozen, on their doorstep. She was scratching the hardened planks of the door with her numb fingers, purple with cold. . . . To feed her Charlotte did what she would never have done for herself. At the market she could be seen begging: an onion, a few frozen potatoes, a piece of pork. She rummaged in the rubbish tank next to the party canteen, not far from the place where the ruler had threatened to shoot her. She found herself unloading railway trucks for a loaf of bread. The child, skeletal to begin with, hovered for several days on the fragile borderline between light and extinction. Then slowly, with a hesitant astonishment, slipped once more into the extraordinary flow of days, words, and smells that everyone called life. . . .

In March, on a day filled with sun and the crunching of snow under the feet of passersby, a woman (her mother? her sister?) came looking for her and, without any explanation, took her away. Charlotte caught up with them on the way out of the village and held out to the child the big doll with flaking cheeks with which the little tzigane had played during the long winter evenings. . . . This doll had originally come from Paris and remained, along with the old newspapers in the "Siberian suitcase," one of the last relics of their former life.

The real famine, Albertine knew, would come in the spring. . . . There was not a single bunch of plants left on the walls of the entrance hall, the market was deserted. In May they fled their *izba,* without really knowing where to go. They walked along a path still heavy with springtime humidity and bent down from time to time to pick fine shoots of sorrel.

It was a kulak who accepted them as day laborers on his farm. He was a strong, lean Siberian with his face half hidden by a beard, through which a few rare words emerged, terse and absolute.

"I'll not pay you anything," he said, making no bones about it. "Bed and board. If I take you on, it's not for your pretty faces. I need hands."

They had no choice. During the first days, on returning, Charlotte would collapse flat out on her pallet, her hands covered with burst blisters. Albertine, who sewed sacks for the coming harvest all day, looked after her as best she could. One evening Charlotte's tiredness was such that, when she met the owner of the farm, she started speaking to him in French. The peasant's beard was stirred with a profound movement, his eyes widened — he was smiling.

"Right, tomorrow you can rest. If your mother wants to go into the town, go ahead. . . ." He took several steps, then turned: "The young people in the village dance every evening, you know. Go and see them if you like. . . ."

As agreed, the peasant paid them nothing. In the autumn, when they were preparing to go back to the town, he showed them a cart with a load covered in a newly homespun cloth.

"He'll drive you," he said, glancing at the old peasant perched on the driver's seat.

Albertine and Charlotte thanked him and hauled themselves up on the edge of the cart, which was laden with crates, sacks, and packages.

"Are you sending all this to market?" asked Charlotte, to fill the awkward silence of these last few minutes.

"No. That's what you've earned."

They had no time to reply. The driver tugged on the reins, the cart pitched and began to move off in the hot dust of the farm track. . . . Beneath the cover Charlotte and her mother discovered three sacks of potatoes, two sacks of corn, a keg of honey, four enormous pumpkins, and several crates of vegetables, beans, and apples. In one corner they caught sight of half a dozen hens with their legs tied; and a cock in their midst, flashing belligerent and angry glances.

"I'm going to dry some bunches of herbs all the same," said Albertine, when she finally succeeded in tearing her eyes from all this treasure. "You never know. . . ."

She died two years later. It was an August evening, calm and transparent. Charlotte was returning from the library, where she had been employed to sort through the mountains of books collected from demolished aristocratic homes. . . . Her mother was seated on a little bench fixed to the wall of the *izba,* her head leaning against the smooth wood of the logs. Her eyes were closed. She must have dozed off and died in her sleep. A light breeze coming from the taiga stirred the pages of the book open on her knees. It was the same little French volume with gilt edges.

They were married in the spring of the following year. He came from a village on the White Sea coast, ten thousand leagues from this Siberian town the civil war had brought him to. Charlotte noticed very quickly that his pride in being a "people's judge" was mingled with a vague unease, whose origin he himself could not have explained at the time. At the wedding supper one of the guests proposed that the death of Lenin be commemorated by one minute's silence. Everyone stood up. . . . Three months after the marriage he was posted to the other end of the empire, to Bukhara. Charlotte was absolutely set on taking the great suitcase filled with old French newspapers. Her husband had nothing against this, but on the train, ill concealing his obstinate unease, he gave her to understand that a frontier more impenetrable than any known mountain range you cared to mention would arise now between her French life and their life. He tried to find the words to express what would soon seem so natural: the iron curtain.

·

6

*C*AMELS IN A SNOWSTORM; frosts that froze the sap in the trees and caused their trunks to burst; Charlotte's numb hands catching huge logs thrown down from the top of a railway truck. . . .

It was thus in our smoke-filled kitchen, during the long winter evenings, that this legendary past was reborn. Outside the snow-covered window there stretched one of the greatest cities in Russia as well as the gray plain of the Volga; out there arose the fortress-buildings of Stalinist architecture. And inside, amid the chaos of an interminable meal and the iridescent tobacco clouds, the shade of this mysterious Frenchwoman, lost beneath the Siberian sky, made its appearance. The television was pouring out the news of the day, transmitting the sessions of the latest Party congress, but this background noise did not make the slightest impact on the conversations of our guests.

Squatting in a corner of this crowded kitchen, with my shoulder against the shelves on which the television was enthroned, I listened to them avidly while trying to make myself invisible. I knew that soon the face of an adult would loom up through the blue fog, and I should hear a cry of simulated indignation: "Hey, just look at him, the little sleepwalker! It's past midnight and he's still not in bed. Go on, off you go! Stir your stumps! We'll send for you when you've grown a beard. . . ."

Banished from the kitchen, I found it hard to get to sleep right away, fascinated by the question that kept returning to my young mind: "Why are they so keen on talking about Charlotte?"

At first I thought I understood why this Frenchwoman was an ideal topic of conversation for my parents and their guests. For it only took memories of the last war to be mentioned for an argument to break out. My father, who had spent four years at the front in the infantry, attributed the victory to those troops mired in the earth who, in his phrase, had irrigated this earth with their blood, from Stalingrad to Berlin. His brother, without wishing to upset him, would then observe that, "as everyone knows," the artillery was the ruling goddess of modern war. The debate would become heated. Little by little the artillerymen would find themselves being labeled "funks," and the infantry, on account of the mud on the roads in war, became the "infectionary." It would be at this moment that their best friend, an ex–fighter pilot, would intervene with his own arguments, and the conversation would plunge into an extremely perilous nosedive. And that was before they went into the respective merits of the fronts they had been on, all three different; let alone the role of Stalin during the war. . . .

This arguing, I sensed, pained them greatly. For they knew that, whatever their own part in the victory had been, the die was cast: their own generation, decimated, massacred, would soon disappear, along with the foot soldier, the gunner, and the pilot. And my mother would precede even them, in accordance with the fate of children born at the beginning of the twenties. At fifteen I would be left alone with my sister. It was as if in their arguments there was an unspoken foreknowledge of this immediate future. . . . Charlotte's life, I believed, reconciled them, offering a neutral territory.

But as I grew older I began to detect quite a different reason for this French predilection in their interminable discussions. It was that Charlotte's advent under the Russian sky was like that of an extraterrestrial being. The cruel history of this immense empire, of its famines, its revolutions, its civil war, was nothing to do with her. . . . We Russians had no choice. But she? Through her eyes they could observe a country they did not recognize, because judged by a foreigner, sometimes naive, often more perspicacious than themselves. Charlotte's eyes reflected a disturbing world where unforced truth abounded — an unfamiliar Russia that they needed to discover.

*   *   *

I listened to them, and I too discovered Charlotte's Russian destiny, but in my own way. Certain details, hardly mentioned, became magnified in my mind and created a whole secret universe. Other events, to which the adults attached considerable importance, passed unnoticed.

Thus, strangely, the horrible images of cannibalism in the villages of the Volga affected me very little. I had just read *Robinson Crusoe,* and Man Friday's fellow countrymen with their joyful rites of anthropophagy had inoculated me, through fiction, against real atrocities.

And the feature of Charlotte's rural past that made the greatest impression on me was not the hard labor at the farm. What I remembered above all was her visit to the young people of the village. She had gone to see them that very evening and had found them engaged in a metaphysical discussion: the topic was what kind of death would befall someone who dared to go to the cemetery on the dot of midnight. Charlotte had smiled and said she was capable of confronting all supernatural powers among the tombs that night. Distractions were few and far between. The young people, secretly hoping for some macabre outcome, had saluted her courage with tumultuous enthusiasm. They only needed to find an object that this harebrained Frenchwoman could leave on one of the tombs in the village cemetery. And it was not easy. For everything that had been proposed could be replaced by a duplicate: scarf, stone, coin. . . . Yes, the wily foreigner could very well go there at dawn and hang up this shawl while everyone else slept. No, a unique object had to be chosen. . . . Next morning what an entire delegation had found, hanging from a cross in the shadiest corner of the cemetery, was "the little Pont-Neuf bag."

It was in picturing this woman's handbag amid the crosses, under the Siberian sky, that I began to have a feeling for the incredible destiny of things. They traveled; beneath their commonplace exterior they logged the different periods of our lives, linking moments that were very far apart.

As for the marriage of my grandmother to the people's judge, doubtless I did not notice all the historical piquancies that the adults could detect in this. Charlotte's love, my grandfather's courtship of her, the couple they made, so unusual in that Siberian country — of all that I grasped only a fragment. Fyodor, his tunic well pressed, his boots gleaming, makes his way toward the place for their crucial rendezvous. A few paces behind him his clerk, the young son of a priest, conscious of the gravity of the moment, walks slowly, carrying an enormous bunch of roses. A people's judge, even when in love, must not look like a mere operatic suitor. Charlotte sees them from afar, understands at once the scene that has been prepared, and with a mischievous smile accepts the bouquet that Fyodor takes from the hands of the clerk. The latter, intimidated but curious, backs away.

Or perhaps this fragment as well: the one and only wedding photo (all the others, those in which my grandfather appeared, would be confiscated at the time of his arrest): their two faces, slightly inclined toward one another, and on the lips of an incredibly young and beautiful Charlotte the smiling reflection of the *"petite pomme"* . . .

Furthermore, in those long nocturnal narratives, all was not always clear to my childish ears. That sudden rush of blood to the head of Charlotte's father, for example . . . One day this respectable and wealthy doctor learns from one of his patients, a senior official in the police, that the big demonstration by workers, which at any minute was about to spill onto the main square at Boyarsk, would be met at one of the crossroads with machine-gun fire. As soon as his patient has left, Dr. Lemonnier removes his white coat and, without summoning his driver, leaps into his carriage and hurtles through the streets to warn the workers.

The massacre did not take place. . . . And I often wondered why this "bourgeois," this privileged man, had acted thus. We were accustomed to seeing the world in black and white: the rich and the poor, the exploiters and the exploited — in a word, the class enemies and the just. Charlotte's father's action confused me. Out of the mass of humanity, so conveniently divided into two, suddenly arose a man, with his unpredictable liberty.

Nor did I understand what had happened at Bukhara. I guessed only that it was a terrible occurrence. It was surely not by chance that the adults only hinted at it, shaking their heads eloquently. It was a kind of taboo, which their narrative skirted around by describing the setting in the following way. First I saw a river flowing over smooth pebbles, then a path running beside the endless desert. And the sun began to dance in Charlotte's eyes, and her cheek was inflamed with the burning of the sand, and the heavens resounded with a neighing. . . . The scene, the sense of which I did not understand but whose physical density I entered, was blotted out. The adults sighed, changed the subject, and poured themselves another glass of vodka.

In the end I sensed that this event, which had occurred in the sands of Central Asia, had marked our family's history forever in a mysterious and very intimate fashion. I also noticed that it was never spoken of when Charlotte's son, my uncle Sergei, was among the guests. . . .

The truth is that if I spied on these nocturnal confidences it was, above all, to explore my grandmother's French past. The Russian side of her life interested me less. I was like that investigator who, in examining a meteorite, is primarily attracted by the little gleaming crystals embedded in its basalt surface. And just as one dreams of a distant journey whose goal is yet unknown, so I dreamed of Charlotte's balcony, of her Atlantis, where I believed I had left a part of myself the previous summer.

2

7

THAT SUMMER I FELT EXTREMELY nervous about encountering the tsar again. . . . Yes, of seeing the young emperor and his wife once more in the streets of Paris. Just as you dread meeting a friend whose doctor has informed you of his imminent death and who, in blissful ignorance, proceeds to tell you all about his plans.

For how could I have traveled with Nicholas and Alexandra if I knew them to be doomed? If I knew that even their daughter Olga would not be spared? And that even the other children, to whom Alexandra had not yet given birth, would meet the same tragic fate?

I was secretly overjoyed that evening when I caught sight of a little collection of poems on my grandmother's lap that she was leafing through as she sat amid the flowers upon her balcony. Had she sensed my unease, remembering the incident of the previous summer? Or did she simply want to read us one of her favorite poems?

I came to sit beside her on the floor itself, resting my elbow on the head of the stone bacchante. My sister stood on the other side, leaning on the handrail, her gaze lost in the warm mist of the steppes.

Charlotte's voice was lyrical as the lines demanded:

> There is a tune, for which I'd gladly part
> With all Rossini, Weber, and Mozart,
> An ancient air, whose languid melody
> Has secret charms that speak only to me . . .

The magic of this poem by Nerval conjured up out of the evening shadows a castle of the time of Louis XIII and the chatelaine, "Fair with dark eyes, in robe of ancient style.". . .

It was then that my sister's voice roused me from my poetic reverie: "And Félix Faure, what became of him?"

She was still standing there, at the corner of the balcony, leaning lightly over the handrail. With absentminded gestures from time to time she plucked at a faded morning glory bloom and tossed it away, watching its gyrations in the nocturnal air. Lost in her young girl's dreams, she had not listened to the reading of the poem. It was the summer of her fifteenth year. . . . Why had she thought about the president? Probably this handsome and imposing man with an elegant mustache and great calm eyes suddenly became a focus, through some capricious play of her amorous daydreams, for her pictured reality of a man's presence. And she asked in Russian — as if better to express the disturbing mystery of this secretly desired presence — "And Félix Faure, what became of him?"

Charlotte threw me a rapid glance with a hint of a smile. Then she closed the book she was holding in her lap, sighed softly, and looked into the distance, toward that horizon where the previous year we had seen Atlantis emerging.

"Some years after the visit of Nicholas II to Paris, the president died. . . ." There was a brief hesitation, an involuntary pause, which only served to increase our attentiveness. "He died suddenly, at the Elysée Palace. In the arms of his mistress, Marguerite Steinheil. . . ."

It was this sentence that sounded the death knell for my childhood. "He died in the arms of his mistress. . . ."

I was overwhelmed by the tragic beauty of these words. A whole new world swept over me.

What struck me above all about this revelation was the setting: this scene of love and death had been played out at the Elysée! At the presidential palace! At the pinnacle of that pyramid of power, of glory, of world fame. . . . I pictured a sumptuous room with tapestries, gilt, rows of mirrors. In the midst of this luxury — a man (the president of the Republic!) and a woman, united in an ardent embrace. . . .

Dumbfounded, I began unconsciously to translate the scene into Russian. That is, to replace the French protagonists with their national equivalents. A series of phantoms, looking cramped in their black suits, appeared before my eyes. Secretaries of the Politburo, masters of the Kremlin: Lenin, Stalin, Khrushchev, Brezhnev. Four very different characters, loved or detested by the population, each of whom had put his stamp on a whole epoch in the history of the empire. Yet they all had one quality in common: at their sides a feminine presence, let alone an amorous one, was inconceivable. It was far easier for us to imagine Stalin in the company of someone like Churchill at Yalta, or with Mao in Moscow, than to picture him with the mother of his children. . . .

"The president died at the Elysée Palace, in the arms of his mistress, Marguerite Steinheil. . . ." This sentence seemed like a coded message coming from another planetary system.

Charlotte went to the Siberian suitcase to look for some of the newspapers of the period, hoping to be able to show us a photo of Madame Steinheil. While I, embroiled in my erotic Franco-Russian translation, recalled a remark that I had heard one evening on the lips of a gangling dunce, a fellow pupil. We were walking along the dark corridors at school after a session of weight lifting, the only subject at which he excelled. Passing the portrait of Lenin, my companion had given a low whistle in a most disrespectful manner and had observed, "You know old Lenin. He didn't have any children, did he? 'Cause he just didn't know how to make love. . . ."

He had used an extremely coarse verb to refer to the sexual activity in which, according to him, Lenin was deficient. A verb I should never have dared to use and which, applied to Vladimir Ilyich, became a monstrous obscenity. Taken aback, I heard the echo of this iconoclastic verb resounding in the long empty corridor. . . .

"Félix Faure . . . the president of the Republic . . . in the arms of his mistress . . ." More than ever Atlantis-France seemed to me a terra incognita where our Russian notions no longer had any currency.

The death of Félix Faure made me aware of my age: I was thirteen; I guessed what "dying in the arms of a woman" meant, and from now on I could be spoken to on such subjects. Furthermore, the courage and total absence of hypocrisy in Charlotte's story demonstrated what I already knew: she was not a grandmother like the others. No Russian babushka would have ventured on such a discussion with her grandson. In this freedom of expression I sensed an unaccustomed perception of the body, of love, of relationships between man and woman — a mysterious "French outlook."

Next morning I went out onto the steppe to brood alone on the fabulous transmutation effected in my life by the death of the president. To my great surprise, rerun in Russian, the scene no longer made a good story. In fact it was impossible to tell! Censored by an inexplicable modesty of words, revised, all of a sudden, by a strange offended morality, when finally told, it swung between pathological obscenity and euphemisms that transformed the pair of lovers into characters in a badly translated sentimental novel.

"No," I said to myself, stretched out in the rippling grass under the warm wind, "it is only in French that he could die in the arms of Marguerite Steinheil. . . ."

Thanks to the lovers of the Elysée Palace, I now grasped the mystery of that young serving maid who, surprised in the bath by her master, gave herself to him with all the terror and fever of a dream finally realized. Yes, before that there had been this bizarre trio I had come across in a novel by Maupassant that I had read in the spring. Throughout the book a Parisian dandy desired the inaccessible love of a female creature, an amalgam of decadent refinements. He sought to gain entry to the heart of this cerebral, indolent courtesan, who was like a fragile orchid, and who always left him to hope in vain. And alongside them — the serving maid, the young woman in her bath with her robust and healthy body. At first reading all I could see was this triangle, which seemed to me artificial and lifeless: for how could the two women even consider one another as rivals . . . ?

From now on I beheld the Parisian trio with new eyes. They became concrete, flesh, palpable — they were alive! I now recognized the blissful dread that caused the young servant maid to shiver when snatched from the bath and carried, all wet, to a bed. I sensed the tickling of the drops meandering over her full breasts, the weight of her haunches in the arms of the man; I even saw the rhythmic stirring of the water in the bath from which her body had just been lifted. Gradually the water grew calm. . . . And the other, the inaccessible *mondaine,* who had previously reminded me of a dried flower between the pages of a book, now revealed an opaque, subterranean sensuality. Her body contained a perfumed warmth, a disturbing fragrance, made up of the throbbing of her blood, the polish of her skin, the alluring languor of her speech.

The fatal love that had caused the heart of the president to burst reshaped the France that I carried inside me. This came mainly from storybooks. But on that memorable evening the literary characters who rubbed shoulders on its highways seemed to be awakening after a long sleep. Before that — however much they had waved their swords, climbed rope ladders, swallowed arsenic, declared their love, traveled in carriages while holding the severed head of their beloved on their knees — they never escaped from their world of fiction. Exotic, brilliant, comic perhaps, they did not move me. Like that curé in Flaubert, the country priest to whom Emma Bovary confessed her torments, I had not been able to understand the woman either: "But what more can she desire, she who has a beautiful house, an industrious husband, and the respect of her neighbors . . . ?"

The Elysée lovers helped me to understand *Madame Bovary.* In a flash of intuition I seized on this detail: the plump fingers of the hairdresser deftly tugging and smoothing Emma's hair. In the cramped salon the air is heavy, the light from the candles that banishes the evening darkness is hazy. This woman, seated before the mirror, has just left her young lover and is now preparing to return home. Yes, I guessed what an adulterous woman might feel in the evening, at the hairdresser's, between the last kiss of a rendezvous at the hotel and the first, very ordinary words that must be addressed to the husband. . . . Without being able to explain it myself, I felt as if I heard a string vibrating in the soul of this woman. My own heart sang out in unison. A smiling voice that came from Charlotte's stories prompted me: *"Emma Bovary, c'est moi!"*

*   *   *

Time passed in our Atlantis according to its own laws. To be precise, it did not pass but rippled around each event described by Charlotte. Each fact, even perfectly accidental ones, became encrusted forever in the daily life of that country. A comet was always crossing its night sky, even though our grandmother, consulting a press cutting, gave us the precise date of this sudden apparition in the heavens: October 17, 1882. We could not picture the Eiffel Tower without seeing the mad Austrian who had leaped from its jagged spire, whose parachute had failed him and who crashed in the midst of a gawking crowd. For us the Père Lachaise was far from being a tranquil cemetery, animated only by the respectful whispers of a few tourists. Not a bit of it: armed men ran among the tombs in all directions, exchanging gun-shots and hiding behind the funerary monuments. Recounted to us once, this battle between the Communards and the Versailles govern-ment troops was forever associated in our minds with the name Père Lachaise. Furthermore we also heard the echo of this shoot-out in the catacombs of Paris. For according to Charlotte, they did battle in those labyrinths too, with bullets shattering the skulls of the dead of several centuries. And if the night sky above Atlantis was lit by the comet and by German zeppelins, the clear blue of day was filled with the regular chirring of a monoplane: a certain Louis Blériot was crossing the channel.

The choice of events was more or less subjective. Their se-quence was chiefly governed by our feverish desire to know, by our random questions. But whatever significance, they never escaped the general rule: the chandelier that fell from the ceiling during the per-formance of *Faust* at the Opéra immediately unleashed its crystalline explosion in all the auditoriums of Paris. For us real theater implied a light tinkling from an enormous glass cluster, ripe enough to be-come detached from the ceiling at the sound of a musical flourish or an alexandrine. . . . And as for real Parisian circus, we knew that the lion tamer was always torn apart by wild beasts, like the "Negro called Delmonico" who was attacked by his seven lionesses.

Charlotte sometimes drew this information from the Siberian suitcase, sometimes from her childhood memories. A number of her stories went back to a still earlier age, related by her uncle or by Albertine, who themselves had inherited them from their parents.

But for us the exact chronology mattered little! Time in Atlantis knew only the marvelous simultaneity of the present. The vibrant baritone of Faust filled the auditorium: "Let me gaze, let me gaze on the form before me . . ."; the chandelier fell; the lionesses hurled themselves at the unfortunate Delmonico; the comet cut through the night sky; the parachutist took off from the Eiffel Tower; two thieves, taking advantage of the summer season carelessness, walked out of the Louvre at night, carrying off the *Mona Lisa;* Prince Borghese stuck out his chest, filled with pride at having won the first Peking–Paris via Moscow car race . . . And somewhere in the half-light of a discreet salon at the Elysée a man with a fine white mustache enfolded his mistress in his arms and suffocated in this last embrace.

This present tense, this time in which actions were repeated indefinitely, was of course an optical illusion. But it was thanks to this illusory perception that we discovered several essential character traits in the inhabitants of our Atlantis. The streets of Paris, in our stories, were constantly shaken by bomb explosions. The anarchists who threw them must have been as numerous as the grisettes or the coachmen in their cabs. For me the names of some of these enemies of the social order will for a long time evoke the roar of an explosion or the sound of gunfire: Ravachol, Sante Caserio . . .

Yes, it was in these tempestuous streets that one of the peculiarities of this people became clear to us: they were always busy making demands; never content with the status quo already achieved; ready at any moment to surge into the thoroughfares of their city, to unseat, to agitate, to insist. In the perfect social calm of our own fatherland these Frenchmen had the look of born rebels, dedicated demonstrators, professional moaners. And the Siberian suitcase containing newspapers that spoke of strikes, assassination attempts, and fights on the barricades seemed itself to be like a great bomb ticking away amid the somnolent tranquillity of Saranza.

And then a few streets further on from the explosions, still in this present, which never passed away, we came upon a quiet little bistro, the name of which Charlotte spelled out to us, smilingly, as she recalled it: Au Ratafia de Neuilly. "This ratafia," she would elaborate, "the patron served it in silver scallop dishes. . . ."

So the people of our Atlantis could feel sentimental attachment to a café, love its name, and discern an atmosphere that was special to it. And for their whole lives retain the memory that it was there, at the corner of a street, that one drank ratafia from silver scallop dishes. Yes, not from thick tumblers, nor from goblets, but from these fine dishes. It was our new discovery: this occult science that linked the place of refreshments, the ritual of the meal, and its psychological tonality.

"In their minds, do their favorite bistros have a soul?" we wondered, "or at least a face of their own?"

There was only one café in Saranza. Despite its pretty name, Snowflake, it did not arouse any special emotion in us, any more than the furniture shop next door or the savings bank opposite. It closed at eight o'clock in the evening, and then it was its dark interior, with the blue eye of a nightlight, which inspired our curiosity. And as for the five or six restaurants in the city on the Volga where our family lived, they were all identical: at seven o'clock precisely the doorkeeper opened the doors to an impatient crowd; and a combination of earsplitting music and the smell of burned fat spilled into the street; at eleven o'clock the same crowd, muted and fuddled, streamed out onto the front steps, near which a flashing police light added a note of fantasy to this immutable rhythm. . . .

"The silver scallop dishes *au Ratafia de Neuilly*," we repeated to ourselves silently.

Charlotte explained the composition of this unusual drink to us. Her account very naturally brought us to the universe of wines. And it was there, enthralled by a colorful tide of *appellations,* aromas, and bouquets, that we became acquainted with these extraordinary entities, each with their nuances that the palate could distinguish. And this too was the work of these builders of barricades! Thinking about the labels on a few bottles displayed on the shelves of the Snowflake, we had to admit that they were all French names: *Shampanskoye, Konyak, Silvaner, Aligoté, Muskat, Kahor. . . .*

Yes, most of all it was this contradiction that left us perplexed: that these anarchists had managed to elaborate such a coherent and complex system of drinks. And what is more, all these innumerable wines, according to Charlotte, formed infinite combinations with cheeses! And the latter in their turn added up to a veritable cheese encyclopedia of tastes, of local colors, of individual humors, almost. . . . Rabelais, who often haunted our evenings on the steppes, had not lied.

We were discovering that a meal, yes, the simple intake of food, could become a theatrical production, a liturgy, an art. As at the Café Anglais on the boulevard des Italiens, where Charlotte's uncle often dined with his friends. It was he who told his niece the story of that incredible bill of ten thousand francs for a hundred . . . frogs! "It was very cold," he recalled; "all the rivers were covered in ice. They had to summon fifty workmen to disembowel that glacier and find the frogs. . . ." I did not know what amazed us most: this unimaginable dish, contrary to all our own gastronomic notions, or the regiment of muzhiks (which is how we pictured them) busy splitting blocks of ice on the frozen Seine.

In truth, we were beginning to lose our heads: the Louvre; *Le Cid* at the Comédie-Française; the barricades; the shoot-out in the catacombs; the Académie Française; the deputies in a boat; and the comet; and the chandeliers, falling one after the other; and the Niagara of wines; and the president's last embrace . . . And the frogs disturbed in their winter sleep! We were up against a people with a fabulous multiplicity of sentiments, attitudes, and viewpoints, as well as manners of speaking, creating, and loving.

And then there was also the celebrated chef, Urbain Dubois, Charlotte told us, who had dedicated a shrimp and asparagus soup to Sarah Bernhardt. This obliged us to picture a borscht being dedicated to someone, like a book. . . . One day we followed a young dandy through the streets of Atlantis; he walked into Chez Weber, a very fashionable café, according to Charlotte's uncle. He ordered what he always ordered: a bunch of grapes and a glass of water. It was Marcel Proust. We contemplated the grapes and the water, which, under our fascinated gaze, became transformed into fare of unequaled elegance. So it was not the variety of wines or the Rabelaisian abundance of food that counted, but . . .

We thought again about that French spirit, the mystery of which we strove to fathom. And Charlotte, as if she desired to make our investigations even more frenzied, was already telling us about the Restaurant Paillard on the rue de la Chaussée d'Antin, where the princesse de Caraman-Chimay eloped one evening with the Gypsy violinist Rigo. . . .

Without daring to believe it yet, I asked myself a silent question: might not this much-sought-after French quintessence have as its source — love? For all roads in our Atlantis seemed to lead to the domain of Cupid.

Saranza was sinking into the aromatic night of the steppes. Its scents were mingled with the perfume that embalmed a woman's body swathed in precious stones and ermine. Charlotte was telling of the escapades of the divine Otero. With incredulous astonishment I contemplated this last great courtesan, all curves on her couch with its capricious shapes. Her extravagant life was devoted only to love. And around this throne buzzed men — some counting the last few louis d'or of their lost fortunes, others slowly raising the barrels of their revolvers to their temples. And even in this final gesture they could display an elegance worthy of Proust's bunch of grapes. One of these unhappy lovers committed suicide on the very spot where he had first set eyes on Caroline Otero!

In this exotic country, moreover, the cult of love knew no social boundaries: far from the boudoirs brimming with luxury, over in the working-class suburb of Belleville, we saw two rival gangs kill one another because of a woman. Sole difference: the beautiful Otero's locks had the sheen of a raven's wing, while the tresses of this disputed lover glowed like ripe corn in the setting sun. The bandits of Belleville called her *"Casque d'or."*

At that moment our critical sense rebelled. We were prepared to believe in the existence of frog eaters, but fancy gangsters slitting one another's throats over a woman's pretty face!

Clearly this was nothing surprising for our Atlantis. Had we not already seen Charlotte's uncle staggering as he emerged from a cab, his eyes dimmed, his arm swathed in a bloodstained kerchief? He had just been fighting a duel in the forest of Marly, defending a lady's honor. . . . And then there was General Boulanger, the fallen dictator: did he not blow his brains out on the grave of his beloved?

One day, returning from a walk, we were all three surprised by a shower of rain. . . . We were strolling in the old streets of Saranza, made up entirely of great *izbas* blackened with age. It was beneath the porch of one of them that we found refuge. The street, stifling with the heat a moment ago, was plunged into a chilly twilight, raked by flurries of hail. It was paved in the old style — with great round granite cobbles. The rain caused them to give off a strong smell of wet stone. The view of the houses was blurred behind a curtain of water — and, thanks to that smell, one could imagine oneself to be in a big city in the evening under autumn rain. Charlotte's voice, at first hardly louder than the sound of the raindrops, seemed like an echo muted by the torrential downpour.

"It was another shower of rain that led me to discover an inscription engraved on the damp wall of a house in the allée des Arbalétriers in Paris. We had taken refuge under a porch, my mother and I, and while we waited for the rain to stop, all we had in front of our eyes was this commemorative plaque. I learned the text by heart: *In this passage, after leaving the Hôtel de Barbette, the duc Louis d'Orléans, brother of King Charles VI, was assassinated by Jean sans Peur, duc de Burgundy, on the night of November 23 to 24, 1407. . . . He was leaving after a visit to the queen, Isabeau de Bavière. . . .*"

Our grandmother fell silent, but in the whispering of the raindrops we could still hear these legendary names woven into a tragic monogram of love and death: Louis d'Orléans, Isabeau de Bavière, Jean sans Peur . . .

Suddenly, without knowing why, I thought of the president. A very very simple, obvious notion: it was that during all those cere-monies in honor of the imperial couple — yes, in the procession on the Champs-Elysées and in front of the tomb of Napoleon and at the Opéra — he had never stopped dreaming of her, his mistress, Mar-guerite Steinheil. He spoke with the tsar, made speeches, replied to the tsarina, exchanged glances with his wife. But she, at every mo-ment, she was there.

The rain streamed onto the mossy roof of the old *izba* that was sheltering us on its steps. I forgot where I was. The city I had once visited in the company of the tsar was transfigured before my eyes. Now I perceived it from the viewpoint of the president in love.

That time, on leaving Saranza, I felt as if I were returning from an expedition. I was bringing back a sum of knowledge; a glimpse of their habits and customs; a description, still fragmentary, of the mys-terious civilization that was reborn each evening in the heart of the steppes.

Every adolescent classifies things, a defensive reflex when faced with the complexity of the adult world as it sucks him in at the end of childhood. I was perhaps more prone to this than most. For the country I had to explore no longer existed, and I had to reconstitute the topography of its high places and its holy places through the thick fog of the past.

I was especially proud of the gallery of human types that I now possessed in my collection. Apart from the president-lover, the deputies in a boat, and a dandy with his bunch of grapes, there were much humbler but no less unusual characters. The children for ex-ample, young mineworkers, their smiles ringed with black. A news vendor crying his wares (we did not dare to imagine a madman run-ning through the streets crying *"Pravda! Pravda!"*). A dog barber who practiced his craft on the quays. A rural constable with his drum. Strikers gathering to be fed "Communist soup." And even a dog turd salesman. I was very proud of knowing that this strange merchandise was used, at the time, to soften leather. . . .

But my greatest initiation that summer was to understand how one could be French. The countless facets of this elusive identity had formed themselves into a living whole. It was a very well ordered mode of existence, despite its eccentric aspects.

France was for me no longer a simple collection of curios but a tangible and solid entity of which a small part had one day been implanted inside me.

8

WHAT I DON'T UNDERSTAND is why she wanted to bury herself out there in that Saranza. Not at all. She could very well have lived here, close to you. . . ."

I almost leaped from my stool beside the television. For I understood so perfectly Charlotte's reasons for being fond of her little provincial town. It would have been so easy to explain her choice to the adults gathered in our kitchen. I would have talked of the dry air of the steppe, whose silent transparency distilled the past. I would have spoken of the dusty streets that led nowhere, as they emerged, all of them, onto the small endless plain. Of the town where history, by decapitating churches and tearing down "architectural excesses," had banished all notion of time. A town where living meant endlessly reliving one's past, even while at the same time mechanically performing routine tasks.

I said nothing. I was afraid of being banished from the kitchen. For some time now I had noticed that the adults tolerated my presence more readily. I seemed, at the age of fourteen, to have won the right to be present at their late-night conversations — on condition that I remained invisible. I was thrilled by this change, and the last thing I wanted to do was to jeopardize such a privilege.

Charlotte's name came up during these winter gatherings just as often as before. Yes, as previously, my grandmother's life offered our guests a topic of conversation that satisfied everyone's self-esteem.

And besides, this young Frenchwoman had the advantage of concentrating within her life span the crucial moments in the history of our country. She had lived under the tsar and survived Stalin's purges; she had come through the war and witnessed the fall of so many idols. In their eyes, her life, traced against the background of the empire's bloodiest century, took on an epic dimension.

And now this Frenchwoman, born at the other end of the world, was blankly contemplating the undulations of the sands beyond the open door of a railway carriage. ("But what the devil dragged her into that wretched desert?" my father's friend, the wartime pilot, had exclaimed one day.) At her side, equally motionless, stood her husband, Fyodor. The draft rushing through the carriage brought no coolness, despite the speed of the train. They remained for a long moment in the light and heat of this embrasure. The wind pumiced their brows like sandpaper. The sun broke up the view into myriad flashes. But they did not move, as if they wanted a painful past to be erased by this scouring and burning. They had just left Bukhara.

It was she too, after their return to Siberia, who spent interminable hours at a dark window, from time to time breathing on the thick layer of hoarfrost to preserve a little melted circle. Through this watery spyhole she saw a white nocturnal street. From time to time a car suddenly came gliding up, approached their house, and after a moment of indecision drove off. Three o'clock in the morning sounded, and a few minutes later she heard the sharp crunch of snow on the front steps. She closed her eyes for a moment, then went to open up. Her husband always came back at this time. . . . People sometimes disappeared at work, sometimes in the middle of the night, from home, after a black car had driven through the snow-covered streets. She was certain that as long as she waited at the window for him, blowing on the hoarfrost, nothing could happen to him. At three o'clock he would stand up, straighten out the files on his desk, and leave, like all the other public officials throughout the empire. They knew that in the Kremlin the master of the country finished his working day at three o'clock. Without thinking, everyone strove to imitate his timetable. And they did not stop to consider that between Moscow and Siberia, spanning several time zones, this "three o'clock in the morning" no longer corresponded to anything:

that Stalin was rising from his bed and filling his first pipe of the day, while in a Siberian town at nightfall his faithful subjects struggled against sleep on chairs that were turning into instruments of torture. From the Kremlin the master seemed to impose his tempo on the passage of time and even on the sun. When he went to bed, all the clocks on the planet showed three o'clock in the morning. At least that was how everyone saw it at the time.

On one occasion Charlotte, exhausted by these nightly vigils, fell asleep several minutes before this planetary hour. A moment later, waking with a start, she heard her husband's footsteps in the children's room. She went in and saw him bending over the bed of their son, this boy with smooth black hair who looked like no one else in the family. . . .

They arrested Fyodor neither in his office in broad daylight nor in the small hours, interrupting his sleep with peremptory drumming on the door. It was on New Year's Eve. He had rigged himself out in the red cloak of Father Christmas, and his face, unrecognizable beneath a long beard, fascinated the children: the boy of twelve and his younger sister — my mother. Charlotte was adjusting the big *shapka* on her husband's head when they came into the apartment. They entered without having to knock; the door was open; guests were expected.

And this scene of an arrest, which had already been repeated millions of times during a single decade in the life of the country, had that evening as its setting the Christmas tree and these two children with their cardboard masks, he the hare, she the squirrel. And at the center of the room this Father Christmas, transfixed, only too able to guess at the outcome and almost happy that the children cannot see the pallor of his cheeks beneath the cotton-wool beard. In a very calm voice Charlotte says to the hare and the squirrel, who are looking at the intruders without removing their masks, "Come into the next room, children. You can set off the Bengal lights."

She had spoken in French. The two policemen exchanged significant glances. . . .

*   *   *

Fyodor was saved by what logically ought to have been his downfall: his wife's nationality. . . . When, some years earlier, people had begun to disappear, family by family, house by house, he had at once thought of this. Inherent in Charlotte were two grave faults, the ones most often imputed to "enemies of the people": "bourgeois" origins and a link to abroad. Married to a "bourgeois element," and worse still a Frenchwoman, he could see himself quite naturally accused of being "a spy in the pay of French and British imperialists." The formula for some time had been standard.

However, it was on just this perfect evidence that the well-tried machinery of repression ground to a halt. For normally those who fabricated a case were supposed to prove that the accused had cunningly and for years concealed his links to abroad. And when they were dealing with a Siberian who spoke only his mother tongue, had never left his fatherland or met a representative of the capitalist world — such a proof, even if totally falsified, called for a certain adeptness.

But Fyodor hid nothing. Charlotte's passport indicated her nationality in black and white: French. Her birthplace, Neuilly-sur-Seine, in its Russian transliteration only served to emphasize her foreignness. Her trips to France, her "bourgeois" cousins who still lived there, her children who spoke French just as well as Russian — it was all too clear. The confessions that were normally false and extracted under torture after weeks of interrogation had this time been vouchsafed willingly from the beginning. The machinery marked time. Fyodor was imprisoned; then, as he became more and more of an embarrassment, posted to the other end of the empire, in a town annexed from Poland.

They spent a week together — the time it took to travel across the country, and a long and chaotic day of moving into a new house. The next day Fyodor set off for Moscow to be reintegrated into the Party, from which he had been promptly expelled. "It'll only take a couple of days," he said to Charlotte, who went with him to the station. Returning home, she noticed that he had left his cigarette case behind. "It doesn't matter," she thought; "in two days' time . . ." And this imminent moment (Fyodor would come into the room, see the cigarette case on the table, and, giving himself a little clout on the forehead, exclaim, "What an idiot! I've been looking everywhere for it. . . ."), yes, this June morning would be the first in a long stream of happy days. . . .

They saw one another again four years later. And Fyodor never did recover his cigarette case, which, in the midst of war, Charlotte exchanged for a loaf of black bread.

The adults talked. The television, with its gung-ho news programs, its reports of the latest achievements of the nation's industry, its Bolshoi concerts, provided a soothing background. The vodka mitigated the bitterness of the past. And I felt that our guests, even new arrivals, all cherished this Frenchwoman who had accepted the destiny of their country without flinching.

I learned a lot from these stories. I now guessed why in our family the New Year's celebrations always had a whiff of anxiety about them, like a sly draft making the doors slam in an empty house at twilight. Despite my father's gaiety, despite the presents, the noise of fireworks, and the glittering of the tree, this impalpable malaise was there. As if amid the toasts, the popping of corks, and the laughter, someone's arrival were expected. I believe that, without admitting it to themselves, our parents even welcomed the snowy and humdrum calm of the first days of January with relief. In any event, it was certainly this moment after the holidays that my sister and I preferred to the holiday itself. . . .

My grandmother's Russian days — those days that, at a given moment, ceased to be a "Russian phase" before a return to France and simply became her life — had for me a secret flavor that the others were not aware of. It was a sort of invisible aura that Charlotte carried within her throughout the past, resurrected in our smoke-filled kitchen. I said to myself with marveling astonishment, "This woman who for months waited at a window covered in ice for the famous three A.M. knock, this woman was the same being, both mysterious and so close to me, who had one day seen silver scallop dishes in a café in Neuilly!"

*　　　*　　　*

Whenever they spoke of Charlotte they never forgot to tell the story of that morning. . . .

It was her son who woke up suddenly in the middle of the night. He jumped out of his folding bed and walked barefoot, holding out his arms in front of him, toward the window. As he crossed the room in the dark he bumped into his sister's bed. Charlotte was not asleep either. She had been lying with her eyes open in the blackness, trying to understand where the dense and monotonous hum might be coming from that seemed to impregnate the walls with a dull throbbing. She felt her body and her head vibrating in this slow and glutinous sound. The children woke and rushed to the window. Charlotte heard her daughter's astonished cry: "Oh look! All those stars! But they're moving. . . ."

Without switching on the light, Charlotte went to join them. In passing she noticed on the table a faint glint of metal: Fyodor's cigarette case. He was due back from Moscow in the morning. She saw rows of luminous dots sliding slowly through the night sky.

"Planes," said the boy, in his calm voice, which never changed in intonation. "Whole squadrons . . ."

"But where are they all flying to like that?" sighed the girl, staring with wide eyes, heavy with sleep.

Charlotte took them both by the shoulders.

"Go to bed! Our air force must be on maneuvers. You know the frontier is very close. Maneuvers, or perhaps training for a fly-past. . . ."

The son gave a little cough and said softly, as if to himself, and still with that calm sadness that was so surprising in this youth, "Or perhaps it's war. . . ."

"Don't say stupid things, Sergei," Charlotte reproved him. "Go to bed this instant. Tomorrow we'll go to the station to meet your father."

Lighting a bedside lamp, she consulted her watch: "Half past two. So, it's already today. . . ."

They did not have time to go to sleep again. The first bombs tore the night apart. The squadrons, which had already been flying over the town for an hour, had as their target regions farther on into the depths of the country, where their assault might have the appearance of an earthquake. It was only toward half past three in the morning that the Germans began to bombard the line of the frontier, clearing the way for their land army. And that sleepy girl, my mother, fascinated by those strange, too well ordered constellations, had found herself in fact in a lightning parenthesis between peace and war.

It was already almost impossible to leave the house. The earth heaved; tiles, one row after another, slid from the roof and smashed with a dry crack on the front steps. The sound of explosions smothered gestures and words in a deafening blanket.

Charlotte finally managed to push the children outside and went out herself, carrying a big suitcase that weighed heavily on her arm. The apartment blocks opposite had no windows left. A curtain was billowing in the wind that had only just arisen. The movement of the pale fabric still had all the lightness of peacetime mornings.

The street that led to the railway station was strewn with shattered glass and broken branches. Sometimes a tree snapped in two barred the way. At one moment they had to skirt an enormous crater. It was at this point that the crowd of refugees became more dense. As they moved away from the hole, the people laden with bags started to push and suddenly noticed one another. They tried to talk, but the blast, lost among the houses, erupted all at once and gagged them with a deafening echo. They waved their arms helplessly and began running again.

When Charlotte saw the station at the end of the road, she could physically feel the life of yesterday slipping away into a past from which there was no return. Only the front wall was still standing, and through the empty sockets of the windows the pale morning sky could be seen. . . .

The message passed along by hundreds of mouths finally penetrated the noise of the bombs. The last train for the east had just left, observing the usual timetable with an absurd precision. The crowd came up against the ruins of the station, stood still; then, crushed by the howling of a plane, scattered into the neighboring streets and under the trees of a public square.

Charlotte, disconcerted, gazed about her. A placard lay at her feet: "Danger! Do not cross the track!" But the track, torn up by explosions, now consisted only of crazed rails, thrown up in a taut curve against the concrete pillar of a viaduct. They pointed toward the sky, and the sleepers seemed like a staircase in a dream that led straight up into the clouds. "Over there. There's a freight train just about to leave." She heard the murmur of her son's calm and almost bored-sounding voice.

In the distance she saw a train of great brown freight cars around which little human figures were busily moving. Charlotte seized the handle of her suitcase, the children grabbed their bags.

As they arrived beside the last car, the train started, and a fearful sigh of joy could be heard greeting its departure. A compact bunch of frightened people were visible between the sliding walls. Charlotte, aware of the desperate slowness of her movements, pushed her children toward this opening that was slowly moving off. The son climbed on board and grabbed the suitcase. Already his sister had to quicken her pace to grasp hold of the boy's hand, which he held out to her. Charlotte seized the child by the waist, lifted her, and managed to heave her on board the crowded car. Now she had to run, while trying to clutch hold of the great iron latch. It only lasted for a second, but she had time to glimpse the petrified faces of the survivors, her daughter's tears, and with a supernatural clarity, the cracked wood of the wall of the car. . . .

She stumbled, fell to her knees. The rest was so swift that she could not believe she had touched the white gravel of the embankment. Two hands squeezed her sides hard, the sky described an abrupt zigzag, and she felt herself propelled into the car. And in a luminous flash she glimpsed the cap of a railwayman, the silhouette of a man profiled for a fraction of a second against the light between the open partitions. . . .

Toward midday the train passed through Minsk. In the thick smoke the sun shone as red as that of another planet. And strange funereal butterflies — great flakes of ash — fluttered in the air. No one could comprehend how in a few hours of war the city could have been transformed into those rows of blackened carcasses.

The train advanced slowly, as if feeling its way, in this carbonized twilight, under a sun that no longer hurt the eyes. They had already become accustomed to this hesitant progress and to the sky filled with the roaring of planes. And even to the strident whistling sound above the freight car, followed by a hail of bullets on the roof.

As they were leaving the charred city, they came upon the remains of a train gutted by bombs. Several cars were overturned on the embankment. Others lay on their sides or were embedded in one another in a monstrous telescoping, blocking the track. Several nurses, sunk into stunned helplessness at the number of bodies lying there, were walking the length of the train. Within its black entrails one could see human shapes; sometimes an arm hung from a broken window. The ground was covered with scattered luggage. What was most surprising was the number of dolls lying on the sleepers and in the grass. . . . One of the carriages still left on the rails retained its enamel plaque, on which the destination could be read. Perplexed, Charlotte realized that it was the train they had missed that morning. Yes, that last train for the east, which had observed the prewar timetable.

At nightfall the train accelerated. Charlotte felt her daughter snuggling against her shoulder and shivering. She got up to free the big suitcase on which they were sitting. She must make ready for the night, take out warm clothes and two bags of biscuits. Charlotte half opened the lid, thrust her hand into the case, and froze, unable to stifle a brief cry, which woke their neighbors.

The suitcase was full of old newspapers! In the panic of that morning she had brought the Siberian suitcase. . . .

Still unable to believe her eyes, she drew out a yellowed page and by the gray light of dusk managed to read, "Deputies and senators, irrespective of faction, had responded with enthusiasm to the summons addressed to them by Messieurs Loubert and Brisson. . . . The representatives of the great bodies of the state were gathered in the Salon Murat. . . ."

With a sleepwalker's gesture Charlotte closed the case again, sat down, and looked about her, gently shaking her head, as if she wanted to deny an indisputable fact.

"I have an old jacket in my bag. And I picked up the bread from the kitchen as well, when we were leaving. . . ."

She recognized her son's voice. He must have sensed her feeling of helplessness.

That night Charlotte slept long enough to have a rapid dream, a mixture of sounds and colors from the old days. . . . Somebody slipping along toward the exit woke her. The train had stopped in the middle of fields. The night air did not have the same black density here as in the town they had fled. The plain stretching out beyond the pale rectangle of the open door held the ash-gray tint of the nights of the north. When her eyes had mastered the darkness, she could make out the shape of a sleeping *izba* beside the track, in the shadow of a copse. And in front of it, in a meadow that bordered on the embankment, she saw a horse. The silence was such that one could hear the light crunching of stems being torn up and the soft tread of hooves on the damp ground. With a bitter serenity that astonished even her, Charlotte sensed a clear thought taking shape and echoing through her mind: "Earlier there was that hell of the burned-out towns: a few hours later — this horse, browsing on the dew-laden grass in the cool of the night. This country is too big for them to conquer. The silence of this boundless plain will resist their bombs. . . ."

Never before had she felt so close to that soil.

During the first months of the war her sleep was punctuated by an endless procession of mutilated bodies, whom she cared for, working fourteen hours a day. In this town, a hundred kilometers from the front line, they brought in the wounded by the trainloads. Charlotte often went to the station with the doctor to meet these trains filled with torn human flesh. She would then sometimes notice on the parallel track another train, filled with freshly mobilized soldiers, setting off in the opposite direction, traveling toward the front.

The round of mutilated bodies did not stop even in her sleep. They passed through her dreams, gathered at the frontier of her nights, waiting for her: the young infantryman with his lower jaw torn off and his tongue hanging out over dirty bandages; another without eyes, without a face. . . . But chiefly all those, ever more numerous, who had lost both arms and legs — horrible limbless trunks, eyes blinded by pain and despair.

Yes, it was these eyes in particular that tore the fragile veil of her dreams. They formed constellations, twinkling in the darkness, followed her everywhere, spoke to her silently.

One night (endless columns of tanks were crossing the town) her sleep was more fragile than ever — a series of brief moments of oblivion followed by reawakening amid the metallic cackling of tank tracks. It was against the pale background of one of these dreams that Charlotte suddenly began to recognize all these constellations of eyes. Yes, she had seen them before, one day in another town. In another life. She woke, surprised at no longer hearing the slightest sound. The tanks had left the street. The silence was deafening. And in that dense and mute darkness Charlotte saw again the eyes of the wounded of the Great War. Her time in the hospital at Neuilly suddenly seemed nearer. "It was yesterday," thought Charlotte.

She got up and went to the window to close it. She stopped in mid-gesture. The white storm (the first snow of this first winter of the war) was carpeting the still black earth in great flurries. The sky, stirred by the waves of snow, drew her thoughts to disturbing profundities. She thought of men's lives. Of their deaths. Of the existence somewhere beneath this tumultuous sky of beings without arms or legs, of their eyes open in the night.

And then life seemed to her like a monotonous sequence of wars, an interminable dressing of ever-open wounds. And the crashing of steel on wet paving stones . . . She felt a snowflake land on her arm. These endless wars, these wounds, and yes, secretly lying in wait in the midst of them, this moment of the first snow.

The stares of the wounded were blotted out in her dreams only twice during the war. The first time when her daughter fell ill with typhus, and bread and milk had to be found at any cost (they had been eating potato peelings for months). The second time was when she received a notification of death from the front. . . . Arriving at the hospital in the morning, she remained there all the night, hoping to be overcome with tiredness, afraid of going home, of seeing the children, of having to speak to them. Around midnight she finally sat down beside the stove, her head against the wall, closed her eyes, and at once began walking along a street. . . . She heard the pavements echoing in the morning, breathed the bright air of a pale, oblique sun. As she walked through this still-sleeping town, at each step she recognized its simple topography: station café, church, market square. . . . She felt a strange joy in reading the street names, in observing the glint of the windows, the foliage in the square behind the church. The person walking beside her asked her to translate one of these names. Then she realized what had made this stroll through the early morning town such a happy one. . . .

Charlotte emerged from sleep with her last words spoken there still moving her lips. And when she understood the complete improbability of her dream — herself and Fyodor in that French town on a bright autumn morning — when she grasped the absolute unreality of this walk, which was nevertheless so simple, she drew a little rectangle of paper from her pocket and read again for the hundredth time the death printed in blurred letters; and her husband's name written by hand in purple ink. Already someone was calling her from the end of the corridor. The new train of wounded was about to arrive.

"Samovars!" That is what my father and his friends in their nocturnal conversations sometimes called these soldiers without arms or legs, these living trunks in whose eyes all the world's despair was concentrated. They were samovars, yes: with bits of thigh that resembled the feet of those copper vessels and stumps of shoulder that looked like the handles.

Our guests spoke of them with an odd mixture of bravado, mockery, and bitterness. The irony and cruelty of the term "samovar" signified that the war was long over, forgotten by some, of no interest to others, to us, the young — born a decade after their victory. And so as not to seem pitiful, it seemed to me, they talked about the past with this rather coarse flippancy, believing in neither God nor the devil, as the Russian saying has it. It was much later that this cynical tone was to reveal its true secret to me: a "samovar" was a soul imprisoned in a lump of amputated flesh; a brain detached from its body, a feeble gaze trapped in the spongy stuff of life. It was this tortured soul the men called a "samovar."

For them, telling the story of Charlotte's life was also a way of not displaying their own wounds and suffering. All the more because her hospital, with its jumble of hundreds of soldiers, coming from all fronts, condensed innumerable destinies, brought together so many personal histories.

For example, there was the soldier who always made an impression on me with his leg stuffed with . . . wood. A shell fragment embedded below his knee had crushed a wooden spoon that he had been carrying down the length of his boot. The wound was not serious, but all the debris had to be extracted. "All those splinters," Charlotte had said.

Another wounded man complained all day long that beneath the plaster his leg was itching "enough to tear your guts out." He writhed, scratching at the white carapace, as if his nails could reach through to the wound. "Get it off," he implored. "It's eating into me. Get it off or I'll smash it with a knife myself." The chief doctor, who did not lay down his scalpel for twelve hours a day, took no notice, believing he was dealing with a whiner. "The samovars never complain," he said to himself. It was Charlotte who finally persuaded him to cut a little opening in the plaster. It was also she who, with tweezers, drew white worms from the bloody flesh and washed the wound.

Everything in me revolted at this story. My body shuddered at the image of decay. I felt the physical touch of death on my skin. And, wide-eyed, I observed the adults who were amused by these episodes, which were all one to them: wood splinters in a wound or worms. . . .

And then there was that wound that would not close. Yet the scar tissue was forming well, and the soldier, calm and serious, remained lying down, unlike others who, scarcely had they been operated on, started to limp about the corridors. The doctor would bend over this leg and shake his head. Beneath the dressing the wound, which the previous day had been covered by a fine glaze of skin, was bleeding again, its dark edges resembling torn lace. "Bizarre," the doctor remarked in surprise, but he could not tarry there any longer. "Make another dressing," he said to the duty nurse, threading his way between the closely packed beds. . . . It was the following night that Charlotte, unintentionally, surprised the wounded man. All the nurses wore shoes with heels that filled the corridors with a busy clatter. Only Charlotte, in her felt bootees, moved noiselessly. He had not heard her come in. She entered the dark room and stopped near the door. The silhouette of the soldier, sitting on his bed, stood out distinctly against the windows lit by the snow. It took Charlotte several seconds to guess: the soldier was rubbing his wound with a sponge. Rolled up on his pillow were the dressings he had just removed. . . . In the morning she spoke to the head doctor. Having had a sleepless night, he stared at her as if through a fog, not understanding. Then, shaking himself out of his torpor, exclaimed in a harsh voice, "What do you want done about it? I'll telephone them at once, and they can take him away. It's self-mutilation. . . ."

"He'll be court-martialed. . . ."

"What about it? He deserves it, doesn't he? While the others are dying in the trenches . . . He . . . He's a deserter!"

There was a moment of silence. The doctor sat down and began to massage his face with palms spotted with tincture of iodine.

"What if we put a plaster cast on him?" said Charlotte.

Behind his hands the doctor's face broke into an angry grimace. He half opened his mouth, then changed his mind. His reddened eyes lit up; he smiled.

"You and your plaster casts. We smash it off one man because it's scratching him. We put it on another because he's scratching himself. You continue to astonish me, Sharlota Norbertovna!"

During his rounds, he examined the wound and in a very natural tone said to the nurses, "We shall have to put a plaster on it. Just one layer. Sharlota will do it before she leaves."

Hope returned when, a year and a half after the first notification of death, she received another. Fyodor could not have been killed twice, she thought, so perhaps he was alive. This double death became a promise of life. Without saying anything to anyone, Charlotte prepared to wait.

He came back, arriving not from the west at the start of the summer, like most of the soldiers, but from the Far East, in September, after the defeat of Japan. . . .

From being a town close to the front line, Saranza was transformed into a peaceful place, reverting to its sleep of the steppes beyond the Volga. Charlotte lived there alone: her son (my uncle Sergei) had entered a military academy; her daughter (my mother) had left for the nearest city, like all the students who wanted to continue their studies.

On a balmy September evening she left the house and walked into the empty street. She wanted to pick some stalks of wild dill at the edge of the steppe for her salted preserves before nightfall. It was on the way back that she saw him. She was carrying a bunch of the tall plants surmounted with yellow umbels. Her dress and her body were permeated with the clarity of the silent fields, with the fluid light of the sunset. The strong scent of the dill and the dry plants clung to her fingers. By now she knew that this life, despite all its pain, could be lived, that one must travel through it slowly; passing from the sunset to the penetrating odor of the stalks; from the infinite calm of the plain to the singing of a bird lost in the sky; yes, going from the sky to that deep reflection of it that she felt within her own breast, as an alert and living presence. And one must even pay heed to the warmth of the dust on this little path leading toward Saranza. . . .

She raised her eyes and saw him. He was walking toward her, still a long way off, far up the road. If Charlotte had welcomed him on the threshold of the room, if he had opened the door and stepped inside, as she had imagined it for so long, as all the soldiers did when they came back from the war, in life or in films, then she would doubtless have uttered a cry, would have hurled herself at him, clinging to his shoulder belt, would have wept. . . .

But he appeared very far away, making himself known little by little, giving his wife the time to come to terms with the road now rendered unrecognizable by the silhouette of a man whose uncertain smile she could already make out. They did not run, they exchanged no words, they did not kiss. It seemed as if they had been walking toward each another for an eternity. The road was empty; the evening light, reflected by the golden foliage of the trees, was of an unreal transparency. Stopping near him, she gently waved her bouquet. He nodded his head, as if to say, "Yes, yes, I understand." He was not wearing a shoulder belt, just one at his waist, with a buckle of tarnished bronze. His boots were red with dust.

Charlotte lived on the ground floor of an old wooden house. From year to year, for a century, the ground had been rising imperceptibly and the house subsiding, so much so that the window of her room scarcely came above the level of the pavement. . . . They entered in silence. Fyodor put down his pack on a stool, made to speak, but said nothing, only cleared his throat, bringing his fingers to his lips. Charlotte began to prepare a meal.

She surprised herself by replying to his questions without thinking (they talked about bread, about ration cards, about life in Saranza); by offering him tea, by smiling when he said, "All the knives in this house need sharpening." But as she took part in this first, still hesitant conversation she was elsewhere. In a profound absence where quite different words were being uttered: "This man with short hair that looks as if it were sprinkled with chalk is my husband. I have not seen him for four years. They buried him twice — first in the battle of Moscow, then in the Ukraine. He is here, he has come back. I ought to weep for joy. I ought to . . . His hair is quite gray. . . ." She guessed that he, too, was far away from their conversation about ration cards. He had come home when the lights of victory had long since gone out. Life was resuming its daily round. He was coming back too late. Like an absentminded man who, invited to lunch, arrives at dinnertime and surprises the mistress of the house as she is saying her farewells to the last of the lingering guests. "I must look very old to him," Charlotte thought suddenly. But not even this idea could disrupt the strange lack of emotion in her heart, this indifference that left her puzzled.

She wept only when she saw his body. After the meal she heated water and brought out a zinc basin, the little child's bath, which she placed in the middle of the room. Fyodor crouched in this gray vessel, whose bottom yielded underfoot, emitting a vibrant sound. And as she poured a trickle of warm water onto the body of her husband, who clumsily rubbed his shoulders and his back, Charlotte began to weep. The tears coursed down her face, whose features remained immobile, and they fell, mixing with the soapy water in the basin.

This body was that of a man she did not know. A body riddled with scars, with gashes — some of them deep, with fleshy edges, like huge voracious lips, some with a smooth shiny surface, like a snail's trail. In one of the shoulder blades a cavity had been dug: Charlotte knew what type of little jagged shell splinters did that. The pink traces of the stitches of a suture surrounded one shoulder, losing themselves in his chest. . . .

Through her tears she viewed the room as if for the first time: a window at ground level; the bunch of dill, already a relic from another epoch in her life; a soldier's pack on the stool near the hall; great boots covered with red dust. And beneath a bare and dim bulb, in the midst of this room half sunk in the ground — this unrecognizable body, as if torn by the wheels of a machine. Stunned words formed unconsciously within her: "this is me, Charlotte Lemonnier, here in this *izba* buried beneath the grass of the steppes, with this man, this soldier, whose body is lacerated with wounds, the father of my children, the man I love so much. . . . this is me, Charlotte Lemonnier . . ."

Across one of Fyodor's eyebrows there was a broad white gash, which, as it grew narrower, made a line across his forehead. It gave him a permanently surprised expression. As if he simply could not manage to get used to this postwar life.

He lived for less than a year. . . . In winter they moved into the apartment where, as children, we were to come and stay with Charlotte every summer. They did not even have time to buy new crockery and cutlery. Fyodor cut the bread with the knife he had brought back from the front, fashioned from a bayonet. . . .

*　　*　　*

As I listened to the adults' stories, this was how I pictured our grand-father during that incredibly brief reunion: a soldier climbs the steps to the *izba*. His gaze is lost in his wife's, and he has just time to say, "You see, I have come back . . . ," before collapsing and dying of his wounds.

9

*T*HAT YEAR FRANCE ENVELOPED me in deep and studious isolation. At the end of the summer I had returned from Saranza, like a young explorer with a thousand and one discoveries in my luggage — from Proust's bunch of grapes to the plaque bearing witness to the tragic death of the duc d'Orléans. In the autumn and particularly during the winter I turned myself into a fanatic of erudition, an archivist obsessively gleaning all possible information about the country whose mystery he had only managed to scratch the surface on his summer excursion.

I read everything of interest about France that our school library possessed. I immersed myself in the much vaster shelves of our city library. I sought to complement the broad outlines of Charlotte's impressionistic stories with a systematic study, progressing from one century to another, from one Louis to the next, from one novelist to his colleagues, disciples, or imitators.

These long days spent in dusty book-lined labyrinths doubtless corresponded to a monkish inclination that everyone feels at that age. One seeks escape before being caught up in the toils of adult life. One remains alone in order to enjoy fantasies about amorous adventures to come. This waiting, this reclusive life, soon becomes painful. Hence the swarming, tribal collectivism of adolescents — a feverish attempt to act out all the scenarios of adult society in advance. Rare are those who at the age of thirteen or fourteen know how to resist the role-playing that is imposed on the loners and the dreamers, with all the cruelty and intolerance of those who were but children yesterday.

It was thanks to my French quest that I managed to preserve my own attentive isolation as an adolescent.

Sometimes the society in miniature of my schoolfellows displayed a careless condescension toward me (I was "not mature," I did not smoke, and I did not tell salacious stories in which the male and female genital organs became characters in their own right); sometimes an aggressiveness, whose collective violence left me stunned. I did not feel I was very different from the others; I did not feel I merited so much hostility. It is true that I did not go into raptures about the films that their mini-society discussed during breaks, and I could not tell apart the football teams of which they were passionate supporters. My ignorance offended them. They perceived it as a challenge. They attacked me with their taunts and with their fists. It was during that winter that I became aware of a disconcerting truth: to harbor this distant past within oneself, to let one's soul live in this legendary Atlantis, was not guiltless. No, it was well and truly a challenge, a provocation in the eyes of those who lived in the present. One day, worn out with the bullying, I pretended to take an interest in the latest match score; I joined in their conversation and mentioned several players' names, learned the previous day. But everyone smelled the imposture. The discussion broke off. The mini-society dispersed. I earned several almost pitying looks. I felt even more undervalued.

After this pathetic attempt I plunged even deeper into my research and my reading. Fleeting glimpses of Atlantis over the years were not enough for me. Henceforth I aspired to know the intimate details of its history. Wandering through the caverns of our ancient library, I sought to throw light on the reasons for that extravagant marriage between Henri I and the Russian princess Anna. I wanted to know what on earth her father, the celebrated Yaroslav the Wise, could have sent as a dowry. And how he managed to transport herds of horses from Kiev to his French son-in-law when he was attacked by the warlike Normans. And how Anna Yaroslavna spent her days in the somber medieval castles, where she so lamented the absence of Russian baths. . . . I was no longer content with the tragic story depicting the death of the duc d'Orléans beneath the windows of the fair Isabeau. No, I now set off in pursuit of his murderer, this Jean sans Peur, whose lineage had to be traced; military exploits verified; dress and weapons reconstructed; landholdings located. . . . I learned by how much maréchal Grouchy's divisions were delayed, those few extra hours more, fatal for Napoleon at Waterloo. . . .

Of course the library, a hostage of ideology, was very unevenly stocked. I only found a single book there on the period of Louis XIV, whereas the shelves next door offered a score of volumes devoted to the Paris Commune and a dozen on the birth of the French Communist Party. But, hungry for knowledge, I contrived to thwart this manipulation of history. I turned to literature. The great French classics were there and, with the exception of a few famous proscribed authors, like Rétif de la Bretonne, or Sade, or Gide, they had in the main escaped censorship.

My youth and my inexperience made a fetishist of me: rather than grasping history's features, I was a collector. And in particular I sought anecdotes, like those recounted to tourists by guides at ancient monuments. In my collection were Théophile Gautier's red waistcoat, worn at the first night of *Hernani;* Balzac's walking sticks; George Sand's hookah, and the scene of her treachery in the arms of a doctor, who was supposed to be attending Musset. I admired her elegance in providing her lover with the subject for *Lorenzaccio.* I never tired of mentally reviewing the sequences, full of images, that my memory recorded, albeit in great disorder. Like the one where Victor Hugo, the grizzled and melancholy patriarch, met Leconte de Lisle under the canopy in a park. "Do you know what I was just thinking about?" the patriarch asked. And, perceiving his interlocutor's confusion, he declared roundly, "I was thinking about what I shall say to God when, very soon perhaps, I enter His Kingdom. . . ." To which Leconte de Lisle, at once ironic and respectful, asserted confidently, "Oh, you will say to him, '*Cher confrère . . .*'"

*　　*　　*

Strangely enough, it was somebody who knew nothing of France, who had never read a single French author — someone who could not, I am sure, have located that country on the map of the world — he was the one who involuntarily helped me to get away from collecting anecdotes by steering my quest into quite a new direction. It was the dunce who had one day told me that if Lenin had no children, it was because he did not know how to make love. . . .

The mini-society of our class treated him with just as much scorn as it did me, but for quite different reasons. They detested him because he presented them with a very unattractive image of adulthood. Two years older than us, and thus at that age the freedoms of which my fellow pupils looked forward to, and yet my friend the dunce scarcely profited from them at all. Pashka, as everyone called him, led the life of those strange muzhiks who cling until their death to an element of childishness that contrasts strongly with their wild and virile physique. They obstinately avoid the city, society, and comfort; they merge into the forest and often end their days there, as hunters or vagabonds.

Pashka brought into the classroom the smells of fish, of snow, and, at the time of the thaw, of clay. He spent whole days squelching about on the banks of the Volga. And if he came to school it was only so as not to upset his mother. Always late, oblivious of the scornful glances of the future adults, he crossed the classroom and slid behind his desk, right at the back. The pupils sniffed pointedly as he passed; the mistress raised her eyes heavenwards, with a sigh. The smell of snow and wet earth slowly filled the room.

Our status as pariahs in the society of our class ended by uniting us. Without becoming friends, properly speaking, we took note of both our solitudes and saw in them, as it were, a sign of recognition. From now on I often found myself accompanying Pashka in his fishing expeditions on the snow-covered shores of the Volga. He bored a hole in the ice with the aid of a powerful brace and bit, cast his line into the hole, and remained motionless above this round opening, which revealed the green thickness of the ice. I would imagine a fish at the far end of this narrow tunnel, sometimes a meter deep, cautiously approaching the bait. . . . Perch with striped backs, speckled pike, roach with bright red tails, all rose up through the bore hole, were released from the hook, and fell onto the snow. After several somersaults their bodies stiffened, frozen by the icy wind. Their dorsal spines became covered in crystals, like fantastic diadems. We spoke little. The great calm of the snowy plains, the silvery sky, and the deep slumber of the great river rendered words useless.

Sometimes Pashka, in his search for a spot with more fish, drew dangerously close to the long slabs of dark ice, humid, undermined by springs. . . . Hearing a crack, I would turn and see my comrade struggling in the water, digging with splayed-out fingers into the grainy snow. Running toward him, a few meters away from the breach, I would lie flat on my stomach and throw him the end of my scarf. Generally Pashka managed to escape before I could help him. Like a porpoise, he hurled himself out of the water and fell with his chest on the ice, then crawled away, leaving a long wet trail. But occasionally, probably just to please me, no doubt, he caught hold of my scarf and allowed himself to be rescued.

After a ducking like this we would go to one of the carcasses of old boats that could be seen, here and there, projecting out of the snowdrifts. We lit great wood fires in their blackened entrails. Pashka removed his large felt boots and his padded trousers and put them close to the flames. Then, with his bare feet resting on a plank, he began to grill the fish.

It was over these wood fires that we became more talkative. He told me of extraordinary fishing exploits (a fish too big to pass through the hole pierced by the brace and bit!); of thaws that, in the deafening breakup of the ice, carried away boats and uprooted trees and even *izbas* with cats clinging to the roof. . . . I told him about tournaments between knights (I had just learnt that the warriors of old, on removing their helmets after a joust, had their faces covered in rust: iron plus sweat. I don't know why, but this detail thrilled me more than the tournament itself). Yes, I talked to him about those manly features accentuated with streaks of rust and about that young hero who sounded his horn three times to summon reinforcements. I knew that, as Pashka paced up and down on the banks of the Volga, in both summer and winter, he secretly dreamed of expanses of open sea. I was glad to find for him in my French collection the terrifying fight between a sailor and an enormous octopus. And, as my erudition was essentially nourished by anecdotes, I told him one suitably in keeping with his passion and our haven in the carcass of an old boat. Once on a perilous sea an English warship met a French vessel, and before embarking on a battle with no quarter, the English captain addressed his historic enemies, cupping his hands around his mouth: "You, Frenchmen, fight for money. But we, subjects of the Queen, we fight for honor!" Then from the French vessel this jovial riposte of the captain's could be heard blowing across in a gust of salt wind: "Each man fights for what he does not have, sir!"

One day he very nearly drowned for real. A whole slab of ice — we were in the midst of the thaw — gave way beneath his feet. Only his head appeared above the water, then an arm, seeking a nonexistent support. With a violent effort he hurled his chest up onto the ice, but the porous surface cracked beneath his weight. The current was already dragging on his legs; his boots were full of water. I did not have time to unroll my muffler; I lay flat on the snow, I crawled; I held out my hand to him. It was at that moment that I saw a brief glimmer of fear pass through his eyes. . . . I believe he would have escaped without my help; he was too seasoned, too close to the forces of nature, to allow himself to be trapped by them. But this time he took my hand without his customary grin.

A few minutes later the fire was burning and Pashka, his legs bare and his body covered only by the long pullover I had lent him while his clothes dried, was prancing about on a plank licked by flames. With his red, skinned fingers he was kneading a lump of clay that he wrapped round the fish before putting it into the embers. . . . Around us was the white desert of the Volga in winter; the willows with fine, trembling branches, which formed transparent thickets all along the bank; and buried under the snow, this boat, half disintegrated, whose timber fed our barbaric wood fire. The dancing of the flames seemed to make the twilight denser, the fleeting sensation of well-being more striking.

Why did I tell him the story on that day rather than any other?

There was no doubt a reason for it, something in our conversation that suggested the subject to me. . . . It was a summary, and indeed a very brief one, of a poem by Hugo that Charlotte had narrated to me long ago, the title of which I could not even recall. . . . Somewhere near the smashed barricades, soldiers were shooting insurgents in the heart of that rebellious Paris, where the paving stones had the extraordinary capacity to rear up suddenly as ramparts. A routine execution, brutal, pitiless. The men stood with their backs to the wall, stared for a moment at the barrels of the rifles aimed at their chests, then raised their eyes toward the lightly racing clouds. And they fell. Their comrades took their places facing the soldiers. . . . Among these condemned men there was a kind of young Gavroche, whose age should have inspired clemency. Alas, no! The officer ordered him to take his place in the fatal waiting line; the child had the same right to die as the adults. "We're going to shoot you as well!" snarled this executioner-in-chief. But a moment before going to the wall the child ran up to the officer and begged him, "Will you allow me to take this watch to my mother? She lives just round the corner from here by the fountain. I will come back, I swear it!" This childish trick touched even the hardened hearts of the soldiery. They guffawed; it seemed really too naive a ruse. The officer, roaring with laughter, declared, "Away with you, run. Make yourself scarce, little good-for-nothing." And they went on laughing as they loaded their rifles. Suddenly their voices were silenced. The child reappeared and, putting himself against the wall beside the adults, called out, "Here I am!"

Throughout my story Pashka hardly seemed to be paying attention. He remained motionless, leaning toward the fire. His face was hidden beneath the turned-down brim of his big fur *shapka*. But when I reached the final scene — the child returns, his face pale and serious, and stands stock-still in front of the soldiers — yes, when I had spoken his final words, "Here I am!" Pashka shuddered and stood up. . . . And something incredible happened. He stepped over the side of the boat and began walking barefoot in the snow. I heard a kind of stifled groaning that was rapidly dispersed over the white plain by the damp wind.

He took several steps, then stopped, sunk up to his knees in a snowdrift. Dumbfounded, I remained for a moment without moving, watching from the boat this great fellow clad in a stretched pullover that billowed in the wind like a short woolen dress. The earflaps on his *shapka* swayed slowly in the cold breeze. His bare legs thrust into the snow fascinated me. No longer understanding anything, I jumped over the side and went up to him. Hearing the crunch of my footsteps, he turned swiftly. His face was contorted in an unhappy grimace. An unaccustomed moisture in his eyes mirrored the flames of our wood fire. He hurried to wipe away these reflections with his sleeve. "Ugh, this smoke!" he complained, blinking his eyelids, and without looking at me, he went back to the boat.

It was there, thrusting his frozen feet toward the embers, that he asked me with an angry insistence, "And after that? They shot him, that fellow, is that right?"

Caught on the hop and finding no enlightenment on this point in my memory, I stammered hesitantly, "Er . . . I don't know exactly. . . ."

"What d'you mean, you don't know? But you told me the whole story!"

"No, but you see, in the poem . . ."

"I don't give a shit about the poem! In real life did they kill him or not?"

He stared at me over the flame with a slightly mad glint in his eyes. His voice came over as both rough and imploring. I sighed, as if to beg Hugo's pardon, and with a firm and clear tone I declared, "No, they didn't shoot him. There was an old sergeant there who was reminded of his own son back at his village. And he shouted, 'Whoever touches the boy will have to answer to me!' And the officer had to let him go. . . ."

Pashka lowered his face and began to extract the fish molded in the clay, poking the embers with a branch. In silence we broke off the crust of baked earth, which came away with the scales, and we ate the tender and burning flesh, sprinkling it with coarse salt.

Nor did we speak as we returned to the city at nightfall. I was still under the spell of the magic that had been wrought, the miracle that had demonstrated to me the overwhelming power of poetry. I sensed that it was not even a question of verbal artifice, nor of a skillful arrangement of words. No! For Hugo's had first been reshaped in Charlotte's retelling long ago and again in the course of my own summary. So, doubly betrayed. . . . And yet the echo of this story, so simple in fact, recounted thousands of kilometers away from the place of its genesis, had succeeded in drawing tears from a young barbarian and driving him naked into the snow. I was secretly proud of having caused a tiny spark to shine from the radiance emitted by Charlotte's native land.

And then, that evening I grasped that it was not anecdotes that I must seek out in my reading. Nor words prettily arranged on a page. It was something much more profound and at the same time much more spontaneous: a deep harmony within the visible world, which, once revealed by the poet, became immortal. Without knowing what name to give it, from now on that is what I pursued from one book to the next. Later I was to learn its name: style. And I could never accept the empty exercises of word jugglers under this name. For in my mind's eye, I would see Pashka's blue legs, thrust into a snowdrift on the banks of the Volga, and the reflections of the flames in his moist eyes. . . . Yes, he was more moved by the fate of the young rebel than by his own narrow escape from drowning an hour before!

Leaving me at a crossroads in the suburb where he lived, Pashka gave me my share of the fish: several long carapaces of clay. Then in a gruff tone, avoiding my eyes, he asked, "And that poem about the men they shot, where's it to be found?"

"I'll bring it to you at school tomorrow. I must have got it copied out at home. . . ."

I said it just like that, finding it hard to contain my joy. It was the happiest day of my youth.

10

$\mathcal{T}$HE TRUTH IS, Charlotte has nothing more to teach me."

The morning I arrived in Saranza this disconcerting thought crossed my mind. I jumped down from the carriage at the little station. I was the only one getting off there. At the other end of the platform I saw my grandmother. She caught sight of me, gave a slight wave of her hand, and came to meet me. It was at that moment, walking toward her, that I had this insight: she had nothing new to teach me about France; she had told me everything, and thanks to my reading, I had accumulated a knowledge possibly vaster than her own. . . . As I kissed her, I felt ashamed of this thought, which had caught me unawares. I saw in it a kind of involuntary betrayal.

In fact I had for months been experiencing a strange torment: that of having learned too much. . . . I was like a thrifty man who hopes to see his amassed savings quickly bring him a wholly different way of life, open up prodigious new horizons, and change his vision of things — right up to his way of walking, of breathing, of speaking to women. The savings continue to accumulate, but the dramatic change is slow in coming.

So it was with the sum of my French knowledge. Not that I would have wanted to derive any profit from it. The interest that my comrade the dunce showed in my stories amply fulfilled me. I was hoping rather for a mysterious click, like that of the spring in a music box: the grinding sound that announces the start of the minuet to be danced by the little figures on the platform. I longed for this medley of dates, names, events, and characters to recast itself into the stuff of a hitherto unseen life, to crystallize into a fundamentally new world. I wanted the France that was grafted onto my heart, that had been studied, explored, and learned, to turn me into a new being.

But the only change at the start of this summer was the absence of my sister, who had gone to continue her studies in Moscow. I was afraid to admit to myself that her departure might make our evening gatherings on the balcony impossible.

The first evening, as if to confirm my fears, I began to question my grandmother about the France of her youth. She replied willingly, believing my curiosity to be sincere. As she spoke, Charlotte continued to darn the lace collar of a blouse. She handled the needle with that touch of artistic elegance one always sees in a woman who is working and at the same time engaged in conversation with a guest she believes to be interested in what she has to say.

Leaning on the handrail of the little balcony, I listened to her. My routine questions drew forth scenes from the past that I had contemplated hundreds of times in my childhood, familiar images, known characters: the dog barber on the quay by the Seine; the imperial procession passing along the Champs Elysées; *la belle* Otéro; the president enfolding his mistress in a fatal embrace. . . . I realized at the time that when Charlotte had repeated all these stories to us every summer, she was responding to our desire to hear a favorite tale once more. That was it precisely. They were simply fairy tales that enchanted our childhood and of which, as with all real tales, we never tired.

I was fourteen that summer. I understood only too well that the time for fairy tales would not return. I had learned too much to let myself be intoxicated by their whirling colorful dance. Strangely, instead of rejoicing at this evident sign of my maturity, that evening I felt nostalgic for my former trusting innocence. My new knowledge, contrary to my expectations, seemed to blot out the pictures I had of France. No sooner did I seek to return to the Atlantis of our youth than a learned voice intervened: I saw pages of books, dates in large print. The voice began to comment, to compare, to quote. And I felt myself stricken with a strange blindness. . . .

At one moment our conversation broke off. I had been listening so inattentively that Charlotte's last remark — it must have been a question — escaped me. Confused, I studied her face, which was raised toward me. In my ears I could hear the melody of the sentence she had just uttered. It was her intonation that helped me to reconstruct the sense. Yes, it was that intonation a storyteller adopts in saying, "No, but you must have heard that one before. I'm not going to weary you with all my old tales . . . ," while secretly hoping that his listeners will urge him on, will assure him that they do not know the story or that they have forgotten it. . . . I shook my head slightly, with a doubtful air. "No, no, I don't think so. Are you sure you've told it to me before?"

I saw a smile light up my grandmother's face. She took up the story. This time I listened alertly. And for the umpteenth time before my eyes appeared a narrow street in medieval Paris, one cold autumn night; and on a wall, that grim plaque that had brought together for all time three destinies and three names from days gone by: Louis d'Orléans, Jean sans Peur, and Isabeau de Bavière. . . .

I do not know why I interrupted her at that moment. No doubt I wanted to show off my erudition to her. But chiefly it was a sudden perception that blinded me: an old lady on a balcony, suspended above the endless steppe, repeating once more a story known by heart; she repeats it with the mechanical precision of a gramophone record, faithful to her more-or-less legendary story that tells of a country that only exists in her memory. . . . Our tête-à-tête in the silence of the evening suddenly seemed to me absurd, and Charlotte's voice reminded me of an automaton's. I seized on the name of the character she had just mentioned and started talking. Jean sans Peur and his shameful conspiracies with the English. Paris, where the butchers became "revolutionaries," laid down the law, and massacred the enemies of Burgundy, or those claimed as such. And the mad king. And the gibbets in the squares of Paris. And the wolves roaming in the suburbs of the city devastated by civil war. And the unimaginable betrayal committed by Isabeau de Bavière, who joined forces with Jean sans Peur and denied the Dauphin, claiming that he was not the king's son. Yes, the fair Isabeau of our childhood . . .

Suddenly I was gasping for breath; I choked myself with my own words; I had too much to say.

After a moment of silence my grandmother nodded gently and said, with absolutely sincerity, "I'm delighted you know your history so well!"

Yet in her voice, full of conviction, I thought I could detect the echo of an unconscious thought: "It is good to know history. But when I spoke of Isabeau and the allée des Arbalétriers, and that autumn night, I had something different in mind. . . ."

She bent over her task, making little thrusts with her needle, precise and regular. I walked through the apartment, went down into the street. A train whistle sounded in the distance. Its tone, softened by the warm air of the evening, had something of a sigh, a lament about it.

Between the apartment block where Charlotte lived and the steppe there was a kind of little wood, very dense, even impenetrable: thickets of brambles, the claws of hazel branches, collapsed trenches full of nettles. And even if we managed to get through these natural obstacles in the course of our games, others, those made by man, barred the way: rows of barbed wire entanglements, the rusty crossed bars of antitank barriers. . . . This place was known as the "Stalinka," after the name of the defensive line built there during the war. They were afraid that the Germans might get that far. But the Volga and, above all, Stalingrad had halted them. . . . The line had been dismantled; what was left of the war materials had ended up abandoned in this wood, which had inherited its name. The "Stalinka," the inhabitants of Saranza would call it, and thus their town seemed to become involved in the great deeds of history.

It was said that the inside of the wood was mined. This deterred even the boldest among us who might have wanted to venture into this no-man's-land that hugged its rusted treasures to itself.

It was beyond the thickets of the Stalinka that the narrow-gauge railway passed; it was like a miniature railway, with a little locomotive, all black with soot, with little cars as well and, as in an optical illusion, the driver dressed in a grease-stained jersey: an apparent giant, leaning out of the window. Each time it was about to cross one of the roads that trailed off toward the horizon, the locomotive emitted its cry, half tender, half plaintive. Doubled by its echo, this signal sounded like the call note of a cuckoo. "The Kukushka" we called it, with a wink, when we caught sight of this train on its narrow track, overrun with dandelion and chamomile. . . .

It was its voice that guided me that evening. I walked round the thickets at the edge of the Stalinka, I saw the last train in a blur slipping into the warm half-light of the dusk. Even this little train gave off the inimitable slightly piquant smell of railways that imperceptibly summons one to go on long journeys. From the distance, from the blue-tinted mist of the evening, I heard a melancholy *coo-coo-oo* floating on the air. I put my foot on the rail, which was gently vibrating from the vanished train. The silent steppe seemed to be awaiting some action, some movement from me.

"How good it was before," a wordless voice said within me. "I believed the Kukushka went off to an unknown destination, to countries not shown on any map, toward snowcapped mountains, toward a nocturnal sea where the paper lanterns on the boats mingled with the stars. Now I know that this train goes from the Saranza brickworks to the station where its trucks are unloaded. Two or three kilometers in all. Some journey! Yes, now that I know this, I'll never again be able to believe that these rails are endless and this evening unique; with the strong scent from the steppe, the immense sky, and my inexplicable and strangely necessary presence here beside this line with its cracked sleepers; at this precise moment, with that *coo-coo-oo* echoing in the violet air. Once upon a time everything seemed so natural. . . ."

That night, before going to sleep, I remembered having finally learned the meaning of the enigmatic formula on the menu for the banquet in honor of the tsar: "Roast bartavels and ortolans, garnished with truffles." Yes, I knew now that they were both game birds, much prized by gourmets. A delicate, tasty, rare dish, but nothing more. In vain I repeated "bartavels and ortolans," as before. The magic that had once filled my lungs with the salt air of Cherbourg had faded. And with a hesitant despair I murmured softly to myself, staring wide-eyed into the darkness, "Part of my life is now behind me!"

From then onward we talked but said nothing. Coming between us we could see the screen that is formed by those smooth words, those echoes of the everyday we give voice to; the verbal liquid with which we feel obliged, without knowing why, to fill the silence. With stupefaction I discovered that talking was in fact the best way of saying nothing about the essential. Whereas to express it one would have to articulate words in quite a different way, whisper them, weave them into the sounds of evening, into the rays of the sunset. Once again I sensed in myself the mysterious gestation of that language so different from words blunted by use, a language in which I could have said softly, meeting Charlotte's gaze, "Why does my heart miss a beat when I hear the distant call of the Kukushka? Why does an autumn morning in Cherbourg a hundred years ago, yes, a moment I have never lived through, in a town I have never visited, why do its lights and breeze seem to me more alive than the days of my real life? Why does your balcony no longer float in the mauve air of the evening above the steppe? The transparency of dreams that once enveloped it is now broken like an alchemist's flask. And the glass splinters grate together to keep us from talking as we used to. . . . Are not your memories, which I now know by heart, a cage that holds you prisoner? Is not our life simply the daily transformation of the fluid and warm present into a collection of frozen memories, like butterflies crucified on their pins in a dusty glass case? And why then do I sense that I would without hesitation exchange this whole collection for the unique sharp taste left on my lips by that little imaginary silver dish in that illusory café at Neuilly? For a single mouthful of Cherbourg's salt breeze? For a single cry of the Kukushka recalled from my childhood?"

But we continued to pour useless words and hollow remarks into the silence, as if into a sieve of the Danaids: "It's hotter than yesterday! Gavrilych is drunk again. . . . The Kukushka hasn't gone past this evening. . . . There's a fire over there on the steppe, look! No, it's a cloud. . . . I'll make some more tea. . . . Today at the market they were selling watermelons from Uzbekistan. . . ."

The unsayable! It was mysteriously linked, I now understood, to the essential. The essential was unsayable. Incommunicable. And everything in this world that tortured me with its silent beauty, everything that needed no words, seemed to me essential. The unsayable was essential.

This equation created a kind of intellectual short circuit in my head. Its conciseness led me that summer to a terrible truth: "People speak because they are afraid of silence. They speak mechanically, whether aloud or to themselves. They are intoxicated by this vocal gruel that ensnares every object and every being. They talk about rain and fine weather; they talk about money, about love, about nothing. And even when they are talking about their most exalted love, they use words uttered a hundred times, threadbare phrases. They talk for the sake of talking. They seek to exorcise silence. . . ."

The alchemist's vessel was broken. Though conscious of the absurdity of our words, we continued our humdrum dialogue: "I think it's going to rain. Look at that big cloud. No, it's a fire on the steppe. . . . That's funny, the Kukushha has gone past earlier than usual. . . . Gavrilych . . . The tea . . . At the market . . ."

Yes, I had lived out a part of my life. Childhood.

In the end, our conversations about the rain and the fine weather that summer were not wholly unjustified. It rained often, and my sadness has colored my memory of those holidays with misty and lukewarm hues.

Sometimes out of the depths of this slow grayness of days, an echo of our evening gatherings in the past surfaced — some photo that I discovered by chance in the Siberian suitcase, the contents of which had long since held no secrets for me. Or from time to time a fleeting detail of the family history, which was as yet unknown to me and which Charlotte offered me with the timid joy of a bankrupt princess, suddenly finding a small coin of fine gold beneath the threadbare lining of her purse.

Thus it was that one day when it was raining hard, as I leafed through the piles of old French newspapers amassed in the suitcase, I lit upon a page that probably came from an illustrated magazine at the turn of the century. It was a reproduction, faintly covered in a brown-and-gray tint, of a painting in that highly wrought realistic style, whose attraction lies in its precise and abundant details. It was through examining these details during the long rainy evening that I retained a memory of the subject. A very disparate column of soldiers, all visibly suffering from exhaustion and old age, was crossing the street of a poor village with bare trees. The soldiers were all of advanced years — old men, it seemed to me, with long white hair escaping from broad-brimmed hats. They were the last able-bodied men in a mass recruitment of a people already engulfed in war. I did not memorize the title of the picture, but it contained the word "last." They were the last to face the enemy, the very last to be able to bear arms. The latter, furthermore, were very rudimentary; some pikes, axes, old sabers. Curious, I scrutinized their clothes; their enormous army boots with large copper buckles; their hats and occasionally a tarnished helmet, like that of the conquistadors; their gnarled fingers, gripping the pike handles. . . . France had always appeared before my eyes in the splendor of her palaces, at the glorious hours of her history, but was suddenly revealed in the shape of this northern village, where low houses huddled behind meager hedges, and where stunted trees shivered in the winter wind. Astonishingly, I felt a close affinity for this muddy road and these old warriors, doomed to fall in an unequal battle. No, there was nothing flamboyant in their demeanor. They were not heroes making a show of their gallantry or their self-sacrifice. They were simple, human. In particular there was one, wearing the old conquistador-style helmet, a very tall old man who walked, leaning on a pike, at the end of the column. His face captivated me with its surprising serenity, bitter and smiling at the same time.

Deep in my adolescent melancholy, I was suddenly overwhelmed with a confused joy. I felt I had understood the calm of this old warrior as he confronted imminent defeat, suffering, and death. Neither a stoic nor a holy fool, he walked with his head held high across this flat, cold, and dull country, which he loved despite everything, and called it his "homeland." He appeared invulnerable. For a fraction of a second my heart seemed to beat in time with his, triumphing over fear, death, and solitude. This defiance felt like a new chord in the living harmony that for me was France. I tried at once to find a name for it. Patriotic pride? Panache? Or the famous *furia francese* that the Italians recognized in French fighters?

As I was calling these labels to mind, I saw that the face of the old soldier was slowly closing and his eyes growing dull. He became once more a figure in an old reproduction of a painting in gray and bister tints. It was as if he had averted his gaze to hide from me that mystery of his, of which I had just caught a glimpse.

Another flash from the past was the woman — the one in a padded jacket and a broad *shapka,* whose photo I had discovered in an album filled with photos dating from our family's French period. I recalled that this photo had disappeared from the album immediately after I had shown an interest in it and spoken about it to Charlotte. I tried to remember why I had failed to obtain a reply at the time. The scene appeared before my eyes: I am showing the photo to my grandmother, and suddenly I see a rapid shadow passing that makes me forget my question: on the wall I cover a strange moth with my hand, a hawkmoth with two heads, two bodies, and four wings.

I told myself that now, four years later, the double hawkmoth no longer held any mystery for me: quite simply two moths coupling. I thought of people coupling, and tried to imagine the movement of their bodies. . . . And suddenly I understood that for months already, possibly years, I had been thinking of nothing but these bodies, entwined, merging. I had been thinking about this without realizing it, at every moment of the day, while speaking of other things. As if the feverish caress of the hawkmoth had been burning my palm the whole time.

Questioning Charlotte to find out who that woman in the padded jacket was now seemed an absolute impossibility. An impenetrable barrier was arising between my grandmother and me: the female body, dreamed of, desired, possessed a thousand times in my thoughts.

That evening, pouring me a cup of tea, Charlotte said in a preoccupied voice, "It's funny, the Kukushka hasn't been past yet. . . ."

Emerging from my reverie, I looked up at her. Our eyes met. . . . We said nothing else to each other until the end of the meal.

The three women changed my outlook, my life. . . .

I had discovered them by chance on the back of a press cutting in the depths of the Siberian suitcase. I was reading yet again the article about the first "Peking–Paris via Moscow" car race, as if to prove to myself that there was nothing new to learn, that Charlotte's France was well and truly exhausted. Absentmindedly I had let the page slip onto the carpet. I had been looking through the balcony's open door. It was a special kind of day at the end of the month of August, cool and sunny, when the chill wind blowing across the Urals brought the first breath of autumn to our steppes. Everything shone in this limpid light. The trees of the Stalinka stood out with fragile clarity against a sky of revitalized blue. The line of the horizon was pure and incisive. With bitter relief I told myself that the end of the holidays was approaching. The end also of a stage in my life, an end marked by this extraordinary discovery: that all my knowledge ensured neither happiness nor privileged access to what was essential. . . . Another revelation also: the whole time I was thinking about the female body, about women's bodies. All other thoughts were complementary, accidental, derivative. Yes, I was facing the fact that being a man meant thinking constantly of women, that a man was nothing but a dreamer about women! And that was what I was turning into. . . .

By a whimsical caprice, the page of the magazine had turned over as it slipped onto the carpet. I picked it up, and as I did so I saw them on the back, these three women from the turn of the century. I had never seen them before, having regarded the reverse side of this press cutting as nonexistent. This unexpected encounter intrigued me. I took the photo closer to the light coming from the balcony. . . .

And suddenly I fell in love with them. With their bodies and with their tender and attentive eyes, which allowed one to guess only too well at the presence of a photographer crouched under a black cloth, behind a tripod.

Their femininity was such as would inevitably touch the heart of a solitary and shy adolescent like myself. It was, in a way, a normative femininity. All three wore long black dresses that enhanced the ample roundness of their bosoms and hugged their hips; but notably, before embracing their legs and spreading into graceful folds around their feet, the fabric sketched the discreet curve of their stomachs. The chaste sensuality of this gently rounded triangle fascinated me!

Yes, their beauty was just what a young, still physically innocent dreamer could endlessly call to mind in his erotic fantasies. It was the image of a "classical" woman. The embodiment of femininity. The vision of the ideal mistress. It was in this light, at any rate, that I contemplated the elegant trio, their great eyes shaded in black; their voluminous hats sporting dark velvet ribbons; their old-fashioned air, which in the portraits of previous generations always seems to us to betoken a certain naïveté, a candid spontaneity lacking in our own contemporaries that both touches us and inspires our confidence.

And I marveled at the neatness of this correspondence: what my lack of experience in love called for was precisely this generic Woman, a woman still devoid of all those sensual particulars that a mature desire would detect in her body.

I contemplated them with a growing uneasiness. Their bodies were inaccessible to me. Oh, the problem was not the physical impossibility of being with them. For a long time my erotic imagination had learned how to thwart this obstacle. I closed my eyes and saw my fair strollers naked. Like a chemist I could reconstruct their flesh by a skillful synthesis, taking the most banal elements: the heaviness of the thigh of that woman who had brushed against me one day in a crowded bus; the curves of sunburned bodies on beaches; all the nudes in paintings. And even my own body! Yes, despite the taboo imposed on nudity in my native land and, with greater reason, on female nudity, I would have known how to reconstitute the elasticity of a breast beneath my fingers and the suppleness of a thigh.

No, the elegant trio were inaccessible to me in quite a different way. . . . When I sought to recreate their era my memory immediately went into action. I remembered Blériot, who around that time was crossing the Channel with his monoplane; Picasso, who was painting the *Demoiselles d'Avignon.* . . . The cacophony of historical facts resounded in my head. But the three women remained immobile, inanimate — three museum exhibits with a label: "The elegant ladies of the belle epoque in the gardens of the Champs-Elysées." Then I tried to make them mine, to turn them into my imaginary mistresses. With my erotic synthesis, I modeled their bodies; they moved, but with all the stiffness of sleepers, whom someone is trying to move around, upright and fully clothed, in a semblance of their waking state. And as if to accentuate this impression of sluggishness, in my dilettante synthesis I dredged up from my memory an image that made me grimace: that bare, flaccid breast, the dead breast of a drunk old woman I had seen one day at the railway station. I shook my head to rid myself of this nauseating vision.

So I had to resign myself to a museum peopled with mummies, with waxworks bearing their labels: "Three elegant ladies," "President Faure and his mistress," "Old soldier in a village in the north.". . . I closed the suitcase.

Leaning on the handrail of the balcony, I let my gaze lose itself in the transparent evening gold above the steppe.

What was the point of their beauty after all? I thought, with a sudden clarity ascendant as the light from this sunset. Yes, what was the point of their fine breasts, their hips, their dresses that hugged their young bodies so prettily? To be so beautiful and to end up thrust into an old suitcase, in a sleepy, dusty town, lost in the middle of an endless plain! In this Saranza, of which, during their lifetime, they hadn't the slightest notion. . . . All that was left of them was this photo, which had survived an unbelievable series of hazards great and small and was only preserved as the back of the page reporting the Peking–Paris car rally. Even Charlotte had no memory of these three feminine figures. I was the only one on this earth to preserve the last thread linking them to the world of the living! My memory was their last refuge, their ultimate abode before final and total oblivion. I was in some sense the god of their trembling universe, of this bit of the Champs-Elysées where their beauty still shone. . . .

I could only offer them the life of puppets. I wound up the spring of my memory, and the elegant trio began their jerky promenade; the president of the Republic embraced Marguerite Steinheil; the duc d'Orléans fell, pierced by perfidious daggers; the old warrior grasped his long pike and stuck out his chest. . . .

"How can it be," I asked with anguish, "that all these passions, griefs, loves, leave so little trace? What an absurdity are the laws of this world in which the lives of such beautiful and desirable women depend on the flutter of a page! For had that page not turned over, I would not have saved them from oblivion, which would have been eternal. What a cosmic blunder is the disappearance of a beautiful woman! Disappearance forever. Complete annihilation. Without shadow. Without reflection, without appeal . . ."

The sun went down over the far-distant steppe. But for a long time the air retained the crystalline luminosity of cool summer evenings. Beyond the wood the cry of the Kukushka rang out, more resonant in this cold air. The foliage of the trees was flecked with a few yellow leaves. The very first. The cry of the little engine rang out again. Already distant, fainter.

It was then that, returning to the memory of the elegant trio, I had this simple thought, this last echo of the sad reflections in which I had just been sunk. "What they had in their lives was an autumn morning, cool and clear, an avenue in the sun strewn with dead leaves, where they paused for a moment, motionless before the lens. Bringing the moment to a standstill . . . Yes, there was in their lives a clear autumn morning. . . ."

I suddenly was transported with all my senses into the moment that the smiles of the elegant trio had captured. I found myself amid the ambience of its autumnal smells; so penetrating was the acrid scent of dead leaves that my nostrils palpitated. I blinked in the sun that shone through the branches. I heard the distant sound of a phaeton bowling over the cobblestones. And the still confused murmuring of a few laughing remarks that the three women exchanged before freezing in front of the photographer . . . Yes, intensely, fully, I was living their time!

The impact of feeling myself beside them on that autumn morning was so great that I tore myself away from its light, almost frightened. I was suddenly afraid of being trapped there forever. Blinded, deafened, I came back into the room and took out the magazine page again. . . .

The surface of the photo seemed to quiver like the wet and vivid colors of a transfer. Its flat perspective suddenly began to deepen, to recede before my eyes. That was how, as a child, I used to contemplate two identical images moving slowly toward each other before blending into a single stereoscopic one. The photo of the elegant trio opened up before me, gradually surrounded me, let me come in under its sky. The branches with broad yellow leaves leaned over me. . . .

My reflections of an hour before (total oblivion, death . . .) no longer had any meaning. I no longer even needed to look at the photo. I closed my eyes, and I even sensed the joy experienced after the idle heat of summer by the three women as they rediscovered the cool of autumn, the seasonal clothes, the pleasures of city life, and no doubt, soon, the rain and the cold that would add to these attractions.

Their bodies, inaccessible a moment ago, lived in me, bathed in the smell of the dead leaves, in the light mist spangled with sunlight. . . . Yes, I sensed in them that imperceptible shiver with which a woman's body greets the fresh autumn, that mixture of delight and dread, that serene melancholy. There was no longer any barrier between these three women and me. Our fusion, I felt, was more loving and more sensual than any physical possession.

I emerged from that autumn morning and found myself under an almost black sky. Exhausted, as if I had just swum across a great river, I looked about me, scarcely recognizing familiar objects. But I nevertheless wanted to retrace my steps to see the three strollers of the belle epoque once more.

The magic I had just experienced now, however, seemed to elude me. My memory unconsciously recreated quite a different scene from the past. I saw a fine man, dressed in black, in the middle of a sumptuous office. The door opened silently; a woman, her face masked by a veil, entered the room. And, very theatrically, the president embraced his mistress. Yes, it was the scene, encountered a thousand times, of the Elysée lovers' secret rendezvous. Summoned up by my memory, they complied by reenacting it one more time, like a hasty vaudeville sketch. But that was no longer enough for me. . . .

The transfiguration of the elegant trio had left me with the hope that the magic could be repeated. I had a clear memory of the very simple sentence that had unleashed it all: "And yet there was in the lives of those three women a cool and sunny morning. . . ." Like a sorcerer's apprentice, I once again pictured the man with the fine mustache in his office at the dark window; and I whispered the magic formula, "And yet there was in his life an autumn evening when he stood before the dark window, beyond which the bare branches stirred in the garden of the Elysée."

I did not notice the moment when the time barrier dissolved. . . . The president stared, unseeing, at the moving reflections of the trees. His lips were so close to the glass that a circle of mist clouded it for a moment. He noticed this and tossed his head slightly in response to his unspoken thoughts. I sensed that he was feeling the strange stiffness of the clothes on his body. He saw himself as a stranger. Yes, as an unknown, tense being that he was obliged to control by his apparent immobility. He thought, no, did not think but sensed, somewhere in the damp darkness beyond the window, the increasingly intimate presence of the woman who would soon enter the room. "The president of the Republic," he said softly, slowly enunciating each syllable. "The Elysée . . ." And suddenly these words, which were so familiar, seemed to him to have no connection with what he was. Intensely he felt he was the man who in a moment would once again thrill to the warm softness of the woman's lips beneath the veil that sparkled with frozen droplets. . . .

For several seconds I could feel these contrasting sensations on my face.

The magic of this transfigured past had simultaneously exalted and shattered me. Sitting on the balcony, I breathed jerkily, my blind gaze lost in the night of the steppes. I was no doubt becoming obsessed with this alchemy of time. Hardly had I returned to myself when I uttered my "open sesame" again: "And yet there was in the life of that old soldier a winter's day. . . ." And I saw the old man wearing a conquistador's helmet. He walked, leaning on his long pike. His face, flushed by the wind, was once more closed in on bitter thoughts: his age and the war that would continue when he was no longer there. Suddenly, in the dull air of that freezing cold day he smelled the odor of a wood fire. This pleasant and somewhat acid aroma mingled with the chill of the hoarfrost in the bare fields. The old man inhaled deeply a raw mouthful of winter air. The ghost of a smile lit up his austere face. He screwed up his eyes slightly. It was him, this man greedily inhaling the icy wind, that smelt of wood smoke. Him. Here. Now. Under this sky . . . The battle in which he was going to take part and the war and even his death seemed to him to be events of no importance. Yes, chapters in an infinitely greater destiny, in which he would be — in which he was already — a participant, albeit for the moment an unconscious one. He breathed deeply; he smiled, with his eyes half shut. He guessed that the moment he was living through now was the start of the destiny he foresaw. . . .

Charlotte came back at nightfall. I knew that from time to time she spent the late afternoon at the cemetery. She weeded the little bed of flowers in front of Fyodor's grave, watered it, cleaned the stele surmounted with a red star. When the day began to draw to a close, she would leave. She would walk slowly, passing through the whole of Saranza, sitting down on a bench occasionally. On those evenings we did not go out onto the balcony. . . .

She came in with some agitation. I heard her footsteps in the corridor, then in the kitchen. Without giving myself the time to consider what I was doing, I went and asked her to tell me about the France of her youth. The way she used to.

Now the moments I had just experienced seemed to me like the experiments of a strange madness, beautiful and frightening at the same time. It was impossible to deny them, for my whole body still felt their luminous echo. I had really lived them! But in a sly spirit of contradiction — a mixture of fear and common sense in revolt — I needed to disavow my discovery, destroy the universe of which I had glimpsed a few fragments. From Charlotte I hoped for a soothing fairy story about the France of her youth. A reminiscence as familiar and bland as a photographic plate, which would help me to forget my passing folly.

She did not respond at once to my request. No doubt she realized that only something serious would have made me disrupt our routine in this way. She must have thought about all our empty conversations for several weeks now, and our traditional stories at sunset, a ritual betrayed that summer.

After a moment's silence she sighed, with a little smile at the corner of her lips: "But what can I tell you? You know everything now. . . . Let me think, I will read you a poem instead. . . ."

I was about to live through the most extraordinary evening of my life. For a long time Charlotte could not lay her hand on the book she was looking for. And with that marvelous abandon with which we sometimes saw her overturn the order of things, she, a woman who was otherwise orderly and punctilious, transformed the night into a long vigil. Piles of books accumulated on the floor. We climbed on the table to explore the upper shelves of the bookcases. The book could not be found.

It was at about two o'clock in the morning that, standing up amid a picturesque disarray of books and furniture, Charlotte exclaimed, "What a fool I am! That poem, I began to read it to you, you and your sister, last summer. Do you remember? And then . . . I can't remember. At any rate, we stopped at the first verse. So it must be here."

And Charlotte bent down to a little cupboard near the door to the balcony, opened it, and beside a straw hat we saw the book.

Seated on the carpet, I listened to her reading. A table lamp placed on the ground lit up her face. On the wall our silhouettes stood out with eerie precision. From time to time a gust of cold air coming from the night steppe burst in through the balcony door. Charlotte's voice carried the tonality of words whose echo can be heard years after their genesis.

Each time its mournful notes sound in my ears
My soul grows younger by two hundred years.
The thirteenth Louis reigns and I behold
A green hill turned by sunset's rays to gold.

A brick-built castle, faced with cornerstones,
With lofty windows, stained in crimson tones,
Stands in a garden where a river fleet
Flows between flowers and swirls about its feet.

A lady at her casement waits the while,
Fair with dark eyes, in robe of ancient style,
I saw her in another life, it seems,
And now remembrance of her haunts my dreams!

We said nothing else to one another during that unusual night. Before going to sleep I thought about the man in my grandmother's country a century and a half earlier, who had had the courage to tell of his "madness" — that moment in a dream more real than any commonsense reality.

The following morning I woke up late. In the next room order had returned. . . . The wind had changed direction and brought the warm breeze from the Caspian. Yesterday's cold weather seemed very remote.

Around midday, without prior agreement, we went out into the steppe. We walked in silence, side by side, skirting round the thickets of the Stalinka. Then we crossed the narrow rails overgrown with wild plants. From afar the Kukushka emitted its whistling call. We saw the little train appear, looking as if it were traveling between tufts of flowers. It drew near, crossed our path, and melted in the heat haze. Charlotte followed it with her eyes, then murmured softly, as she started walking again, "In my childhood I had occasion to take a train that was a bit like a cousin to our Kukushka. This one carried passengers, and with its little carriages it wound its way slowly through Provence. We used to go and stay with an aunt who lived in . . . I can no longer remember the name of the town. What I do remember is the sun flooding the hillsides; the loud, dry chirruping of the cicadas when we stopped in sleepy little stations. And on those hills, as far as the eye could see, stretched fields of lavender. . . . Yes, the sun, the cicadas, and the intense blue; and the scent that came in through the open windows on the breeze . . ."

I walked beside her in silence. I sensed that "Kukushka" would henceforth be the first word in our new language. The new language that would say the unsayable.

Two days later I left Saranza. For the first time in my life the silence of the last moments before the train pulled out did not become embarrassing. Through the window I gazed at Charlotte on the platform, amid people gesticulating like deaf-mutes, for fear of not being understood by those departing. Charlotte was silent. Catching my eye, she smiled softly. We had no need of words.

3

11

*T*HAT AUTUMN THERE were only a few days between the time when, ashamed to admit it to myself, I was rejoicing at my mother's absence — she had gone into hospital, "just for tests" she told us — and the afternoon when, coming out of school, I learned of her death.

The day after she left for the hospital an agreeable lack of constraint became established in our apartment. My father stayed in front of the television till one o'clock in the morning. And I, savoring this prelude to adult freedom, sought to delay my return to the house each day a little longer: nine o'clock, half past nine, then ten o'clock . . .

I spent these evenings at a crossroads that, in the autumn dusk and with a slight effort of the imagination, created a surprising illusion: that of a rainy evening in a metropolis in the West. It was a unique spot amidst the monotonous broad avenues of our city. The streets that met here branched out like the radii of a circle, leaving the front of each apartment block truncated in the form of a trapezium. I had learned that Napoleon ordered this configuration where streets met in Paris to avoid collisions between carriages . . .

The denser the darkness, the more complete my illusion became. Knowing that one of these buildings housed the local museum of atheism and the walls of others concealed overcrowded communal apartments — all this hardly troubled me at all. I contemplated the yellow and blue watercolor sketch of windows in the rain, the reflections of the street lamps on the oily asphalt, the silhouettes of the bare trees. I was alone, free. I was happy. Whispering, I talked to myself in French. In front of these trapezium-shaped facades the sound of that language seemed to me very natural. Would the magic I had discovered that summer materialize in some encounter? Each woman who came toward me seemed to want to talk to me. Each extra half hour of night that I gained gave my French mirage more substance. I no longer belonged either to my time or to my country. On this little nocturnal circus I felt wonderfully foreign to myself.

Now the sun wearied me, daytime became a useless waiting period before my true life, the evening. . . .

However, it was in broad daylight, blinded by the glitter of the first hoarfrost, that I learned the news. As I walked past the cheerful crowd of pupils, who still displayed the same disdainful hostility toward me, a voice rang out.

"Have you heard? His mother's dead."

I intercepted several inquisitive glances. I recognized the one who had spoken — the son of one of our neighbors. . . .

It was the lack of concern in the remark that gave me time to grasp the inconceivable situation: my mother was dead. All the events of the past days suddenly fitted together into a coherent picture: my father's frequent absences, his silence, the arrival, two days before, of my sister (although it was not the university vacation time, I now realized). . . .

It was Charlotte who opened the door to me. She had arrived from Saranza that very morning. So they all knew! While I was "the child we won't say anything to at the moment." And this child, unaware of everything, had continued to pace up and down at his "French" crossroads, imagining himself to be adult, free, mysterious. This sobering thought was the first my mother's death gave rise to. This then gave way to shame: while my mother was dying, I, in selfish contentment, had been reveling in my freedom, recreating the Parisian autumn under the windows of the museum of atheism!

During these sad days and on the day of the funeral Charlotte was the only one who did not weep. Her face impassive, her eyes calm, she saw to all the household tasks, greeted visitors, settled in relatives who came from other towns. Her dry manner displeased people. . . .

"You can come to me whenever you want," she said to me in parting. I nodded my head, picturing Saranza again, the balcony, the suitcase stuffed with old French newspapers. Again I felt ashamed: while we were telling each other stories, life had continued with its real joys and its real sorrows. My mother had gone on working, already ill, suffering without admitting it to anyone, knowing herself to be doomed but never betraying it by word or gesture. And all the while we had spent days on end talking about the elegant ladies of the belle epoque. . . .

It was with concealed relief that I saw Charlotte leave. I felt myself to be covertly implicated in my mother's death. Yes, I bore the vague responsibility for it that a spectator feels when his gaze causes a tightrope walker to stumble or even to fall. It was Charlotte who had taught me to pick out Parisian silhouettes in the midst of a great industrial city on the Volga; it was she who had imprisoned me in this fantasy of the past, from whence I cast absentminded glances at real life.

Real life was the layer of stagnant water that, with a shudder, I had caught sight of at the bottom of the grave on the day of the burial. Under a fine autumn rain, they lowered the coffin slowly into the mixture of water and mud. . . .

Real life also made itself felt with the arrival of my aunt, my father's elder sister. She lived in a workers' district where the population got up at five o'clock in the morning and streamed in to the gates of the gigantic factories in the city. This woman brought with her a ponderous and powerful breath of Russian life — a strange amalgam of cruelty, compassion, drunkenness, anarchy, invincible joie de vivre, tears, willing slavery, stupid obstinacy, and unexpected delicacy. . . . With growing astonishment, I discovered a universe previously eclipsed by Charlotte's France.

My aunt was concerned that my father would take to drinking, a fatal move for the men she had known in her life. Each time she came to see us she repeated, "Whatever you do, Nikolai, keep off the bitter stuff!" That is to say, vodka. He would agree mechanically, without hearing her, then shaking his head energetically, he would declaim: "But it's me who should have died first. That's for sure. With this, you know. . . ."

And he would touch his bald head with his palm. I knew that above his left ear he had a "hole" — a place covered only with fine, smooth skin that pulsated rhythmically. My mother had always been afraid that if involved in a brawl, my father might be killed by a simple flick of the finger. . . .

He did not start drinking. But in February, the time of the last winter frosts, the harshest of all, he collapsed in a snowy alleyway one evening, felled by a heart attack. The militiamen who later found him stretched out in the snow thought he was a drunkard and took him to the sobering-up station. Only the following morning would the error be discovered. . . .

Once again real life, with its arrogant power, came to challenge my fantasies. A single sound sufficed: they had transported his body in a van covered with cloth, which was as cold inside as outside; as the body was placed on the table, there was a thud like a block of ice hitting wood. . . .

I could not lie to myself. Amid a great turmoil of exposed thoughts and unflinching admissions — in my soul — the disappearance of my parents had not left incurable scars. Yes, I admitted during these secret tête-à-têtes with myself, my suffering was not inordinate.

And if on occasion I wept, I was not really mourning their loss. Mine were tears of helplessness at the realization of a stupefying truth: a whole generation of dead, of wounded, of those whose youth had been stolen from them. Tens of millions of human beings whose lives had been blotted out. Those who had fallen on the field of battle at least had the privilege of a heroic death. But those who came back, and who disappeared ten or twenty years after the war, appeared to die quite "normally," of "old age." You had to come very close to my father to see the slightly concave mark above his ear where the blood throbbed. You had to know my mother very well to discern in her that child transfixed in front of the dark window on that first morning of war under a sky with strange rumbling stars. To see in her as well that pale skeletal adolescent, choking as she wolfed down potato peelings. . . .

I viewed their lives through a mist of tears. I saw my father, on a warm June evening, coming home after demobilization to his native village. He recognized everything: the forest, the river, the curve in the road. And then there was that unknown place, that black street made up of two rows of *izbas,* all burned to a cinder. And not a living soul. Only the merry notes of a cuckoo, keeping time with the burning throbbing of the blood above his ear.

I saw my mother, a student who had just passed her university entrance exams, this petrified young girl standing frozen to attention before a wall of disdainful faces — a Party commission assembled to judge her "crime." She had known that Charlotte's nationality, yes, her "Frenchness," was a terrible blemish during that period of the struggle against "cosmopolitanism." Filling in the questionnaire form before the examination she had written, with a trembling hand, "Mother — of Russian nationality" . . .

And they had met, these two human beings, so different, yet so alike in their mangled youth. And we were born, my sister and I, and life had continued, despite the wars, the burned villages, the camps.

Yes, if I wept, it was for their silent resignation. They bore no grudge against anyone, demanded no reparations. They lived and tried to make us happy. My father had passed his whole life shuttling back and forth across the endless spaces between the Volga and the Urals, erecting high-tension cables with his team. My mother, expelled from university following her crime, had never had the courage to renew the attempt. She had become a translator in one of the great factories in our city, as if this technical and impersonal French exonerated her from her criminal Frenchness.

I viewed these two lives — at the same time banal and extraordinary — and felt a confused rage mounting within me, against whom, I did not really know. Yes, I did know: against Charlotte! Against the serenity of her French universe. Against the useless refinement of that imaginary past: what madness to be thinking about three creatures featured on a press cutting from the turn of the century or to try to recreate the states of mind of a president in love! While forgetting about the soldier who was saved by the winter itself when he packed his fractured skull in a shell of ice, thus staunching the blood. While forgetting that if I was alive it was thanks to that train that had slowly edged its way past the carriages filled with crushed human flesh, a train that carried Charlotte and her children away to refuge in the protective depths of Russia. . . . That propaganda catchphrase — "Twenty million people died so that you might live!" — had always left me indifferent. Suddenly this patriotic refrain acquired a new and grievous meaning for me. And a very personal one.

Russia, like a bear after a long winter, was awakening within me. A pitiless, beautiful, absurd, unique Russia. A Russia pitted against the rest of the world by its somber destiny.

Yes, if I had occasion to weep at the death of my parents, it was because I felt Russian. And the French graft in my heart began, at times, to give me great pain.

My father's sister, my aunt, had also unwittingly contributed to this turnabout. . . .

She moved into our apartment with her two sons, my young cousins, happy to leave her crowded communal apartment in the workers' district. Far from seeking to impose some other way of life on us and to eradicate the traces of our previous existence, she simply lived as she could. And the eccentricity of our family — its very discreet Frenchness, as remote from France as my mother's technical translations — faded away of its own accord.

My aunt was a true product of the Stalinist era. Stalin had been dead for twenty years, but she had not changed. It was not that she had any great love for the Generalissimo. Her first husband had been killed in the murderous shambles of the first days of the war. My aunt knew where the guilt for this catastrophic start lay, and she would tell anyone who was prepared to listen. The father of her two children, whom she had never married, had spent eight years in a camp. "Because of his wagging tongue," she would say.

No, her "Stalinism" lay chiefly in her manner of speaking, of dressing, of looking other people in the eye as if we had always been in the thick of war, as if the radio were still capable of announcing in solemn and funereal tones, "After heroic and bitter resistance, our armies have yielded the city of Kiev. . . . have yielded the city of Smolensk. . . . have yielded the city of . . . ," with everyone's faces frozen as they followed the inexorable advance on Moscow. . . . She still lived as she did in the years when neighbors would exchange silent glances, indicating a house with a movement of the eyebrows — after a whole family had been taken away in the night in a black car. . . .

She wore a great brown shawl and an old coat of coarse cloth; in winter, felt boots; in summer, walking shoes with thick soles. I would not have been at all surprised to have seen her donning a military tunic and putting on a soldier's boots. And when she put the cups on the table, her big hands looked as if they were handling shell cases on the conveyor belt of an armaments factory, as they had done during the war. . . .

Sometimes the father of her children, whom I called by his patronymic, Dmitrich, came to see us, and then our kitchen rang with his raucous voice, which sounded as if it was gradually getting warmed up after several years of winter. Neither my aunt nor he had anything more to lose, and they were afraid of nothing. They talked about everything with an aggressive and desperate forthrightness. He drank a lot, but his eyes remained clear: his jaws simply clamped more and more tightly together, as if better from time to time to spit out the occasional fierce oath from the camps. It was he who made me drink my first glass of vodka. And it was thanks to him that I was able to picture the invisible Russia — a continent encircled by barbed wire and watchtowers. In this forbidden country the simplest words took on a fearful significance, burned the throat like the "bitter stuff" that I drank from a thick glass tumbler.

One day he talked about a little lake in the midst of the taiga, frozen eleven months of the year. At the behest of the camp commander its bed was turned into a cemetery: it was easier than digging into the permafrost. The prisoners died by the score. . . .

"We went there one day in autumn: we had ten or fifteen to dump in the drink. And then I saw them, all the others, the last lot. Naked; we made a bit from their gear. Yeah, butt-naked, under the ice, not rotted at all. I tell you, it was like a hunk of *kholodets!*"

So *kholodets,* that meat in aspic, of which there was a plateful on our table at that moment, became a terrible word — ice, flesh, and death congealed into one trenchant sound.

What caused me most pain during the course of their nocturnal confessions was the indestructible love for Russia that these revelations inspired in me. My intellect, struggling with the bite of the vodka, rebelled: "This country is monstrous! Evil, torture, suffering, self-mutilation, are the favorite pastimes of its inhabitants. And still I love it? I love it for its absurdity. For its monstrosities. I see in it a higher meaning that no logical reasoning can penetrate. . . ."

This love was a continual heartbreak. The blacker the Russia I was discovering turned out to be, the more violent my attachment became. As if to love it, one had to tear out one's eyes, plug one's ears, stop oneself thinking.

One evening I heard my aunt and her lover talking about Beria. . . .

In the old days, from our guests' conversations, I had learned what this terrible name concealed. They uttered it with scorn, but not without a note of awe. Being too young, I could not understand the disturbing zone of darkness in this tyrant's life. I grasped only that some human weakness was involved. They referred to it in hushed tones, and that was generally when they noticed my presence and banished me from the kitchen. . . .

These days there were three of us in our kitchen. Three adults. Certainly my aunt and Dmitrich had nothing to hide from me. They talked; and through the blue fog of tobacco, through the drunkenness, I pictured a great black car with smoked glass windows. Despite its imposing size, it had the look of a curb-crawling taxi. It traveled with a furtive slowness, almost stopping, then moving off rapidly, as if to catch up with someone. Intrigued, I observed its comings and goings along the streets of Moscow. Suddenly I guessed the purpose of them: the black car was following women. Beautiful young ones. It studied them from its opaque windows, advanced in time with their footsteps. Then it let them go. Or sometimes, finally making up its mind, dived up a side street after them. . . .

Dmitrich had no reason to spare me. He recounted everything without mincing his words. On the backseat of the car sprawled a rotund figure, bald, with a pince-nez buried in a fat face. Beria. He selected the passing woman's body that aroused his desire, then, his henchmen arrested the woman. Those were the days when not even a pretext was needed. Carried off to his residence, the woman was raped, having been broken with the aid of alcohol, threats, torture. . . .

Dmitrich did not say — he did not know himself — what happened to these women afterward. Nobody ever saw them again.

I spent several sleepless nights, staring into space. I was thinking about Beria and those condemned women with only one night to live. My brain was on fire. I felt an acid, metallic taste in my mouth. I pictured myself as the father, or the fiancé, or the husband of that young woman pursued by the black car. Yes, for several seconds, for as long as I could bear it, I inhabited the skin of this man, was in his anguish, in his tears, in his useless, powerless anger, in his resignation. For everyone knew how these women disappeared! I felt a knot in my stomach, a horrible spasm of grief. I opened the hinged windowpane, I scooped up the layer of snow that clung to its edge, I rubbed my face with it. This provided temporary relief. Now I saw a fat man, lurking behind the smoked glass of the car, silhouettes of women reflected in the lenses of his pince-nez. He picked them, felt them, appraised their attractions. . . .

And I hated myself! For I could not help admiring this stalker of women. Yes, within me there was someone who — with dread, with repulsion, with shame — reveled in the power of the man with the pince-nez. All women belonged to him! He cruised around the vastness of Moscow as if in the middle of a harem. And what fascinated me most was his indifference. He had no need to be loved, he did not care what the women he chose might feel toward him. He selected a woman, desired her, possessed her the same day. Then forgot her. And all the cries, lamentations, sobs, groans, supplications, and curses that he had occasion to hear were for him only spices that added to the savor of the rape.

I lost consciousness at the start of my fourth sleepless night. Just before fainting I felt I had grasped the fevered thought of one of those raped women, who must have realized that whatever happened she would not be allowed to leave. This thought, which cut through her enforced intoxication, her pain, her disgust, resounded in my head and threw me to the ground.

When I came to, I felt different. Calmer, stronger. Like a patient after an operation, I progressed slowly from one word to the next. I needed to put everything in order again. In the darkness I murmured short sentences that took stock of my new state: "So, within me there is someone who can contemplate these rapes. While I order it to be silent, it is still there. Beria has taught me that everything is allowed. Russia knows no limits, neither in goodness nor in evil. Especially not in evil. And here I was, fascinated by this hunter of women's bodies. And hating myself for it. I felt one with this brutalized woman, crushed by the weight of sweaty flesh, guessing her last clear thought: the thought of the death that will follow this hideous coupling. I longed to die at the same time as her. How could I go on living while carrying within myself this other me that admires Beria. . . ."

Yes, I was Russian. Now I understood, in a still confused fashion, what that meant. Carrying within one's soul all those human beings disfigured by grief, those burned villages, those lakes filled with naked corpses. Knowing the resignation of a human herd violated by a despot. And the horror of feeling oneself participating in this crime. And the wild desire to reenact all these stories from the past — so as to eradicate from them the suffering, injustice, and death. Yes, to catch the black car in the streets of Moscow and destroy it beneath one's giant palm. Then, while holding one's breath, to watch the young woman pushing open the door of her house, going up the stairs . . . Remaking history. Purifying the world. Hunting down evil. Giving all these people refuge in one's heart, so as to be able to release them one day into a world liberated from evil. But meanwhile sharing the sorrow that oppresses them. Detesting oneself for every lapse. Pushing this commitment to the point of delirium, to the point of fainting. Living very mundanely on the edge of the abyss. Yes, that's what Russia is.

Thus it was that in my juvenile confusion, I latched onto my new identity. I was Russian. It became life itself for me, and one, I believed, that would erase forever my French illusion.

But this life quickly revealed its chief characteristic (which daily routine prevents us from seeing) — its total improbability.

Formerly I had lived in books. I moved from one character to another, following the logic of an amorous intrigue or of a war. But one March evening, so warm that my aunt had opened our kitchen window, I learned that in this life there was no logic, no coherence. And that perhaps only death was predictable.

That evening I learned about what my parents had always hidden from me. That murky episode in central Asia: Charlotte, the armed men, the jostling, the shouting. I had only a hazy and childish memory of their accounts from the old days. The adults' words had been so obscure!

This time their clarity blinded me. In a very matter-of-fact voice, while emptying the steaming potatoes into a dish, my aunt remarked, addressing our guest, who was sitting beside Dmitrich, "Of course down there they don't live like us. Imagine, they pray to their god five times a day! And what's more, they eat without a table. Yes, all on the ground. Well, on a carpet. And without spoons; with their fingers!"

The guest, mainly to make conversation, argued back in reasonable tones, "We-ell, 'not like us' is pitching it a bit high. I was in Tashkent last summer. You know, it's not so different from here. . . ."

"And their desert — have you been there?" (She raised her voice, happy to have hit upon a good talking point, so that the supper promised to be lively and convivial.) "Yes, in the desert? His grandmother, for example" — my aunt motioned with her chin in my direction — "that Sherl . . . Shourl . . . anyway that Frenchwoman, her. It was no joke what happened to her down there. Those *basmachi,* those bandits who wouldn't have anything to do with the Soviets, they caught her on the road; she was still very young, and they raped her, just like wild animals! All of them, one after the other. There were maybe six or seven. And you say, 'They're just like us.' . . . Then they shot her in the head with a bullet. The murderer missed his aim, thank goodness. And the farmer who was carrying her in his cart, they slit his throat like a sheep. And you say, 'It's just like here.'"

"Hang on. You're talking about ancient history," interrupted Dmitrich.

And they continued arguing, while drinking vodka and eating. Outside the open window you could hear the tranquil sounds of our courtyard. The evening air was blue, soft. They went on talking without noticing that frozen to my chair, I was holding my breath, seeing nothing, failing to understand the sense of anything else they said. Finally I stepped out of the kitchen like a sleepwalker. I went out into the street and walked through the melting snow, more alien to that clear spring evening than a Martian.

It was not that I was terrified by the episode in the desert. Told in that matter-of-fact way, it could never, I sensed, shake off that layer of words and everyday gestures. Its sharp edge would remain blunted by the fat fingers seizing a gherkin; by the bobbing up and down of the Adam's apple in our guest's neck as he swallowed his vodka; by the merry squeals of the children in the courtyard. It was like that human arm I had seen one day on a motorway beside two cars rammed into one another. A torn-off arm that someone had wrapped in a piece of newspaper while waiting for the arrival of the ambulances. The printer's typeface, and the photos stuck to the bloody flesh, made it almost neutral. . . .

No, what had really shattered me was the improbability of life. The previous week I was learning the mystery of Beria, his harem of raped and murdered women. And now it was the rape of that young Frenchwoman, whom I could never, it seemed to me, recognize as Charlotte.

It was too much all at once. The gratuitous, absurdly obvious coincidence confused my thoughts. I told myself that in a novel, after that appalling tale of women abducted in the heart of Moscow, the reader would have been left to recover his spirits over long pages. He could have prepared himself for the appearance of a hero who would bring the tyrant down. But life did not bother about the coherence of subject matter. It spilled out its contents in disorder, pell-mell. In its clumsiness it spoiled the purity of our compassion and compromised our just anger. Life, in fact, was an endless rough draft, in which events, badly organized, encroached on one another, in which the characters were too numerous and prevented one another from speaking, suffering, being loved or hated individually.

I was struggling between these two tragic stories. Beria and the young women whose lives ended with their rapist's last gasp of pleasure; and Charlotte, young, unrecognizable, hurled down onto the sand, beaten, tortured. I felt myself overcome by a strange numbness. I was disillusioned, and I reproached myself for this obtuse indifference.

That night all my earlier musings on the reassuring incoherence of life seemed to me false. In a half-waking reverie I again saw the arm wrapped in a newspaper. . . . No. It was a hundred times more alarming in that banal package! Reality, with all its implausibility, by far exceeded fiction. I shook my head to drive away the vision of the little blisters in the newspaper stuck to the bloody skin. Suddenly without any interference, clear, sharply etched in the translucent desert air, another vision became fixed in my eyes. That of a young woman's body stretched out on the sand. A body already inert, despite the unbridled convulsions of the men who hurled themselves savagely upon it. The ceiling turned green as I stared at it. The pain was so great that within my breast I felt the burning shape of my heart. The pillow beneath my neck was as hard and rough as the sand. . . .

I began to slap myself, at first holding back the blows, then without pity. I struck myself until my swollen face, wet with tears, disgusted me with its sticky surface. Until that other one, which lurked within me, fell totally silent. Then, stumbling over the pillow I had knocked down in my agitation, I approached the window. The cold air calmed my puffed-up face.

"I am Russian," I said softly, all of a sudden.

12

*I*T WAS THANKS TO THAT BODY, young and with a still innocent sensuality, that I was cured. Yes, one day in April I felt I was finally liberated from the most painful winter of my youth, from its sorrows, from the deaths, and from the burden of the revelations it had brought.

But the most important thing was that my French implant no longer seemed to exist. As if I had succeeded in stifling that second heart within my breast. The last day of its death throes coincided with the April afternoon that for me was to mark the start of a life without specters. . . .

I saw her from behind, standing under the trees at a table made of thick, unplaned pine planks. An instructor was watching her movements and from time to time threw a glance at the stopwatch he was clutching in his palm.

She must have been the same age as me, fifteen, this young girl, whose body, impregnated with sun, had dazzled me. She was busy dismantling an automatic rifle and then reassembling it as quickly as possible. These were the paramilitary competitions that several of the city schools took part in. We stepped up to the table in turn, awaited the signal from the instructor, and hurled ourselves at the Kalashnikov, stripping its weighty bulk. The dismantled pieces were spread out on the planks and a moment later, in a droll reverse sequence of movements, reassembled. Some of us dropped the black spring on the ground, others confused the order of assembly. . . . As for her, I thought at first that she was dancing up and down in front of the table. Wearing a tunic and a khaki skirt, a forage cap perched on her russet curls, she made her body undulate in time with her drill. She must have practiced a great deal to be able to handle the slippery bulk of the gun with such dexterity.

I gazed at her, dumbfounded. Everything in her was so simple and so alive. Her hips, responding to the actions of her arms, swayed gently. Her full golden legs quivered. She took pleasure in her own agility, which even allowed her superfluous movements — like the rhythmic arching of her pretty, muscular buttocks. Yes, she was dancing. And even without seeing her face, I guessed she was smiling.

I fell in love with this young russet-haired stranger. It was of course a very physical desire, a carnal wonderment at the contrast between her still childishly fragile waist and her already womanly torso. . . . I performed my own dismantling-assembly routine with all my limbs in a state of numbness. I took more than three minutes, and thus ended up near the bottom of the class. . . . But beyond the desire to embrace this body, to feel its smooth, bronzed surface beneath my fingers, I experienced a new and nameless happiness.

There was this table with thick planks placed at the edge of a wood. The sun and the smell of the last of the snow taking refuge in the shadows of the thickets. Everything was blessedly simple. And luminous. Like this body, with its still insouciant femininity. Like my desire. Like the commands of the instructor. No shadow of the past troubled the clarity of this moment. I breathed, felt desire, carried out orders mechanically. And with unspeakable joy I felt the clot of my painful and confused winter reflections dissolving in my mind. . . . The young russet-haired girl swayed her hips gently before the automatic rifle. The sun lit up the contours of her body through the fine fabric of her tunic. Her fiery locks curled up over the cap. And it was as if from the depths of a well, in a dull and melancholy echo, those grotesque names rang out: Marguerite Steinheil, Isabeau de Bavière. . . . I found it hard to believe that my life had once been made up of these dusty relics. I had lived without sunlight, without desire — in the twilight of books. In search of a phantom country, a mirage of a France of yesteryear, peopled with ghosts. . . .

The instructor uttered a cry of delight and showed his stop-watch to everybody: "One minute fifteen seconds!" It was the best time. The redhead turned round, radiant. She took off her cap and shook her head. Her hair caught fire in the sunlight, her freckles flashed like sparks. I closed my eyes.

And the next day, for the first time in my life, I was discovering the very singular sensual pleasure of squeezing a firearm, a Kalashnikov, and feeling its nervous shuddering against my shoulder. And seeing in the distance a plywood figure target riddled with holes. Yes, its insistent quivering and its male power were for me of a profoundly sensual nature.

Furthermore, from the first burst of fire my head was filled with a buzzing silence. The person on my left had fired first, deafening me. The incessant clatter in my ears, the iridescent flurries of sunlight in my eyelashes, the wild smell of the earth beneath my body — I was at the peak of happiness.

For at last I was coming back to life. Living in the happy simplicity of orderly actions: shooting, marching in file, eating millet kasha from aluminum mess tins. Letting oneself be carried along in a collective movement directed by others, by those who knew the supreme objective, who generously relieved us of all the burden of responsibility, making us light, transparent, clear. The objective was simple and unequivocal too: to defend the fatherland. I could not wait to lose myself in this monumental goal, to dissolve into the marvelously irresponsible mass of my comrades. I hurled practice grenades; I shot; I pitched a tent. Happy. Blissful. Healthy. And that adolescent in an old house at the edge of the steppe, who had spent entire days meditating on the life and death of three women seen in a pile of old newspapers, seemed increasingly unreal. If I had been introduced to this dreamer I would doubtless not have recognized him. I would not have recognized myself. . . .

The next day the instructor took us to watch the arrival of a column of tanks. What we made out first was a gray cloud growing larger on the horizon. Then a mighty vibration spread through the soles of our shoes. The earth shook. And the cloud, turning yellow, rose as high as the sun and eclipsed it. All sounds disappeared, shrouded by the metallic din of the caterpillar tracks. The first gun thrust through the wall of dust, the commander's tank loomed, then the second, the third . . . And, before stopping, the tanks described a tight arc, so as to line up side by side. Then their tracks clattered even more furiously, tearing up the grass in long slices.

Hypnotized by the power of the empire, I had a sudden vision of the terrestrial globe and how these tanks — our tanks! — could strip it entirely bare. A brief command would have sufficed. I took a pride in this, such as I had never felt before. . . .

And the soldiers who emerged from the turrets fascinated me with their serene virility. They were all alike, carved from the same firm and healthy material. I guessed that they would have been invulnerable to the morbid thoughts that had tortured me during the winter. No, all that mental sludge would not have remained for a single second in the clear stream of their thinking, simple and direct, like the orders they executed. I was terribly jealous of their life. It was exposed there, under the sun, without a spot of shadow. Their strength, the male smell of their bodies, their tunics covered in dust. And the presence, somewhere, of the young russet-haired girl, of that adolescent-woman, of that amorous promise. I had only one wish now: to be able one day to emerge from the narrow turret of a tank, leap down onto its tracks, then onto the soft earth, and to walk with pleasantly weary steps toward the promise of a woman.

This life, actually a very Soviet life on whose margins I had always lived, now exalted me. To blend into its easygoing and collectivist routine suddenly seemed to me like a brilliant solution. To live the life of everybody else! To drive a tank; then, when demobilized, to pour molten steel amid the machines in a great factory beside the Volga; to go to the stadium every Saturday to watch a football match. But above all to know that this succession of days, tranquil and predictable, was crowned by a grand messianic project — the communism that, one day, would make us all perpetually happy, clear as crystal in our thoughts, strictly equal. . . .

It was then that, almost grazing the forest treetops, the fighter aircraft hurtled over our heads. Flying in groups of three, they caused the exploded sky to fall in about our ears. They surged past, wave after wave, ripping the air, their decibels cutting into my brain.

Later, in the silence of evening, I spent a long time gazing at the empty plain, with the dark streaks of torn-up grass here and there. I said to myself that once upon a time there had been a child who had imagined a fabulous city arising above that misty horizon. . . . That child was no more. I was cured.

After that memorable April day the mini-society at school accepted me. They welcomed me with that condescending magnanimity that people have toward neophytes, the born-again, or enthusiastic penitents. That is what I was. At every opportunity I was eager to show them that my singularity had been put behind me for good. That I was like them. And furthermore, ready for anything in order to expiate my eccentricity.

The mini-society itself had also changed, meanwhile. Imitating the world of adults more and more closely, it had divided itself into several tribes. Yes, almost into social classes. I could distinguish three. They already foreshadowed the future of these adolescents, yesterday still united in a homogeneous little pack. There was now a group of "proletarians." The most numerous, they came for the most part from the workers' families, who provided manual labor for the workshops of the enormous river port. There was in addition a core of students who were good at mathematics, future *tekhnars* who, having previously been lumped together with the proletarians and dominated by them, increasingly stood out from them, as they occupied the scholastic front ranks. Finally, the most exclusive and the most elitist, as well as the most restrained, that coterie in which one could detect the budding intelligentsia.

In each of these classes I became one of them. My intermediate presence was appreciated by them all. There was even a time when I believed myself irreplaceable. Thanks to . . . France.

For, cured of France, I now dined out on her. I was happy to be able to pass on my whole stock of anecdotes, accumulated over the years, to those who had now accepted me among them. My stories found favor. Battles in the catacombs; frogs' legs paid for in gold; entire streets in Paris devoted to the sale of love — these subjects earned me the reputation of an established storyteller.

I talked, and I felt my recovery to be complete. The bouts of that madness that had earlier plunged me into the vertiginous sensation of the past did not recur. France became simply a source of stories — entertaining and exotic in the eyes of my fellow pupils, arousing when I described love *à la française,* but overall little different from the funny and often smutty stories that we told one another during the breaks, as we puffed on our hasty cigarettes.

I noticed fairly quickly that it was necessary to season my French stories according to the tastes of my listeners. The same story would change in tone according to whether I was telling it to the "proletarians," the *"tekhnars,"* or the "intellectuals." Proud of my talent as a raconteur, I varied genres, adapted my style, chose my words. Thus, to please the first group, I dwelled at length on the torrid frolics of the president and Marguerite. A man, and what's more a president of the Republic, who died from too much lovemaking — this picture alone had them in ecstasy. The *tekhnars,* on the other hand, were more interested in the twists and turns of psychological intrigue. They wanted to know what happened to Marguerite after her erotic masterstroke. So I talked about the mysterious double murder in the impasse Ronsin; about that terrible May morning when Marguerite's husband was discovered, garrotted with the aid of a curtain cord; and likewise her mother-in-law, also choked, but on her own false teeth. . . . Nor did I fail to point out that her husband, a painter by profession, had been overwhelmed with official commissions, while his wife had never forgone friendships in high places. According to one version, it was one of the late Félix Faure's successors, evidently a minister, who had been surprised by her husband. . . .

As for the intellectuals, the subject seemed to leave my new friends cold. Some of them even yawned from time to time, to show their lack of interest. They only abandoned this assumed indifference when they found a pretext to make a play on words. The name of French President "Faure" quickly fell victim to a pun: in Russian, giving *foru* means giving odds to a rival. The laughter, knowingly blasé, erupted. I realized that the language spoken in this narrow circle was made up almost exclusively of twisted words, punning riddles, camp remarks, and turns of phrase known only to its members. With a mixture of admiration and anguish, it became clear to me that their language had no need of the world about us, the sun, the wind. And I was soon contriving to imitate these word jugglers with ease. . . .

The only person who did not appreciate my turnabout was Pashka, the dunce, whose fishing expeditions I once used to share in. From time to time he would approach our group and listen to us, and when I embarked on telling my French stories he would stare at me with a suspicious air.

One day the gathering round me was more numerous than usual. My story must have been particularly interesting. I was talking (summarizing the novel by that poor Spivalski, who was accused of all the mortal sins and killed in Paris) about the two lovers who had spent a long night in an almost empty train, fleeing across the dying empire of the tsars. The next day they parted forever. . . .

On this occasion my listeners belonged to all three castes — sons of proletarians, future engineers, and intelligentsia. I described the passionate embraces in the depths of a sleeping compartment as the train hurtled through dead villages and over burned bridges. They listened to me avidly. It was certainly easier for them to picture this pair of lovers in a train than a president of the Republic with his beloved in a palace. . . . And to satisfy the aficionados of wordplay I described the train stopping in a provincial town: the hero lowered the window and asked the few people who were walking alongside the track what the name of the place was. But no one could tell him. It was a town without a name! A town peopled with strangers. A sigh of satisfaction arose from the group of aesthetes. And then in a cunning flashback, I returned to the compartment, to talk again of the restless love of my crazy travelers. . . .

It was at that moment that above the crowd I saw Pashka's tousled head appearing. Pashka listened for several minutes, then growled, easily drowning my voice with his rough bass. "You've got these fools with their tongues hanging out over your pack of fibs!"

No one would have dared to contradict Pashka in a solo confrontation. But the crowd has a courage of its own. Snorts of indignation came in response.

In order to cool tempers I said in a conciliatory tone, "They're not fibs, Pashka! It's an autobiographical novel. This guy really did escape from Russia with his mistress after the Revolution, and then in Paris he was murdered. . . ."

"Right. So why don't you tell them what happened at the station?"

I was left openmouthed. Now I remembered having already told this story to my friend, the dunce. In the morning the two lovers had found themselves beside the Black Sea, in a deserted café, in a town buried in snow. They drank scalding tea by a window covered with hoarfrost. . . . Several years later when they met again in Paris they admitted to one another that those few hours that morning were more dear to them than all the transports of love in their lives. Yes, that dull, gray morning; the muffled sounds of the foghorns; and their complicit presence at the height of the murderous storm of history. . . .

It was that station café that Pashka was speaking of. . . . The school bell rescued me from my embarrassment. My listeners stubbed out their cigarettes and streamed into the classroom. While I, abashed, told myself that none of my styles — not the one I adopted when speaking to the *prolos,* nor the one for the *tekhnars,* nor even the verbal acrobatics that the intellectuals adored — no, none of these ways of speaking could have recreated the mysterious charm of that snowy morning on the edge of the abyss of the times. The light, the silence . . . Furthermore none of my fellow students would have been interested! It was too simple: without erotic attractions, without intrigue, without wordplay.

As I went home from school I remembered that when telling my comrades the story of the French president in love, I had never yet spoken of his silent vigil beside the black window at the Elysée. He alone, facing the autumn night, and — somewhere out there in that world of darkness and rain — a woman with her face hidden beneath a veil that sparkled with mist. But who would have listened to me if I had ventured to speak of that moist veil in the autumn night?

Pashka tried again two or three times, and always clumsily, to tear me away from my new friends. To no avail. One day he invited me to go fishing on the Volga. I refused in the presence of everybody, with a vaguely scornful air. He remained for several seconds in front of our group—alone, hesitant, strangely frail despite his broad shoulders. . . . On another occasion he caught up with me on the journey home and asked me to bring him Spivalski's book. I promised I would. The next day I had forgotten all about it. . . .

I was too absorbed in a new collective pleasure: the Mountain of Joy.

That was the name given in our city to an enormous open-air dance floor situated on the summit of a hill high above the Volga. We scarcely knew how to dance. But it was clear that our rhythmic gyrations had only one objective: to hold a girl's body in our arms, to touch it, to tame it. On our evening excursions to the Mountain, castes and coteries no longer existed. In the feverishness of our desire we were all equal. Only the young soldiers on leave formed a group apart. I observed them jealously.

One evening I heard someone calling me. The voice seemed to come from the foliage on the trees. I looked up and there was Pashka! The square dance floor was surrounded by a high wooden fence. Outside, wild vegetation grew thickets somewhere between a park run to seed and a forest. It was on a broad branch of a maple tree, above the fence, that I saw him. . . .

I had just left the dance floor after having clumsily bumped against my partner's breasts. . . . It was the first time I had danced with such a buxom girl. My palms, resting on her back, were all moist. Caught out by an unexpected flourish from the band, I made a false move, and my chest pressed against hers. The effect was more powerful than an electric shock! The soft elasticity of a female breast overwhelmed me. I continued to shuffle without hearing the music: instead of the dancing girl's fair face, all I saw was a shining oval.

When the band stopped playing, she walked away without saying a word, visibly piqued. I crossed the floor, sliding between couples, as if I were walking on ice, and went out.

I needed to be alone, to recover my spirits. I walked along the path that ran beside the dance floor. The wind coming from the Volga cooled my burning brow. "But suppose it was her, my partner herself," I thought suddenly, "who chose to bump into me on purpose?" Yes, perhaps she had wanted me to feel her bosom and was sending me a signal that in my naïveté and my timidity I had failed to decode. Had I missed the chance of a lifetime?

Like a child that has just broken a cup and closes its eyes, hoping that this momentary darkness will put everything back together again, I screwed up my eyes: why couldn't the band play the same number again and I find my partner again and repeat all the same movements? I had never felt and would never again feel so intensely the intimate proximity and at the same time, the most irretrievable remoteness of a female body. . . .

It was in the midst of this emotional disarray that I heard the voice of Pashka, hidden in the foliage. I looked up. He was smiling at me, half stretched out along a thick branch: "Climb up! I'll make room for you," he said, folding up his legs.

Clumsy and heavy in the city, as soon as he was in the wild Pashka was transfigured. On that branch he looked like a big cat, resting before its nightly prowl. . . .

In any other circumstances I would have ignored his invitation. But his position was too unusual, and in addition I felt I had been caught in flagrante delicto. I felt as if he had intercepted my feverish thoughts from his branch! He held his hand out to me, and I hauled myself up beside him. The tree was a veritable observation post.

Seen from above, the swaying of hundreds of entwined bodies had quite a different look to it. It seemed at one and the same time absurd (all these creatures pawing the ground!) and endowed with a certain logic. Bodies circulated, coalesced for the space of a dance, separated, sometimes remained glued to one another during several numbers. From our tree, at a single glance, I could take in all the little emotional games unfolding on the dance floor. Rivalries, challenges, betrayals, loves at first sight, breakups, explanations, potential brawls quickly brought under control by the vigilant keepers of order. But above all, it was desire that was visible through the veil of the music and the ritual of the dance. Within that human tide I located the girl whose breasts I had brushed against. For a moment I followed her trajectory from one partner to another. . . .

In short, I felt all this whirling about reminded me insidiously of something. "Life!" a silent voice suddenly suggested to me, and my lips repeated silently, "Life . . ." The same mingling of bodies driven by desire and hiding it under innumerable pretenses. Life . . . "And where am I, myself, at this moment?" I asked myself, sensing that the answer to this question would shed light on an extraordinary truth, which would explain everything once and for all.

Shouts rang out beside the path. I recognized my classmates returning to the city. I seized the branch, ready to jump. Pashka's voice, tinged with embittered resignation, rang out uncertainly: "Wait! Look, they're going to switch off the floodlights. There'll be masses of stars! If we climb higher we'll see Sagittarius. . . ."

I was not listening to him. I jumped to the ground. The earth, ribbed with thick roots, bruised the soles of my feet violently. I ran to catch up with my classmates, who were moving off, gesticulating. I wanted to tell them, as quickly as possible, about my partner with the beautiful bosom, to hear their remarks, to deafen myself with words. I was in a hurry to get back to life. And with cruel glee I parodied the strange question that had formed inside my head a moment before: "Where am I? Where was I? On a branch beside that idiot, Pashka, obviously. On the edge of real life!"

By a freakish coincidence (I already knew that reality is made up of implausible repetitions of the kind that novelists hound down as serious faults) we met again the next day, with that unease experienced by two companions who at night have exchanged grave, exalted, and emotional confidences, have revealed themselves to the very intimate core of their souls, and who meet again in the morning by the mundane and skeptical light of day.

I wandered around outside the still-closed dance floor. I wanted to be the first partner for the dancer of the night before. I wanted time to go into reverse and glue my broken cup back together again.

Pashka appeared in the scrub of the park, saw me, hesitated for a second, then walked toward me. He was laden with his fishing gear. Under his arm he carried a big loaf of black bread from which he tore off and ate pieces, chewing them with relish. Once more I felt I had been caught in flagrante delicto. He inspected me, scrutinizing my light-colored shirt wide open at the neck, my fashionable trousers, very flared at the bottom. Then, tossing his head as a sign of good-bye, he moved off. I heaved a sigh of relief. But suddenly Pashka turned and called out to me in a slightly coarse voice, "Here, come with me, I'll show you something! Come on, you won't be sorry. . . ."

I followed him with a hesitant tread.

We went down toward the Volga, walked beside the port with its enormous cranes, its workshops, its corrugated iron warehouses. Farther downstream we made our way into a broad wasteland littered with old barges; with misty metallic constructions; with pyramids of lengthy, rotten tree trunks. Pashka hid his lines and nets under one of these worm-eaten boles and began to jump from one boat to another. There was also an abandoned landing stage, and several pontoon bridges that yielded buoyantly beneath our feet. In following Pashka, I had not in fact noticed the moment when we left dry land to find ourselves on this floating island of abandoned craft. I held on to a broken handrail, leaped into a kind of junk, stepped over its side, slipped on the wet timbers of a raft. . . .

We finally found ourselves in a channel that had steep banks all covered in flowering elder trees. Its surface, from one shore to the other, was hidden under the hulks of ancient vessels packed close together, side by side, in fantastic disorder.

We settled ourselves on the thwart of a little boat. Above it arose the side of a barge that bore traces of fire. Craning my neck, I noticed up there, on the deck of the barge, a rope strung out near the cabin: several fragments of faded cloth undulated gently — washing that had been hanging out to dry for years. . . .

The evening was warm, misty. The smell of the water mingled with the insipid emanations from the elder trees. From time to time a vessel that we could see passing in the distance in the middle of the Volga sent a series of lazy waves into our channel. Our boat began to pitch up and down, rubbing against the black side of the barge. The whole half-submerged graveyard came to life. One could hear the grating of a cable, the lapping of the water under a pontoon, the lisping of the reeds.

"They are great, all these bulwarks!" I exclaimed, using a word whose maritime application was only vaguely known to me.

Pashka gave me a rather confused glance. I got up, in a hurry to return to the Mountain of Joy. . . . But my friend tugged me forcefully by the sleeve to make me sit down and announced in a nervous whisper, "Hang on! They're coming!"

I heard the sound of footsteps, the click of heels on the wet clay of the bank, then a tattoo on the wood of a footbridge. Finally a metallic hammering right above us on the deck of the barge. . . . And already muffled voices reaching to us from its bowels.

Pashka stood up straight and pressed himself against the side of the barge. It was only then that I noticed the three portholes. Their panes were broken and blocked up from the inside with pieces of plywood. The surfaces of these were covered in fine holes made by a knife blade. Without leaving his porthole, my friend gestured with his hand, inviting me to imitate him. Clinging onto a steel projection that ran the length of the side, I glued myself to the left-hand porthole. The one in the center remained unoccupied.

What I saw through the crack was at the same time banal and extraordinary. A woman, of whom I could only see her head in profile and the upper part of her body, seemed to be leaning with her elbows on a table, her arms parallel, her hands motionless. Her face appeared calm and even drowsy. Only her presence here, on this barge, seemed surprising. Although after all . . . She kept gently nodding her head, which had fair, curly hair, as if she were continually agreeing with an invisible speaker.

I moved away from my porthole and glanced at Pashka. I was perplexed. "But after all, what's there to see?" But he had his palms stuck to the flaking surface of the barge, and his forehead against the plywood.

Then I moved to the neighboring porthole, peering into one of the cracks that perforated the wood that blocked it.

It was as if our boat were sinking, going to the bottom of that cluttered canal, and the side of the barge, on the other hand, were hurtling up toward the sky. Feverishly I let myself be magnetized by its rough metal, while trying to keep within my sight the vision that had just blinded me.

It was a woman's buttocks, white, nude, massive. Yes, the haunches of a kneeling woman, still seen in profile, her legs, her thighs, the breadth of which terrified me; and the start of her back, cut off by the field of vision allowed by the crack. Behind that enormous backside there was a soldier, also on his knees, his trousers unbuttoned, his tunic in disorder. He was grasping the hips of the woman and drawing them toward him, as if he wanted to be swallowed up into that mass of flesh, which at the same time he kept thrusting away from him with violent shudders of his whole body.

Our boat began to slip away beneath my feet. A vessel sailing up the Volga had sent its waves into our channel. One of them managed to unbalance me. In saving myself from falling I took a step to the left and found myself by the first porthole. I pressed my forehead against its steel frame. In the crack appeared the woman with curly hair and an indifferent and somnolent face, the one I had seen at first; leaning on what resembled a tablecloth, dressed in a white blouse, she continued acquiescing with little nods of her head and was distractedly examining her fingers. . . .

This first porthole. And the second. The woman whose eyelids were heavy with sleep, her dress and her hairstyle very ordinary. And the other. This naked, erect backside; this white flesh into which there plunged a man who seemed slender beside her; those broad thighs; that heavy movement of the hips. In my shocked young head no link could associate these two images. Impossible to join this upper half of a woman's body to that lower half!

My excitement was such that the side of the barge suddenly seemed to me to be stretched out horizontally. Lying flat on the surface like a lizard, I moved toward the porthole with the naked woman. She was still there, but the powerful curve of her flesh was now motionless. The soldier, now facing me, was buttoning himself up with limp and clumsy movements. And another one, smaller than the first, was kneeling down beside the white backside. His movements, on the other hand, were of a nervous and fearful rapidity. But as soon as he began wrestling, pushing the heavy white hemispheres with his belly, you could not have told him apart from the first one. There was no difference in their actions.

My eyes were already filling with black needles. My legs were giving way. And my heart, pressed against the rusty metal, was making the whole vessel vibrate with its deep, breathless echoes. A new series of little waves shook the boat. The side of the barge became vertical again, and, losing my lizard's agility, I slid toward the first porthole. The woman in the white blouse was nodding her head mechanically while examining her hands. I saw her scratching one nail with another, to remove the layer of varnish. . . .

Their footsteps resounded in reverse order this time: the hammering of the heels on the deck; the tattoo on the planks of the footbridge; the slapping of the wet clay. Without looking at me, Pashka stepped over the side of our boat, bounded onto a half-submerged pontoon, then onto a landing stage. I followed him, jumping limply like a rag doll on strings.

Reaching the bank, he sat down, removed his shoes, rolled up his trousers to the knees, and walked into the water, parting the long stems of the reeds. He thrust aside the duckweed and splashed water over his face for a long time, uttering groans of pleasure, which in the distance could have been taken for cries of distress.

It was a great day in her life. On that June evening she was, for the first time in her life, going to give herself to one of her young friends, to one of those dancers who shuffled on the dance floor at the Mountain of Joy.

She was rather frail. Her face had the neutral features that pass unnoticed in the crowd. The color of her pale russet hair could only be detected by daylight. Under the floodlights of the Mountain or in the bluish glow of the street lamps she appeared simply blond.

I had discovered this erotic custom just a few days ago. In the human swarm at the dance floor I saw groups forming — a swirling knot of adolescents came together, wriggling, getting excited, and as they left, they would scatter to be initiated into what sometimes seemed to me stupidly simple, sometimes fabulously mysterious and profound: love.

She must have been passed over in one of those groups. Like the others, she had been secretly drinking among the bushes that covered the slopes of the Mountain. Then, when their excited little circle had exploded into couples, she was left alone: the accidents of arithmetic did not provide her with a partner. The couples had vanished. Drunkenness was already overtaking her. She was not used to alcohol and had drunk too much, out of eagerness, out of fear of not matching up to the others, and also from the desire to overcome her nervousness on this great day. . . . She had come back onto the floor, not knowing what to do with her body now, every fiber of which was filled with impatient excitement. But already they were beginning to switch off the floodlights.

All this I was to guess later. . . . That night I simply saw a girl pacing up and down in a corner of the park at night, walking round the wan pool of light from a street lamp. Like a moth held prisoner by a ray of light. Her gait surprised me. She moved forward as if on a tightrope, with steps that were at once floating and tense. I could see that in every one of her movements she was struggling against drunkenness. Her face had a fixed expression. Her whole being was mobilized in this single effort — not to fall over, to let nothing be suspected, to continue walking round on this circle of light until the black trees stopped swaying and leaping when she approached them, waving their noisy branches.

I went toward her. I entered the blue circle of the street lamp. Her body (black skirt, light top) suddenly focused all my desire. Yes, she instantly became the woman I had always desired. Despite her breathless frailty, despite her features being blurred with drunkenness, despite everything in her body and her face that should have displeased me but which at that moment I found so beautiful.

Making her rounds, she bumped into me and lifted her eyes. I saw a succession of masks on her face — fear, anger, a smile. It was the smile that triumphed, a vague smile that seemed to be directed at someone other than myself. She took my arm. We descended from the Mountain.

At first she talked without stopping. Her tipsy young voice would not remain steady. She whispered, then almost shouted. Clinging to my arm, she stumbled from time to time and let fly an oath, then put her hand to her lips with affected haste. Or else she suddenly broke away from me with an offended air, only to snuggle against my shoulder a moment later. I guessed that my companion was now acting out a love scene rehearsed long ago — a performance intended to show her partner she was somebody special. But in her intoxication she was confusing the sequence of these little interludes. While I, a bad actor, remained dumb, enthralled by this feminine presence, suddenly so accessible; and above all by the staggering ease with which this body was about to offer itself to me. I had always believed that such an offer would be preceded by a long emotional journey, by a thousand speeches, by subtle flirting. I was silent as I felt a little feminine breast squeezed against my arm. Next my nocturnal companion, jabbering animatedly, rejected the advance of a overly forward phantom and puffed out her cheeks for several seconds to show that she was sulking; then she enveloped her imaginary lover in what she believed was a languorous look, but which was simply blurred with the wine and the excitement.

I led her toward the only place that could accommodate our love — toward that floating island where at the beginning of the summer Pashka and I had spied on the prostitute and the soldiers.

In the darkness I must have taken a wrong turn. After wandering for a long time amid sleeping boats we stopped on a kind of old ferry — its ramp had broken supports and was half sunk in the water.

Abruptly she fell silent. Her drunkenness must have been gradually wearing off. I remained motionless, confronting her tense expectation in the darkness. I did not know what I was supposed to do. Kneeling down, I felt the boards, and threw into the water first a tangle of worn ropes, then a bundle of dried seaweed. It was by accident that, busy with my clearing up, I brushed her leg. My fingers, slipping over her skin, gave her goose bumps. . . .

She remained silent until it was over. Her eyes closed, she seemed absent, abandoning to me her body that quaked with little shivers. . . . I must have hurt her badly with my hasty actions. This act, so dreamed of, blundered into a series of clumsy, thwarted manipulations. Love was apparently like a hasty, nervous excavation. The knees and the elbows stuck out with a strange anatomical stiffness.

The pleasure was like the flame of a match in an icy wind — a fire that has just enough time to burn your fingers before going out, leaving a blinding spot in your eyes.

I tried to kiss her (I believed that one should do so at this moment); beneath my mouth I felt her lip being bitten hard. . . .

And what frightened me the most was that a second later I no longer needed either her lips or her erect breast in her gaping blouse, or her slender thighs, over which she had pulled down her skirt with a rapid movement. Her body was becoming indifferent to me, useless. Sunk in my dull physical contentment, I was self-sufficient. "Why is she still stretched out like that, half naked?" I wondered, irritated. I felt the uneven boards beneath my back, several splinters burning in my palm. The wind had the heavy taste of stagnant water.

In this nocturnal interval there may well have been a fleeting moment of oblivion, a lightning sleep of several minutes. For I did not see the ship approaching. When we opened our eyes, all its white enormity, glittering with lights, was already looming above us. I had thought that our refuge was located deep in one of the countless bays cluttered up with rusty wrecks. But the opposite had occurred. In the darkness we had reached the tip of a headland that projected almost into the middle of the river. . . . The brightly lit passenger ship, cruising slowly down the Volga, suddenly rose up above our old ferryboat, towering with its three decks. Human silhouettes were outlined against the somber sky. They were dancing on the top deck by the blaze of the lights. The warm flow of a tango spilled over us, enveloped us. The cabin windows, more discreetly lit, seemed to lean over, allowing us to enter their intimacy. . . . The swell caused by the riverboat was so powerful that our raft swung in a half circle, a swirling glissade that made us giddy. The ship with its light and its music seemed to be circling round us. . . . It was at that moment that she squeezed my hand and pressed herself against me. It seemed as if the hot-blooded denseness of her body could be concentrated entirely in my hands, like the trembling body of a bird. Her arms and her waist had the suppleness of that armful of water lilies I had picked one day, embracing several slippery stems in the water. . . .

But already the ship was melting into the darkness. The echo of the tango faded. On its voyage toward Astrakhan, it carried the night with it. The sky around our ferry was filling with a hesitant pallor. I found it strange to see us in the middle of a great river at the timid birth of that day on the damp timbers of a raft. And along the shore the outlines of the port slowly took shape.

She did not wait for me. Without looking at me, she began to jump from one boat to the next. She was escaping with the shy haste of a young ballerina after a muffed exit. As I followed her leaping flight my heart stood still. At any moment she could slip on the wet wood, be betrayed by a broken footbridge, fall between two boats whose sides would close over her head. The concentration of my gaze sustained her in her acrobatics through the morning mist.

A moment later I saw her walking along the shore. In the silence the sand crunched softly beneath her feet. . . . Here was a woman to whom I had felt so close a quarter of an hour before, who was now leaving. I experienced a pain quite new to me; a woman was leaving, breaking the invisible ties that still bound us. And there on that deserted shore she was transformed into an extraordinary being — a woman I love who is becoming independent of me again, a stranger to me, and who will soon be speaking to other people, smiling. . . . Living!

She turned, hearing me running after her. I saw her pale face, her hair that I now noticed was of a very light auburn color. Unsmiling, she looked at me in silence. I no longer remembered what I had wanted to say to her while listening, a moment before, to the wet sand crunching beneath her heels. "I love you" would have been a lie I could not utter. Alone her crumpled black skirt, and her arms, childishly slender, meant more to me than all the "I love you"s in the world. To suggest to her that we should meet again that day or the next was unthinkable. Our night must remain unique. Like the passing of the riverboat, like our momentary sleep, like her body in the cool of the great somnolent river.

I tried to tell her. I spoke, at random, of the crunching of the sand under her feet; of her solitude on this shore; of her fragility that night, which had reminded me of the stems of water lilies. I felt suddenly and with an acute happiness that I must also tell her about Charlotte's balcony, about our evenings on the steppes, about the elegant trio on an autumn morning on the Champs-Elysées. . . .

Her face screwed up into an expression at once scornful and anxious. Her lips trembled.

"Are you sick or what?" she said, interrupting me in that slightly nasal tone that girls on the Mountain of Joy adopted to rebuff unwanted attention.

I stood stock-still. She went off, climbing toward the first buildings of the port, and soon plunging into their massive shadow. The workers were beginning to appear at the gates of their workshops.

Some days later, in the nocturnal gathering at the Mountain, I heard a conversation between my classmates, who had not noticed that I was close by. One of the girls in their little circle had complained, they were saying, about her partner who did not know how to make love (they expressed the notion much more crudely); and apparently she had confided some comic details ("killing," said one of them) of his behavior. I was listening to them in the hope of some erotic revelations. Suddenly the name of the despised partner was mentioned — "Frantsuz" — it was my nickname, of which I was generally proud. "Frantsuz" — the Russian for a Frenchman. Through their laughter I picked up a quiet exchange of remarks between two friends, in the manner of a secret agreement: "Let's take care of her tonight, after the dancing. Us two. Agreed?"

I guessed they were still talking about her. I left my corner and went toward the exit. They saw me. "Frantsuz! Frantsuz . . ." The whispering accompanied me for a moment, then was lost in the first surge of the music.

The next day, without warning anyone, I left for Saranza.

13

I WAS GOING TO THAT SLEEPY LITTLE TOWN, lost in the middle of the steppes, to destroy France. I must put an end to Charlotte's France, which had made of me a strange mutant, incapable of living in the real world.

In my mind this destruction had to resemble a long cry, a howl of rage that would best express my whole revolt. So far this howl was welling up without words. They would come, I was sure of it, as soon as Charlotte's calm eyes rested on me. For the moment I was shouting silently. There were only images hurtling by in a chaotic and motley flood.

I saw the gleam of a pince-nez in the well-upholstered shadows of a huge black car. Beria was choosing a woman's body for the night. And our neighbor across the street, a quiet, smiling pensioner, was watering the flowers on his balcony, listening to the warbling of a transistor. And in our kitchen a man with his arms covered in tattoos was speaking of a frozen lake filled with naked corpses. And none of the people in the third-class carriage that was taking me toward Saranza seemed to notice these shattering paradoxes. They got on with their lives, calmly.

In my cry I wanted to spill out these images over Charlotte. I awaited a response from her. I wanted her to explain herself, to justify herself. For it was she who had passed on to me this French sensibility — her own — condemning me to live painfully between two worlds.

I would speak to her of my father with the hole in his head, that little crater where his life pulsed. And of my mother, from whom we had inherited the fear of an unexpected ring at the door on the eve of holidays. Both of them dead. Unconsciously I resented her for her calm during my mother's burial. And for the life, so European in its good sense and neatness, that she led at Saranza. I found in her the West personified, that rational and cold West against which Russians harbor an incurable grudge. That Europe which looks down condescendingly from the stronghold of its civilization on our barbarian miseries . . . the wars in which we died by the million, the revolutions whose scenarios it wrote for us. . . . In my juvenile rebellion there was a large dose of this innate mistrust.

The French implant, which I thought had atrophied, was still within me and was preventing me from seeing. It split reality in two. As it had done with the body of that woman I had spied on through two different portholes: there was one woman in a white blouse, calm and very ordinary — and the other — that immense backside, whose potent carnality rendered the rest of the body almost useless.

And yet I knew that the two women were only one. Just like my shattered reality. It was my French illusion that confused my vision, like an intoxication, giving the world a deceptively lifelike mirage as its double. . . .

My cry was ripening. The images I would find words for swirled in my eyes more and more rapidly: Beria murmuring to the driver, "Faster! Catch that one! Let me see . . ."; and a man in a Father Christmas costume, my grandfather Fyodor, arrested on New Year's Eve; and my father's charred village; and the slender arms of my beloved — childlike arms with blue veins; and that erect backside with its animal power; and that woman removing red varnish from her nails while the lower part of her body is possessed; and the little Pont-Neuf bag; and the "Verdun"; and all that French nonsense that was ruining my youth!

At Saranza station I remained on the platform for a moment. From force of habit I was looking for Charlotte's silhouette. Then with scornful anger I called myself a fool. No one was waiting for me this time. My grandmother had not the slightest inkling that I was coming! Furthermore, the train that brought me had no connection with the one I used to take each summer to come to this town. I had arrived in Saranza not in the morning but in the evening. And the incredibly long train, too long and massive for this little provincial station, moved off heavily, traveling to Tashkent, near the Asiatic border of the empire. Urgench, Bukhara, Samarkand, the echo of the forward stops reverberated in my head, awakening a yearning for the Orient, which is mournful and profound for every Russian.

This time everything was different.

The door was unlocked. It was still the period when one only locked one's apartment at night. I pushed it open, as in a dream. I had pictured this moment so clearly I thought I knew word for word what I was going to say to Charlotte, what I was going to accuse her of. . . .

However, as I heard the imperceptible click of the door, as familiar to me as the voice of a friend, and breathed the light and pleasant aroma that always hung on the air in Charlotte's apartment, I felt my head emptying of words. Only a few snatches of my prepared howl still rang in my ears: "Beria! And that old man calmly watering his gladioli. And that woman cut in two! And the forgotten war! And your rape! And that Siberian suitcase, filled with old French scraps of paper, which I drag about like a prisoner's ball and chain! And our Russia, which you, a Frenchwoman, do not understand and will never understand! And my beloved, whom those two young swine are going to 'take care of'!"

She did not hear me come in. I saw her sitting before the balcony door. Her face was bent over a light-colored garment spread out on her lap, her needle flashing (I do not know why, but in my memory Charlotte was always engaged in darning a lace collar). . . .

I heard her voice. It was not singing, but rather a slow recitation, a melodious murmur interrupted by pauses, which kept time with the flow of her silent thoughts. Yes, a French song, half hummed, half spoken. In the overheated torpor of the evening her notes gave an impression of freshness, like the thin resonance of a harpsichord. I listened to the words, and for several seconds I had the feeling of listening to an unknown foreign language — a language that meant nothing to me. After a minute I recognized it as French. . . . Charlotte was crooning very slowly, sighing from time to time, letting the bottomless silence of the steppe intervene between two verses of her recitation.

It was the song whose charm I had discovered while still a very young child, and which now focused all my rancor on her.

> At each corner of the bed
> Periwinkles in a bunch . . .

"Yes. That's just the kind of French sentimentality that is choking my life!" I thought angrily.

> We'd sleep together there
> Till the world comes to an end. . . .

No, I could not listen to these words anymore!

I entered the room and announced with deliberate abruptness, in Russian, "It's me! I'll bet you weren't expecting me!"

To my amazement, to my chagrin as well, the look Charlotte gave me was quite calm. I read in her eyes the faultless self-control that is acquired through coping daily with grief, anguish, danger.

Having established, via a few discreet and apparently humdrum questions, that I had not come as the bearer of bad tidings, she went to the hall and telephoned my aunt to tell her of my arrival. And once again Charlotte surprised me by the ease with which she spoke to this woman, who was so different from her. Her voice, the same voice that a moment ago had been softly crooning an old French song, took on a slightly rough accent, and in a few words she managed to explain everything, arrange everything, putting my escapade on the same level with our regular summer reunions.

"She's trying to mimic us," I thought, as I listened to her talking. "She's parodying us." Charlotte's calm and that very Russian voice only served to exacerbate my bitterness.

I began to lie in wait for each and every word. One of them was going to unleash my explosion. Charlotte would offer me her *boules de neige,* our favorite dessert, and then I could let fly against all her French fripperies. Or else, trying to recreate the atmosphere of our evenings together in the old days, she would start talking about her childhood, that's right, about some dog barber on a quay beside the Seine. . . .

But Charlotte was silent. She paid very little attention to me. As if my presence had not in the least disturbed the atmosphere of one more ordinary evening in her life. From time to time she caught my eye and smiled at me, and then her face became blank again.

Our supper astonished me by its simplicity. There were no *boules de neige,* nor any of our childhood treats. I was amazed to realize that this black bread and weak tea was Charlotte's normal fare.

After the meal I waited for her on the balcony. The same garlands of flowers, the same endless steppe beneath the heat haze. And between two rosebushes — the face of the stone bacchante. I had a sudden impulse to hurl this head over the handrail, to snatch at the flowers, to shatter the stillness of the plain with my cry. Yes, and now Charlotte would come and sit on her little chair and spread out a piece of fabric on her lap. . . .

She did appear, but instead of settling down on her low seat she came and leaned on the handrail beside me. This was how my sister and I used to stand in the old days, side by side, watching the steppe as it sank slowly into the night and listening to our grandmother's stories.

Yes, she rested her elbows on the cracked wood, gazing at the endless plain that was tinged with transparent violet light. And suddenly, without looking at me, she began to speak in a remote and pensive voice, which seemed to be addressing both me and someone else besides.

"You know, it's strange. . . . A week ago I met a woman at the cemetery. Her son is buried in the same row as your grandfather. We talked about them, their deaths and the war. What else can one talk about in the presence of graves? Her son was wounded a month before the end of the war. Our soldiers were already advancing on Berlin. Every day she prayed that they would keep her son in the hospital one more week, three more days (she was a believer — or was turning into one during that waiting time). . . . He was killed in Berlin, during the very last of the fighting. Actually on the streets of Berlin. She told me all that very simply. Even her tears were simple as she told me how she prayed. . . . And do you know what her story reminded me of? A wounded soldier in our hospital. He was afraid to go back to the front, and every night he reopened his wound with a sponge. I surprised him doing it and told the head doctor. We put a plaster cast on this wounded man, and some time later when his leg was healed, he went back to the front. . . . At the time, you see, it all seemed so clear, so right. And now I feel a bit lost. Yes, my life is behind me, and suddenly everything has to be reconsidered. Perhaps it may seem silly to you, but from time to time I ask myself, 'Suppose I sent him to his death, that young soldier?' I tell myself that probably somewhere in the heart of Russia there was a woman who was praying every day that they would keep him in the hospital for as long as possible. Yes, like that woman at the cemetery. I don't know. . . . I can't forget that mother's face. It's quite untrue, you see, but now it seems to me as if there was a little note of reproach in her voice. I don't know how to explain all that to myself. . . ."

She fell silent and remained quite still for a long moment, her eyes wide open; the pupils seemed to retain the light of the sunset, now faded. Transfixed, I watched her sideways, without being able to turn my head, change the position of my arms, or relax my crossed fingers. . . .

"I'll go and make your bed," she said finally, leaving the balcony.

I stood up and glanced around in amazement. Charlotte's little chair, the lamp with its turquoise shade, the stone bacchante with her melancholy smile, the narrow balcony poised above the nocturnal steppe — all suddenly seemed so fragile! I was bewildered to recall my desire to destroy this ephemeral setting. Now the balcony was tiny — as if I were observing it from a great distance — yes, tiny and defenseless.

The next day a dry burning wind invaded Saranza. At the corners of the streets baked hard by the sun there arose little tornadoes of dust. And their appearance was followed by an explosion of sound — a military band struck up on the central square, and the hot gusts carried snatches of their valiant uproar all the way to Charlotte's house. Then the silence abruptly returned, and one could hear the grating of sand against the windowpanes and the feverish buzzing of a fly. It was the first day of maneuvers that were taking place several kilometers away from Saranza.

We walked for a long time. First of all crossing the town, then out over the steppe. Charlotte spoke with the same calm and detached voice as the previous evening on the balcony. Her story mingled with the merry tumult of the band, then suddenly the wind dropped, and her words resounded with a strange clarity in the emptiness of sun and silence.

She told of her brief stay in Moscow two years after the war. . . . One fine afternoon in May as she was walking along the network of lanes in the Presnya district, which led down toward the Moskva River, she felt she was convalescing, recovering from the war, from fear, and even, without daring to admit it to herself, from Fyodor's death, or rather from her obsession with his absence. . . . On the corner of a street, she heard a snatch of a remark as two women passed close by her in conversation, "Samovars . . ." said one of them.

"The good tea in the old days," thought Charlotte, echoing them. Then as she emerged onto the square, in front of the market, with its wooden booths, its kiosks, and its fencing of thick planks, she realized that she had been mistaken. A man without legs, installed in a kind of box on wheels, advanced toward her, his one arm outstretched.

"Now then, my lovely, spare a little ruble for the invalid."

Instinctively Charlotte turned away from him, so much did this stranger resemble a man rising from the earth. It was then she perceived that the outskirts of the market were swarming with disabled soldiers — with these "samovars." Trundling along in their boxes, some equipped with little wheels with rubber tires, some with simple ball bearings, they confronted people at the exit, asking them for money or tobacco. Some people gave, some hurried past, yet others let fly with a curse, adding in reproving tones, "The state supports you already. . . . Shame on you!" The samovars were almost all young, several of them visibly drunk. All had piercing, slightly mad eyes. . . . Three or four boxes came hurtling toward Charlotte. The soldiers thrust their sticks down against the trampled soil of the square, writhing as they propelled themselves along with violent convulsions of their whole bodies. Despite their pain it almost looked like a game.

Charlotte stopped, hastily withdrew a bill from her bag, and gave it to the first one to reach her. He could not take hold of it — his only hand, his left hand, had lost its fingers. He thrust the bill into the bottom of his box, then suddenly pitched over on his seat and, reaching out with his stump toward Charlotte, brushed against her ankle. And looked up at her with a demented and bitter gaze. . . .

She did not have time to grasp what occurred next. She saw another disabled man, but this time with two good arms, suddenly appear beside the first one and brutally snatch the crumpled bill from the one-armed man's box. Charlotte uttered a cry, and opened her bag again. But the soldier who had just caressed her foot seemed resigned. Turning his back on his aggressor, he was already making his way up a steeply sloping little alley, the top of which was open to the sky. Charlotte remained undecided for a moment — should she go after him? Give him more money? She saw several more samovars steering their boxes in her direction. She felt a terrible unease. Fear, shame as well. An abrupt raucous cry cut through the dull hubbub that hung over the square.

Charlotte turned rapidly: it was a vision swifter than a lightning flash. The one-armed man in his box on wheels came hurtling down the sloping alley with a thunderous grinding of ball bearings. His stump pushed repeatedly against the ground, steering his crazy descent. And in his mouth, which was twisted into a horrible grimace, there quivered a knife, clenched between his teeth. The cripple who had stolen his money had just enough time to grasp his stick. The one-armed man's box crashed into his own. Blood gushed. Charlotte saw two other samovars racing toward the one-armed man, who turned his head from side to side as he lacerated the body of his enemy. Other knives appeared, flashing between teeth. The yelling spread all around. Boxes collided with one another. Passersby, petrified by what was now becoming a general battle, did not dare to intervene. Another soldier rolled down the slope of the street at full tilt, his blade between his teeth, and plunged into the terrifying confusion of mutilated bodies. . . . Charlotte tried to get closer, but the fighting was taking place almost at ground level — you would have had to go on all fours to come between them. Already the militiamen were running up, emitting shrill whistle blasts. The bystanders came to themselves. Some hurried away. Others withdrew to the shade of the poplar trees to watch the end of the fighting. Charlotte saw one woman bend over and pick up a samovar from the pile of bodies, repeating in a tearful voice, "Lyosha! You promised me not to come here anymore! You promised!" And she went off, carrying the crippled man like a child. Charlotte tried to see if her one-armed man was still there. One of the militiamen pushed her away. . . .

We were walking in a straight line farther and farther from Saranza. The uproar of the military band had been absorbed into the silence of the steppe. All we heard now was the rustling of plants in the wind. And it was in that great space of light and heat that Charlotte's voice broke the silence once more.

"No, they weren't fighting over that stolen money. Not at all. Everybody understood that. They were fighting to . . . to be revenged on life. Its cruelty, its stupidity. And on that May sky above their heads . . . They were fighting as if they wanted to defy someone. The one who had combined within a single life the spring sky and their crippled bodies . . ."

"Stalin? God?" I was on the point of asking, but the air of the steppe made the words rough, hard to articulate.

We had never walked this far before. Saranza had long since sunk into the flickering haze of the horizon. This excursion with no end in view was vital to us. At my back I could feel, almost physically, the shade of a little square in Moscow. . . .

Finally we came upon a railway embankment. The line marked a surrealist frontier in this infinite space, whose only defining features were the sun and the sky. Curiously, on the other side of the tracks the terrain changed. We had to skirt several ravines, gigantic faults lined inside with sand, before descending into a valley. Suddenly, through the willow thickets there came a glint of water. We exchanged smiles and exclaimed with a single voice, "Sumra!"

It was a remote tributary of the Volga, one of those modest streams, lost in the immensity of the steppe, whose existence is known only because they flow into the great river.

We remained in the shade of the willows until evening. . . . It was on the road home that Charlotte finished her story.

"The authorities finally grew tired of all those cripples on the square, their shouting and their brawling. But above all, they were giving the great victory a bad image. You see, people prefer a soldier either to be gallant and smiling or else . . . dead on the field of honor. But these men . . . In short, one day several lorries drove up, and the militiamen began to snatch the samovars out of their boxes and throw them into the trucks. The way you throw logs onto a cart. A Muscovite told me they took them to an island, in the northern lakes. They had fixed up a former leper hospital for it. . . . In autumn I tried to find out about this place. I thought I might be able to go and work there. But when I went to that region in the spring they told me that there wasn't a single cripple left on the island and that the leper hospital was closed for good. . . . It was a very beautiful spot. Pine trees as far as the eye could see, great lakes, and above all, very pure air. . . ."

After we had been walking for an hour Charlotte gave me a little wry smile.

"Wait, I'm going to sit down for a moment. . . ."

She sat down on the dry grass and stretched out her legs. I walked on automatically for a few paces and turned round. Once again, as if from an unfamiliar perspective or from a great height, I saw a woman with white hair, wearing a very simple dress of pale satin, a woman seated on the ground in the midst of this immensity that stretches from the Black Sea to Mongolia, and which is known as "the steppe." My grandmother . . . I saw her with that inexplicable detachment that the previous evening I had taken for a kind of optical illusion caused by my nervous tension. I felt I had a glimpse of that vertiginous disorientation that must be a common experience for Charlotte: an almost cosmic alienation. There she was under this violet sky: she seemed totally alone on this planet, there on the mauve grass, under the first stars. And her France and her youth were more remote from her than the pale moon — left behind in another galaxy, under another sky. . . .

She raised her face. Her eyes seemed larger than usual to me. She spoke in French. The resonance of this language gave off vibrations like a last message from that distant galaxy.

"You know, Alyosha, sometimes it seems to me that I understand nothing about the life of this country. Yes. That I am still a foreigner. After living here for almost half a century. Those 'samovars' . . . I don't understand. There were people laughing as they watched them fight!"

She made a movement to stand up. I hastened toward her, holding out my hand. She smiled at me, taking hold of my arm. And as I leaned toward her, she murmured several brief words in a firm and solemn tone that surprised me. It is probably because I mentally translated them into Russian that I have remembered them. They made a long sentence, whereas Charlotte's French captured everything in a single image: the one-armed samovar sitting with his back against the trunk of an immense pine tree, silently watching the reflection of the waves fading behind the trees . . .

In the Russian translation, which my memory retained, Charlotte's voice added in a tone of justification, "Yet sometimes I tell myself that I understand this country better than the Russians themselves. For I have carried that soldier's face with me over so many years. . . . I have felt his solitude beside the lake. . . ."

She got up and walked on slowly, leaning on my arm. In my body and in my breathing I could feel the disappearance of that aggressive and nervous adolescent who had arrived in Saranza the previous day.

That is how our summer began, my last summer spent in Charlotte's house. The next day I woke up with the feeling that I was myself at last. A great calm, at the same time both bitter and serene, spread through me. I no longer had to struggle between my Russian and my French identities. I accepted myself.

*   *   *

Now we spent almost all our days on the banks of the Sumra. We set off very early in the morning, carrying with us a big gourd of water, bread, cheese. In the evening, taking advantage of the first cool breeze, we would return.

Once the path was known to us, it did not seem so long. In the sun-drenched monotony of the steppe we discerned hundreds of features, landmarks that quickly became familiar to us. A block of granite on which mica glittered in the sun from a long way off. A strip of sand that resembled a miniature desert. The area covered with brambles that had to be avoided. When Saranza disappeared from sight we knew that soon the line of the embankment would emerge from the horizon, the rails would gleam. And once this frontier was crossed we had almost arrived: beyond the ravines that cut into the steppes with their abrupt gullies, we already sensed the presence of the river. It seemed to be waiting for us. . . .

Charlotte would settle down with a book in the shade of the willows, a step away from the stream, while I would swim and dive until exhausted, several times crossing the river, which was narrow and not very deep. Along its shores there was a string of little islands, covered with thick grass, where there was just enough room to stretch out and imagine oneself to be on a desert island in the middle of the ocean. . . .

Then, lying on the sand, I listened to the bottomless silence of the steppe. . . . Our conversations started spontaneously and seemed to flow from the sunny babbling of the Sumra, from the rustling of the long leaves of the willows. Charlotte, her hands resting on the open book, would gaze across the river toward the plain scorched by the sun and begin to talk, sometimes replying to my questions, sometimes anticipating them intuitively as she spoke.

It was during those long summer afternoons, in the midst of the steppe, where every plant resonated with dryness and heat, that I learned what had previously been concealed from me in Charlotte's life. And also what my childish intelligence had not managed to grasp.

I learned that he really was her first lover, the first man in her life, that Great War soldier who had slipped the little pebble known as "Verdun" into her hand. Only they had not met on the day of the solemn parade on July 14, 1919: it was two years later, some months before Charlotte's departure for Russia. I learned also that this soldier was very far from being the mustached hero, glittering with medals, of our naive imaginings. He turned out rather to have been thin, with a pale face and sad eyes. He had frequent coughing fits. His lungs had been scorched in the course of one of the first gas attacks. And he did not step out of the ranks of the great parade to approach Charlotte and give her the "Verdun." He had handed this talisman to her at the station, the day of her departure for Moscow, certain of seeing her again soon.

One day she spoke to me about the rape. . . . Her calm voice had that tone that seemed to be saying, "Of course you already know what happened. . . . It's no secret to you." I confirmed this implication by repeating briefly, "Yes, yes," with studied nonchalance. I was very much afraid, after this story, that I might get up and see a different Charlotte, a different face, bearing the indelible expression of a violated woman. But it was chiefly this blinding vision that lodged itself in my brain.

A man in a turban, wearing a kind of long coat, very thick and very hot, particularly in the midst of the desert sands that lie all about him. Veiled eyes, like two razor blades; the copper-colored sunburn of his round face, glistening with sweat. He is young. With feverish gestures, he tries to grasp the curved dagger that hangs from his belt, on the other side from the rifle. These few seconds seem interminable. For the desert and the man with his hasty movements are seen only with a tiny fraction of her vision — the chink between her eyelashes. A woman lying on the ground, her dress torn, her disheveled hair half buried in the sand, looks as if she is embedded forever in this empty landscape. There is a strand of red across her left temple. But she is alive. The bullet has torn the skin under her hair and buried itself in the sand. The man twists round to grasp at his weapon. He would like the death to be more physical — the throat cut, a surge of blood soaking the sand. But the dagger he is reaching for slid round to the other side when, just now, with the folds of his long garment open, he was writhing on the crushed body. . . . He pulls at his belt angrily, throwing hate-filled glances at the transfixed face of the woman. Suddenly he hears a whinny. He turns. His companions are galloping already far away; their silhouettes, at the top of a ridge, stand out clearly against the sky. And all at once he feels oddly alone: himself, the desert in the evening light, the dying woman. He spits angrily, kicks the inert body with his pointed boot, and leaps onto the saddle with the agility of a caracal. When the sound of the hoofbeats has died away, the woman, slowly, opens her eyes. And she begins to breathe hesitantly, as if she had lost the habit. The air tastes of stone and blood. . . .

Charlotte's voice mingled with the soft sighing of the willows. She fell silent. I thought of the rage of that young Uzbek: "He needed to slit her throat at any price, reduce her to lifeless flesh!" And, with what was already a man's perception, I understood that this was not mere cruelty. I recalled the first minutes after the act of love, when the body, desired a moment ago, suddenly became useless, unpleasant to see and to touch, almost hostile. I remembered my young companion on our raft that night: it was true; I resented her because I no longer desired her; because I was disappointed; because I could feel her there, clinging to my shoulder. . . . And pursuing my thought to its logical conclusion, laying bare the male egoism that both frightened and tempted me, I said to myself, "It's true: after love the woman should disappear!" And I again pictured that hand feverishly reaching for the dagger.

I stood up abruptly and turned toward Charlotte. I was going to ask her the question that had tortured me for months, which I had formulated and reformulated in my mind a thousand times: "Tell me, in a word, in a sentence. Love. What is it?"

But Charlotte, doubtless anticipating what would have been a much more logical question, spoke first: "And do you know what saved me? . . . Did no one ever tell you?"

I looked at her. Telling me about the rape had left no mark at all on her features. There was simply the flickering of shadow and sunlight through the leaves of the willows that brushed against her face.

She had been saved by a *saiga,* that desert antelope with enor-

mous nostrils, like an elephant's trunk cut short, and — in astonishing contrast — huge, timid, and gentle eyes. Charlotte had often seen
herds of them bounding across the desert. . . . When she was finally
able to get up she saw a *saiga* slowly crawling along a sand dune.
Charlotte followed it, without thinking, instinctively — the animal
was the only beacon in the midst of the endless undulations of the
sands. As if in a dream (the lilac sky had the deceptive emptiness of
visions), she managed to draw close to the animal. The *saiga* did not
run away. In the hazy light of dusk Charlotte saw dark patches on the
sand — blood. The animal collapsed, then, lunging violently with its
head, picked itself up from the ground, staggered on long, trembling
legs, made several uncoordinated leaps. Fell again. It had been mor-
tally wounded. By the same men who had almost killed her? Perhaps.
It was spring. The night was icy cold. Charlotte curled up, pressing
her body against the animal's back. The *saiga* did not move anymore.
Shivers ran across its skin. Its sibilant breathing was like human sighs,
like whispered words. Numb with cold and pain, Charlotte woke fre-
quently, aware of this murmuring, which was obstinately trying to
say something. In one of these waking moments, in the middle of
the night, she was amazed to see a star, close at hand, shining in the
sand. A star fallen from the sky. . . . Charlotte leaned toward this luminous dot. It was the great open eye of the *saiga* — with a glorious,
fragile constellation reflected in its tear-filled globe. . . . She did not
notice the moment when the heartbeats of this living creature,
which kept her alive, stopped. . . . In the morning the desert was glittering with hoarfrost. Charlotte remained standing for several minutes before the motionless body scattered with crystals. Then, slowly,
she scaled the dune that the beast had not managed to cross the previous evening. When she reached the crest she uttered an "Oh" that
rang out in the morning air. A lake, pink with the first rays, stretched
out at her feet. It was this water that the *saiga* was trying to reach. . . .
They found Charlotte sitting on the shore that same evening.

In the streets of Saranza, at nightfall, she added this emotional
epilogue to her story: "Your grandfather," she said softly, "never referred to that business. Never . . . And he loved your uncle Sergei as
if he were his own son. Even more, perhaps. It's hard for a man to ac-

cept that his first child is the result of a rape. Especially as Sergei, you know, doesn't look like anyone else in the family. No, he never spoke about it. . . ."

I sensed her voice shaking slightly. "She loved Fyodor," I thought quite simply. "It was he who made it possible for this country, where she has suffered so much, to be her own. And she still loves him. After all these years without him. She loves him out here on the steppes at night, in this Russian immensity. She loves him. . . ."

Love appeared to me anew in all its sorrowful simplicity. Inexplicable. Inexpressible. Like that constellation reflected in the eye of a wounded animal in the middle of a desert covered in ice.

It was a chance slip of the tongue that revealed an unsettling reality to me: the way I was speaking French was no longer the same. . . .

In asking Charlotte a question that day, I got my words twisted. I must have come up against one of those pairs of words, a deceptive pair, of which there are many in French. Yes, it was couples along the lines of "mitigate-militate" or "prefabricate-prevaricate." In the old days my verbal clumsiness with such perfidious duos, some as fraught with risk as *"luxe-luxure"* ("luxury-lewdness"), used to provoke mockery from my sister and discreet corrections from Charlotte.

This time I did not need prompting with the appropriate word. After a second of hesitation I corrected myself. But much more shocking than this momentary hesitation was a devastating revelation: I was speaking a foreign language!

So the months of my rebellion had left their mark. It was not that henceforth I found it hard to express myself in French. But the break was there. As a child I had absorbed all the sounds of Charlotte's language. I swam in them, without wondering why that glint in the grass, that colored, scented, living brilliance, sometimes existed in the masculine and had a crunchy, fragile, crystalline identity, imposed, it seemed, by one of its names, *tsvetok;* and was sometimes enveloped in a velvety, feltlike, and feminine aura, becoming *une fleur.*

I was later reminded of the story of the millipede that, when questioned about its dancing technique, immediately muddled the — normally instinctive — movements of its innumerable limbs.

My case was not quite as desperate. But from the day of my slip, the question of technique became unavoidable. Now French became a tool whose capacity I measured as I was speaking. Yes. An instrument independent of me, which I would employ, even as I became aware from time to time of the strangeness of this activity.

My discovery, disconcerting though it was, gave me a penetrating insight into style. This language-tool, employed, sharpened, perfected, was, I told myself, nothing other than literary composition. I had already sensed that the anecdotes about France with which I had amused my fellow pupils throughout that year were the first draft for this novelist's language: had I not manipulated it to please sometimes the "proletarians" and sometimes the "aesthetes"? Literature was now revealed as being perpetual amazement at the flow of words into which the world dissolved. French, my grandmaternal tongue, was, I saw now, the supreme language of amazement.

Ever since that particular day in the distant past, spent beside a little river, lost in the midst of the steppe, occasionally when I am in midconversation in French I recall my surprise of long ago: a gray-haired lady with great calm eyes and her grandson are seated at the heart of the empty plain, beneath the burning sun, very Russian in the endlessness of its isolation, and they are speaking in French, the most natural thing in the world. . . . I see this scene again and I am amazed to be speaking French. Then I stumble and feel as if the cat had got my French. Strangely, or rather quite logically, it is at moments like this, when I find myself between two languages, that I believe I can see and feel more intensely than ever.

Perhaps it was on that same day, when I said *précepteur* (tutor) instead of *percepteur* (tax collector) and thus entered a silent zone between two languages, that I also noticed Charlotte's beauty. . . .

The idea of this beauty at first seemed to me improbable. In Russia at that time every woman reaching the age of fifty was transformed into a "babushka" — a being in whom it would have been absurd to look for femininity, let alone beauty. And as for stating, "My grandmother is beautiful" . . .

Yet Charlotte, who must have been sixty-four or sixty-five at the time, was beautiful. Settling down at the bottom of the steep, sandy bank of the Sumra, she read beneath the branches of the willows that covered her dress with a network of shadow and sunlight. Her silver hair was gathered at the nape of her neck. Her eyes looked at me from time to time with a faint smile. I tried to understand what it was in this face, in this very simple dress, that radiated the beauty whose existence I was almost embarrassed to recognize.

No. Charlotte was not "a woman who does not look her age." Nor did her features have that haggard prettiness seen in the "well-cared-for" faces of women who wage unending war on wrinkles. She did not seek to camouflage her age, but her aging did not provoke the shrinking that emaciates the features and withers the body. I took in with my eyes the silvery gleam of her hair, the lines of her face, her arms lightly tanned, her bare feet almost touching the lazy rippling of the Sumra. . . . And with an unwonted joy I observed that there was no strict boundary between the flowered fabric of her dress and the shadows dappled with sunlight. The contours of her body merged imperceptibly into the luminosity of the air; her eyes, in the manner of a watercolor, mingled with the warm brilliance of the sky; the movements of her fingers turning the pages wove themselves into the undulation of the long willow branches. . . . So it was this fusion that hid the mystery of her beauty!

Yes, her face and her body were not tensed, fearful of the arrival of old age; they absorbed sun and wind; the bitter scents of the steppe; the freshness of the willow groves. And her presence conferred an astonishing harmony on this desert space. Charlotte was there, and in the monotony of the plain scorched by the heat, an elusive consonance was formed: the melodious gurgling of the stream, the tart smell of the wet clay and the aromatic one of the dry plants; the play of shadow and light beneath the branches. A unique moment, inimitable in the blurred sequence of days, of years, of ages. . . .

A moment that did not pass away.

I was discovering Charlotte's beauty. And almost at the same moment her isolation.

That day, lying on the shore, I was listening to her talking about the book she took on our excursions. Ever since my slip of the tongue, I could not prevent myself taking note, while keeping up with the conversation, of the way in which my grandmother employed French. I compared her style with that of the authors I was reading and with that of the rare French newspapers that got through into our country. I knew all the distinctive features of her French, her favorite expressions, her personal syntax, her vocabulary, and even the patina of time that her sentences bore — the belle epoque flavor. . . .

On this occasion, more than all these linguistic observations, a surprising thought came into my mind: "For half a century this style has lived in complete isolation, very rarely spoken, grappling with a reality foreign to its nature, like a plant striving to grow on a bare rock face. . . ." And yet Charlotte's French had retained an extraordinary vigor, rich and pure, that amber transparency that wine acquires with aging. This style had survived Siberian snowstorms, the burning sands in the desert of central Asia. And it resonates still on the banks of this river in the midst of the endless steppe. . . .

It was then that this woman's isolation came into focus in all its shattering and mundane simplicity. "She has no one to talk to," I said to myself with stupefaction. "No one to talk to in French . . ." I suddenly understood what might be the significance for Charlotte of these few weeks that we spent together each summer. I understood that this French, this fabric of sentences that seemed so natural to me, would be frozen, when I left, for a whole year; replaced by Russian, by the rustling of pages, by silence. And I pictured Charlotte alone, walking along the dim streets of Saranza buried under the snow. . . .

The next day I saw my grandmother talking to Gavrilych, the drunkard and scandalizer of our courtyard. The babushkas' bench was empty — the man's arrival must have driven them away. The children hid behind the poplar trees. The inhabitants at their windows watched the scene with interest: the strange Frenchwoman who dared to approach the monster. I thought again of my grandmother's isolation. I felt a pricking in my eyelids: "This is what her life is. This courtyard, this drunkard Gavrilych, this huge black *izba* across the yard. With all those families piled on top of one another . . ." Charlotte came in, a bit out of breath but smiling, her eyes veiled in tears of joy.

"Do you know," she said to me in Russian, as if she had not had the time to switch from one language to the other, "Gavrilych has been talking to me about the war; he was defending Stalingrad on the same front as your father. He often speaks to me about it. He was describing a battle on the banks of the Volga. They were fighting to take a hill back from the Germans. He said he had never before seen such a chaos of tanks in flames, mangled corpses, bloody earth. That evening on the hilltop he was one of a dozen survivors. He went down to the Volga; he was dying of thirst. And there, on the shore, he saw the water, very calm, white sand, reeds, and young fish leaping as he approached. Just like the days of his childhood in his own village . . ."

I listened to her, and Russia, the country of her isolation, no longer seemed to me hostile to her "Frenchness." Touched, I said to myself that this big man, drunk, with his fierce gaze, this Gavrilych would not have dared to talk to anyone else about his feelings. They would have laughed in his face: Stalingrad, the war, and then all at once these reeds, and young fish! No one else in that courtyard would have even taken the trouble to listen to him: what can a drunkard tell you that is interesting? He had spoken to Charlotte. With confidence, with the certainty of being understood. This Frenchwoman was closer to him at that moment than all those people who were staring at him and counting on a free show. He had stared at them darkly, grumbling privately to himself, "There they all are, like in a circus. . . ." All at once he had seen Charlotte crossing the courtyard with a bag of provisions. He had straightened himself up and greeted her. A minute later, with a face that seemed to have grown lighter, he was telling her, "And you know, Sharlota Norbertovna, it was no longer the earth under our feet but hacked-up meat. I've never seen anything like it, not since the start of the war. And then, that evening, when we had finished with the Germans, I went down toward the Volga. And there, how can I tell you . . ."

That morning when we went out, we walked past the great black *izba*. It was already alive with a dense hum. One could hear the angry hissing of oil on a stove, the female and male duet of a quarrel, the jumble of the voices and music from several radios. . . . I glanced at Charlotte, raising my eyebrows with a mocking grimace. She had no difficulty in guessing the significance of my smile. But the great stirring anthill seemed not to interest her.

It was only when we began walking over the steppe that she spoke: "Last winter," she said, "I took some medicines to dear old Frossia, you know, that babushka who is always the first one to make herself scarce as soon as Gavrilych is sighted. . . . It was very cold that day. I had great difficulty in opening the door of their *izba*. . . ."

Charlotte continued her story, and with growing amazement, I sensed that her plain words were redolent of sounds, smells, light veiled by the fog of the great frosts. . . . She shook the door handle, and the door opened reluctantly, breaking a frame of ice, with a shrill creaking. She found herself inside the great wooden house, facing a staircase black with age. The treads uttered plaintive groans under her feet. The corridors were cluttered with old cupboards, with great cardboard boxes piled high along the walls, with bikes, with dull mirrors that opened up surprising perspectives in this cavernous space. The smell of burning wood hovered between the dark walls and mingled with the cold that Charlotte carried in the folds of her coat. . . . It was at the end of the corridor on the first floor that my grandmother saw her. A young woman with a baby in her arms was standing near a window covered in scrolls of ice. Without moving, her head slightly inclined, she was watching the dancing flames in the open door of a great stove that occupied the corner of the corridor. Outside the frosted window the winter dusk was slowly drawing in, blue and clear. . . .

Charlotte was silent for a moment, then continued in a slightly hesitant voice, "Of course, it was an illusion, you know. . . . But her face was so pale, so fine. . . . Almost like the ice flowers that covered the windowpane. Yes, as if her features had been lifted out of those hoarfrost ornaments. I have never seen such a fragile beauty. Yes, like an icon sketched on ice. . . ."

We walked in silence for a long time. The steppe was slowly unfolding before us with the resonant chirruping of cicadas. But that
dry sound and the heat did not prevent me from feeling in my lungs
the freezing air of the great black *izba*. I saw the window covered
with hoarfrost, the glittering blue of the crystals, the young woman
with her child. Charlotte had spoken in French. French had gone inside that *izba*, which had always alarmed me with its somber, heavy,
and very Russian life. And within its depths a window had lit up. Yes,
she had spoken in French. She could have spoken in Russian. That
would have taken nothing away from her recreation of the moment.
So a kind of intermediary language did exist. A universal language! I
thought again about that "between two languages" that I had discovered, thanks to my slip of the tongue, and I thought of the "language
of amazement." . . .

That day, for the first time, the inspiring thought crossed my
mind: Suppose one could express this language in writing?

One afternoon we spent on the banks of the Sumra, I surprised myself thinking about Charlotte's death. Or rather, on the contrary, I
was thinking about the impossibility of her death. . . .

The heat had been particularly intense that day. Charlotte had
removed her espadrilles and, lifting her dress up to her knees, was
paddling in the water. Perched on one of the little islands, I watched
her walking along, following the shore. Once again I felt as if I were
observing her and the beach of white sand and the steppe from a
great distance. Yes, as if I were suspended in the basket of a hot air
balloon. This is the way (I was to learn much later) that we perceive
the places and the faces that subconsciously we are already locating in
the past. I was looking at her from that illusory height, from that future toward which all my young energies tended. She walked in the
water with the dreamy carelessness of an adolescent girl. Her book,
open, was left behind on the grass, under the willows. Suddenly in a
single brilliant illumination I reviewed Charlotte's life in its entirety.
It was like a throbbing sequence of lightning flashes: France at the
turn of the century; Siberia; the desert; and again endless snows; the

war; Saranza . . . I had never before had the opportunity to examine the life of a living person in this way — from one end to the other — and to say: this life is closed. There would be nothing in Charlotte's life other than Saranza, this steppe. And death.

I stood up on my island, I stared at this woman who was walking slowly in the current of the Sumra. And with an unfamiliar joy that suddenly filled my lungs, I whispered, "No, she won't die." And at once I longed to understand whence this serene assurance came, this confidence, which was so strange, especially in the year marked by the death of my parents.

But instead of a logical explanation I saw a flood of moments streaming by in a dazzling disorder: a morning filled with sunlit mist in an imaginary Paris; the breeze redolent of lavender filling a railway carriage; the cry of the Kukushka in the warm evening air; that distant moment of the first snow that Charlotte had watched swirling around on that terrible night of the war; and also this present moment — this slim woman, with a white scarf over her gray hair, a woman strolling absentmindedly in the clear water of a river that flows through the heart of the endless steppe. . . .

These visions seemed to me both ephemeral and endowed with a kind of eternity. I felt an intoxicating certainty; in a mysterious way they made Charlotte's death impossible. I sensed that the encounter with the young woman beside the frosted window in the black *izba* — the icon on the ice! — and even Gavrilych's story — the reeds, the young fish, an evening in the war — yes, even these brief flashes of illumination contributed to the impossibility of her death. And the most wonderful thing was that there was no need to prove it, to explain it, to argue it. I looked at Charlotte, climbing onto the bank to sit in her favorite spot under the willows, and I repeated to myself, as if it were something luminously obvious: "No, all those moments will never disappear. . . ."

When I came beside her, my grandmother looked up and said to me, "This morning, you know, I copied out two different translations of a sonnet by Baudelaire for you. Listen, I'm going to read them to you. It will amuse you. . . ."

Thinking that I was in for one of those stylistic curiosities that Charlotte liked to unearth for me in her reading, often in the form of a riddle, I concentrated, eager to show off my knowledge of French literature. I did not dream that this sonnet by Baudelaire would be a veritable liberation for me.

It is true that Woman, during those summer months, had imposed herself on all my senses like a ceaseless oppression. Without knowing it, I was living through that painful transition that lies between the very first experience of physical love, often barely sketched in, and those that will follow. This is often a more delicate path to travel than the one that leads from innocence to the first knowledge of a woman's body.

Even in the marooned town that was Saranza, this multifarious woman, elusive, innumerable, was strangely present. More insinuating, more discreet than in the big cities, but all the more provocative. Like, for example, the girl whom I passed one day in an empty street, dusty and scorched by the sun. She was tall, well built, with that healthy physical robustness that one finds in the provinces. Her blouse clung to powerful rounded breasts. Her miniskirt hugged the very full tops of her thighs. The pointed heels of her glossy white shoes made her gait a little strained. Her fashionable clothes, her makeup, and this stilted gait lent an almost surrealist air to her appearance in the empty street. But above all there was this almost brutish physical superabundance of her body, of her movements! On this afternoon of silent heat. In this sleepy little town. Why? To what end? I could not prevent myself glancing furtively behind me: yes, her strong calves, polished by sunburn, her thighs, the two hemispheres of her buttocks moving with suppleness at each step. Bewildered, I told myself that somewhere in this dead Saranza there must be a room, a bed, where this body would stretch out and, parting its legs, welcome another body into its groin. This obvious thought plunged me into boundless amazement. How simultaneously natural and improbable it all was!

Or again the plump, bare woman's arm that appeared at a window one evening. A little winding street, overhung with still, heavy foliage — and this very white, very rounded arm, uncovered to the shoulder, which had swayed for a few seconds, the time it took to draw a muslin curtain over the darkness of the room. And I do not know by what intuition I had recognized the somewhat excited impatience of this gesture, and had understood on what interior this naked woman's arm was drawing the curtain. . . . I even felt the smooth coolness of the arm on my lips.

At each of these encounters, an insistent summons rang out in my head: I must seduce them at once, these unknown women, make them mine, fit their flesh into my rosary of dreamed-of bodies. For each missed opportunity was a defeat, an irremediable loss, an emptiness that other bodies would only partially be able to fill. At such moments my fever became unbearable!

I had never dared to embark on this subject with Charlotte. Still less to talk to her about the woman cut in two on the barge, or my night with the young drunken dancer. Did she guess at my turmoil herself? Certainly. Without actually picturing that prostitute seen through the portholes, or the young redhead on the old ferry, it seems to me that she identified with great precision "where I was at" in my experience of love. Unconsciously, through my questions, my evasions, my feigned indifference over certain delicate subjects — my silences, even — I was painting my own portrait as apprentice lover. But I was not aware of it, like someone who forgets that his shadow is projecting onto a wall the gestures he is trying to hide.

Thus, hearing Charlotte speak of Baudelaire, I thought it was mere coincidence when in the first stanza of his sonnet, this feminine presence was sketched:

> When, with closed eyes, on some warm autumn night,
> I breathe your bosom's sultry fragrances,
> Enchanted shores unfold their promontories,
> Dazed by a sun monotonously bright.

"You see," my grandmother continued, in a mixture of Russian and French, for she had to quote the texts of the translations, "In

Bryussov the first line is rendered as: 'On an autumn evening, with eyes closed . . .'

"In Balmont: 'When, closing my eyes, on a stifling summer's night . . .'

"In my opinion both of them are simplifying Baudelaire. In his sonnet, you see, the 'warm autumn night' is a very particular moment, yes, in mid-autumn, suddenly, like a blessing, this warm night, unique, a parenthesis of light amid the rains and miseries of life. In their translations they have traduced Baudelaire's idea: 'an autumn evening,' 'a summer's night,' is flat. It has no soul. While in his text this moment makes magic possible, you know, a bit like those warm days just before the winter."

Charlotte elaborated her commentary at every stage with the lightly assumed dilettantism that disguised her often very broad knowledge, which she was afraid to flaunt. But now all I was hearing was the melody of her voice, sometimes in Russian, sometimes in French.

In place of my obsession with female flesh, with that omnipresent womanhood whose inexhaustible multiplicity harassed me, I had a feeling of great relief. This had the transparency of that "warm autumn night." And the serenity of a slow, almost melancholy contemplation of a woman's beautiful body, stretched out in the blissful lassitude of love. A body whose physical reality is reflected in a series of reminiscences, scents, lights . . .

Before the storm reached us, the river became swollen. We shook ourselves, hearing the stream already lapping among the roots of the willows. The sky became purple, black. The steppe, bristling, froze into blinding, livid scenes. A piquant, acid smell assailed us with the chill of the first showers. And Charlotte, as she folded the napkin on which we had taken our lunch, rounded off her exposition: "But in the end, in the last line, there is a real paradox of translation. Bryussov excels Baudelaire! Yes, Baudelaire talks of 'the song of mariners' on that island that is born of 'your bosom's sultry fragrances.' And Bryussov, in translating him, gives 'the voices of sailors calling in several tongues.' What is wonderful is that the Russian can convey that with a single adjective. These cries in different languages are much more alive than the 'song of mariners,' which is rather mawkishly romantic, you have to admit. It's what we were saying the other day, you see: the translator of prose is the slave of the author, and the translator of poetry is his rival. Besides, in this sonnet . . ."

She did not have the time to finish her sentence. The water streamed under our feet, carrying away my clothes, several sheets of paper, and one of Charlotte's espadrilles. The sky, gorged with rain, burst upon the steppe. We rushed to rescue what we still could. I seized my trousers and my shirt, which had happily caught on the branches of the willows as they floated along, and I just managed to fish out Charlotte's espadrille. Then the sheets of paper — they were the recopied translations. The downpour quickly turned them into little balls spotted with ink.

We did not notice our fear — the violence of the thunder's deafening clatter drove out all thought. The cloudburst isolated us inside the shivering confines of our bodies. With a thrilling keenness we felt our hearts laid bare, drowned in this deluge that merged heaven and earth.

A few minutes later the sun shone. From the top of the bank we contemplated the steppe. Shining, quivering with a thousand iridescent sparks, it seemed to be breathing. We exchanged smiling looks. Charlotte had lost her white headscarf; her wet hair was streaming in swarthy braids on her shoulders. Raindrops glittered on her eyelashes. Her dress, quite soaked, clung to her body. "She is young. And very beautiful. In spite of everything," declared that involuntary voice within me that disobeys and embarrasses us with its uncompromising frankness, but which reveals what is censored by considered speech.

We stopped at the railway embankment. In the distance we could see a long freight train approaching. Often a panting train would stop at this point, barring our path for a brief moment. This obstruction, due no doubt to some points or a signal, would amuse us. The cars rose up in a gigantic wall, covered in dust. A dense wave of heat was given off by their sides exposed to the sun. And the silence of the steppe was only broken by the distant hooting of the locomotive. Each time I was tempted not to wait for it to move off, and to cross the track by slipping under a car, Charlotte would restrain me, saying she had just heard the whistle. Sometimes when our wait was really becoming too long, we climbed onto the open deck, which freight cars had at that time, and got off on the other side of the track. These few seconds were filled with gleeful nervousness: what if the train set off and took us to an unknown and fabulous destination?

This time we could not wait. Soaked as we were, we needed to reach home before nightfall. I climbed up first and held out my hand to Charlotte, who stepped up onto the footboard. Just at that moment the train moved off. We ran across the deck. I could still have jumped. But not Charlotte . . . We stood facing the embrasure, which was filling with an increasingly biting draft. The line of our footpath vanished in the immensity of the steppe.

We were not at all worried. We knew that one station or another would halt the progress of our train. It seemed to me that Charlotte was in some ways quite pleased with our unexpected adventure. She gazed at the plain, revived by the storm. Her hair, blowing in the wind, spread across her face. She flung it aside from time to time with a rapid gesture. Despite the sun, a little fine rain began to fall at intervals. Charlotte smiled at me through this shining veil.

What suddenly struck me on this lurching deck in the middle of the steppe was like the wonder experienced by a child who, after long, fruitless study, discovers a character or an object that has been camouflaged in the cleverly jumbled lines of a drawing. Now he sees it, and the arabesques of the drawing acquire a new meaning, a new life. . . .

It was the same with my internal perception. All at once I saw! Or rather I felt, with all my being, the luminous tie that linked this moment full of iridescent reflections to other moments I had inhabited in the past: that evening long ago with Charlotte, the melancholy cry of the Kukushka; then that Parisian morning, shrouded in my imagination in sunlit mist; that moment at night on the raft with my first lover, when the great riverboat towered above our entwined bodies; and the evening gatherings of my childhood, lived, it already seemed, in another life. . . . Linked together thus, these moments formed a singular universe, with its own rhythm, its particular air and sun. Another planet, almost. A planet where the death of this woman with her big gray eyes became inconceivable. Where a woman's body was reflected in a series of dreamed moments. Where my "language of amazement" would be comprehensible to others.

This planet was the same world that was unfolding as our car hurtled along. Yes, the same station where the train finally came to a halt. The same empty platform, washed by the downpour. Those same rare passersby with their mundane concerns. The same world, but seen differently.

As I helped Charlotte to step down, I tried to grasp this "differently." Yes, to see this other planet, one would have to behave in a special way. But how?

"Come, we're going to have something to eat," my grandmother said, drawing me away from my musings, and she set off for the restaurant located in one of the wings of the station.

The room was empty, the tables were not laid. We sat down near an open window, through which a square lined with trees could be seen. On the front of the apartment blocks were visible long strips of red calico with their customary slogans glorifying the Party, the Fatherland, and Peace. . . . A waiter came up and told us in a sullen voice that the storm had cut off their electricity and that the restaurant was therefore closing. I was already about to get up, but Charlotte insisted with extreme politeness, which, with its old-fashioned turns of phrase that I knew to be borrowed from French, always impressed Russians. The man hesitated for a second, then went away with a visibly disconcerted air.

He brought us a dish astonishing in its simplicity. A plate with a dozen rounds of sausage and a huge pickled cucumber, cut into fine slices. But above all, he put in front of us a bottle of wine. I had never had a dinner like it. The waiter himself must have grasped the unusual couple we made and the strangeness of this cold meal. He smiled and stammered some remarks about the weather, as if to excuse the welcome he had just given us.

We remained alone in the room. The wind coming in at the window smelled of wet foliage. The sky layered itself into gray-and-purple clouds, lit by the setting sun. From time to time the wheels of a car squealed on the wet asphalt. Each mouthful of wine gave these sounds and colors a new density: the cool heaviness of the trees, the shining windows washed by the rain, the red of the slogans on the facades, the wet squealing of the wheels, the sky still stormy. I felt that, little by little, what we were living through in this empty room was becoming detached from the present moment, from that station, from that unknown town, from its daily life. . . .

Heavy foliage, long splashes of red on the facades, squealing tires, sky gray and purple. I turned to Charlotte. She was no longer there.

And it is no longer the restaurant in the station lost in the middle of the steppe. But a café in Paris — and outside the window a spring evening. The gray-and-purple sky, still stormy, the squealing of cars on the wet asphalt, the fresh exuberance of the chestnut trees, the red of the blinds belonging to the restaurant on the opposite side of the square. And I, twenty years later, I, who have just recognized this combination of colors and have just relived the giddiness of the moment regained. A young woman facing me is keeping up a conversation about nothing with a very French grace. I watch her smiling face, and occasionally I punctuate her words with a nod of my head. This woman is very close to me. I love her voice, her way of thinking. I know the harmony of her body. . . . "And what if I were to speak to her about that moment twenty years ago, in the middle of the steppe, in that empty station?" I ask myself, and I know that I will not do it.

On that distant evening, twenty years ago, Charlotte is already getting up, adjusting her hair in the reflection of the open window, and we leave. And on my lips, with the pleasant sharpness of the wine, these words, never ventured upon, fade away: "If she is so beautiful still, despite her white hair and having lived so many years, it is because all these moments of light and beauty have been filtered through her eyes, her face, her body. . . ."

Charlotte leaves the station. I follow her, drunk with my unsayable revelation. And night falls over the steppe. The night that has lasted for twenty years in the Saranza of my childhood.

I saw Charlotte for a few hours ten years later, before I went abroad. I arrived very late in the evening, and I was due to leave again for Moscow early in the morning. It was an icy night at the end of autumn. For Charlotte it brought together the troubled memories of all the departures in her life; all the nights of farewells. . . . We did not sleep. She went to make the tea, and I paced up and down in her apartment, which seemed to me strangely small and very touching, through the constancy of familiar objects.

I was twenty-five. I was ecstatic about my trip. I already knew that I was going away for a long time. Or rather that my visit to Europe would be extended far beyond the planned two weeks. It seemed to me that my departure would shake the calm of our stagnant empire; that its inhabitants would all talk of nothing but my exile; that a new era would begin from my first action, from my first words uttered on the other side of the frontier. I was already living off the procession of new faces I would meet; the dazzle of dreamed-of landscapes; the stimulus of danger.

It was with the conceited egoism of youth that I said to her, in rather jocular tones, "But you could go abroad as well! To France, for example . . . Wouldn't that tempt you, eh?"

The expression on her face did not change. She simply lowered her eyes. I heard the whistling melody of the kettle, the tinkling of snow crystals against the black windowpane.

"When I went to Siberia in 1922," she finally said to me with a weary smile, "half, or maybe a third of that journey, you know, I made on foot. That was as far as from here to Paris. Do you see, I wouldn't need your airplanes at all. . . ."

She smiled again, looking me in the eye. But despite the tone of voice she assumed, I sensed within her voice a deep note of bitterness. Embarrassed, I took a cigarette and went out onto the balcony. . . .

It was there, above the frozen darkness of the steppe, that I believed I had finally understood what France meant to her.

4

14

*I*T WAS IN FRANCE that I almost forgot Charlotte's France forever. . . .

Autumn had come, and twenty years now separated me from those times spent in Saranza. I became aware of this interval — of the poignant "twenty years on" — the day our radio station made its last broadcast in Russian. That evening, leaving the newsroom, I pictured an endless expanse yawning between this German city and Russia, asleep under the snows. Henceforth all that nocturnal space, which on the previous evening was still alive with the sound of our voices, would fade, it seemed to me, into the muffled cracking of the empty airwaves. . . . The goal of our dissident, subversive broadcasts had been achieved. The snowbound empire was waking up, opening itself up to the rest of the world. The country would soon change its name, its regime, its history, its frontiers. Another country would be born. We were no longer needed. The station was being closed. My colleagues exchanged artificially noisy and warm farewells and departed, each in his own direction. Some wanted to rebuild their lives on the spot, others to pack their bags and go to America. Yet others, the least realistic, dreamed of a return that would take them back into the blizzard of twenty years ago. . . . Nobody had any illusions. We knew that it was not just a radio station that was disappearing but our era itself. All that we had said, written, thought, fought against, defended, all that we had loved, detested, feared — all those things belonged to that era. We were left with a vacuum, like waxwork figures in a cabinet of curiosities, relics of a defunct empire.

On board the train taking me to Paris I tried to find words to describe all the years spent far away from Saranza. Exile as a mode of existence? Brute necessity of life? A life half lived and mainly wasted? The meaning of those years seemed to me obscure. So I tried to convert them into what men consider to be sound values in life: recollections of dramatic changes of scene ("In those years I have seen the whole world!" I said to myself with childish arrogance); the bodies of women they have loved. . . .

But the recollections remained drab, the bodies strangely inert. Or occasionally they emerged from the dimness of memory with the wild insistence of a shop dummy's eyes.

Those years were nothing more than a long journey for which I managed from time to time to find a goal. I would invent it just as I was leaving a place or already en route; or sometimes on arrival, when I had to explain my presence that day, in one particular town, in one particular country rather than another.

A journey from one nowhere to another, yes. As soon as the place where I was staying began to exert a hold on me, to establish me in its pleasant daily routine, I had to leave at once. My journey knew only two moments: arrival in an unknown town and departure from a town whose facades hardly trembled as I looked at them. . . . When I had arrived in Munich six months before, as I walked out of the railway station, I was already prudently telling myself that I must find a hotel, then an apartment, as close as possible to my new work at the radio. . . .

That morning, in Paris, I had the fleeting illusion of a real return: in a street not far from the station, a street still hardly awake in that misty dawn, I saw an open window and the interior of a room that exuded a simple, everyday, but for me mysterious calmness, with a lamp lit on the table, an old dark wood chest of drawers, a picture on the wall coming slightly unstuck. The warmth of this glimpsed intimacy seemed to me suddenly both ancient and familiar, so much so that I shivered. To climb the stair, knock at the door, recognize a face, be recognized. . . . I hastened to banish this sensation of redis-

covery, which struck me then as nothing other than a vagrant's sentimental moment of weakness.

Life was rapidly exhausted. Time stagnated, measurable from now on
only by the wearing out of heels on the wet asphalt, the succession
of sounds, soon learned by heart, that the drafts carried along the
corridors of the hotel from dawn till dusk. The window of my room
looked out on an apartment block under demolition. A wall covered
with wallpaper stood there amid the rubble. Fixed to this colored surface a mirror, without a frame, reflected the delicate and ephemeral
depth of the sky. Each morning I wondered whether I was going to
see this reflection again when I drew open my curtains. The daily
suspense gave a rhythm to the stagnant time, to which I was becoming more and more accustomed. And even the idea that one day I
must quit this life, that I must make a break with what little still
bound me to those autumn days, to that city, kill myself, perhaps —
even such a notion soon became habitual. . . . And then one morning — when I heard the dry sound of collapsing masonry, and outside the curtains, in the place of the wall, I saw an empty space
smoking with dust — the idea seemed to me like a marvelous way of
leaving the game.

I remembered it several days later. . . . I was sitting on a bench in the
middle of a boulevard soaked in drizzle. Through the numbness of a
fever I felt within myself a kind of silent dialogue between a frightened child and a man: the adult, himself troubled, was trying to reas-
sure the child, speaking in a falsely cheerful tone. The encouraging
voice told me that I could get up and return to the café; drink another glass of wine and stay out of the cold for an hour. Or go down
into the clammy warmth of the Métro. Or even try to spend another
night at the hotel without having anything left to pay with. Or if
need be, walk into that pharmacy at the corner of the boulevard and
sit down on a leather chair, stay still, say nothing, and when people
gather round me, whisper very softly, "Leave me in peace for a moment, in this light and this warmth. I will go soon, I promise
you. . . ."

The keen air above the boulevard condensed and began to fall as a fine, dogged rain. I got up. The reassuring voice had fallen silent. I felt as if my head were wrapped in a cloud of red-hot cotton wool. I dodged a passerby who was walking along holding a little girl by the hand. I was afraid I might alarm the child with my inflamed face, and the cold shivers shaking me. . . . Wanting to cross the road, I stumbled against the edge of the pavement and waved my arms like a tightrope walker. A car braked and just avoided me. I felt a brief grazing of the door handle against my hand. The driver took the trouble to lower his window and hurl an oath at me. I saw his scowl, but his words reached me with a strange cotton-wool slowness. At the same moment a thought dazzled me with its simplicity: "That's what I need. That impact, that encounter with metal, but much more violent. An impact that would shatter my head, my throat, my chest. That impact, and then instant, final silence." Several whistle blasts pierced the fog of the fever that burned my face. Absurdly, I got the idea that a policeman might have set off in pursuit of me. I sped up my pace, floundering on a saturated patch of lawn. I could not breathe. My vision broke up into a multitude of sharp-edged facets. I had an urge to burrow in the ground like an animal.

I was drawn in by a misty void, which opened up into a broad avenue, beyond a wide-open gate. It seemed to be floating between two lines of trees, in the dull air of the twilight. Almost at once the avenue was filled with strident whistle blasts. I turned into a narrower path, skidded on a smooth stone slab, and plunged between strange gray cubes. Finally, without strength, I crouched behind one of them. The whistle blasts rang out for a moment, then fell silent. From a long way off I heard the grating sound of the gate's metal bars. On the porous wall of the cube I read these words, without immediately grasping the sense of them: *Plot held in perpetuity. Number . . . Year 18 . . .*

Somewhere behind the trees a whistle blast rang out, followed by a conversation. Two men, two keepers, were walking up the avenue.

I got up slowly. And through the weariness and the torpor of the start of my illness, I felt a flicker of a smile on my lips; "mockery must enter into the nature of the things of this world. By the same token as the law of gravity. . . ."

All the gates of the cemetery were now closed. I walked round the family vault behind which I had collapsed. The glass door yielded easily. The interior seemed to me almost spacious. Apart from the dust and a few dead leaves, the paving was clean and dry. My legs would not support me any longer. I sat down, and then stretched out full length. In the darkness my head brushed against a wooden object. I touched it. It was a prie-dieu. I rested my neck on its faded velvet. Oddly, its surface seemed warm, as if someone had just been kneeling on it. . . .

For the first two days I left my refuge only to go and look for bread and to wash. I returned at once, stretched out, and sank into a feverish numbness from which I was only roused for a few minutes by the whistle blasts at closing time. The great gate creaked in the fog, the world was reduced to these walls of soft porous stone, which I could touch if I spread out my arms in the form of a cross; to the reflection of the ground glass panes of the door; and to the resonant silence, which I believed I could hear beneath the paving stones, beneath my body. . . .

I rapidly became confused about the sequence of dates and days. I remember only that one afternoon I finally felt a little better. Walking slowly, screwing up my eyes in the returning sunlight, I was going back . . . home. Home! Yes, that was my thought: I surprised myself thinking it, and started to laugh, choking in a fit of coughing that made the passersby turn. This family tomb more than a century old, in the least-visited part of the cemetery, where there were no famous tombs to honor — my "home." With amazement I told myself I had not used the word since my childhood. . . .

It was during that afternoon, by the light of the autumn sun shining into my vault, that I read the inscriptions on the marble tablets fixed to its walls. It was, in fact, a little chapel belonging to the Belval and Castelot families. And the laconic epitaphs on the tablets retraced their history in outline.

I was still too weak. I read one or two inscriptions and then sat down on the paving stones, breathing as if after a great effort, my head buzzing with giddiness. *Born September 27, 1837, at Bordeaux. Died June 4, 1888, in Paris.* Perhaps it was the dates that made me giddy. I took note of their time as acutely as if I were hallucinating. *Born the 6th March 1849. Recalled to God the 12th December 1901.* The intervals between these dates became filled with sounds, with silhouettes, mixing history and literature. There was a flow of images, the vivid and very concrete sharpness of which was almost painful. I thought I could hear the rustling of a lady's long dress as she stepped into a cab. In this simple action of times past she embodied all those anonymous women who had lived, loved, and suffered; who had seen this sky, breathed this air. . . . Now I felt physically the cramped stiffness of a dignitary in his black suit: the sun, the great square of a provincial town, the speeches, the brand new republican emblems. . . . Now the wars, the revolutions, the swarming crowds, the great holidays, all fused for a second into one character, one explosion, one voice, one song, one salvo, one poem, one sensation — and the flow of time resumed its course between the date of birth and the date of death. She was born *August 26, 1861, at Biarritz. Deceased February 11, 1922, at Vincennes.*

I progressed slowly from one epitaph to the next: *Captain of the Empress's Dragoons. Divisional General. Painter of History, attached to the French armies: Africa, Italy, Syria, Mexico. Intendant General. Section President of the Conseil d'Etat. Woman of letters. Former Public Auditor to the Senate. Lieutenant in the 224th Infantry Regiment. Croix de Guerre with palms. Died for France.* . . . They were the shades of an empire once resplendent at all four corners of the world. . . . The most recent inscription was also the shortest: *Françoise, November 2, 1952–May 10, 1969.* Sixteen years old; any other words would have been excessive.

I sat down on the paving stones and closed my eyes. I sensed the vibrant density of all those lives in myself. And without trying to formulate my thoughts, I murmured, "I feel the climate of their days and of their deaths. And the mystery of that birth at Biarritz on August 26, 1861. The inconceivable individuality of that birth, precisely at Biarritz, that day, more than a century ago. And I feel the fragility of that face that disappeared on May 10, 1969, I feel it like an emotion that I myself have lived through intensely. . . . These unknown lives are close to me."

I left in the middle of the night. The stone wall was not high at that point. But the hem of my coat caught on one of the iron spikes set in the top of the wall. I almost fell head first. In the darkness the blue eye of a street lamp described a question mark. I fell on a thick layer of dead leaves. My descent seemed to take a very long time; I had the impression of landing in an unknown town. Its houses at this night hour resembled the monuments of an abandoned city. Its air smelled of wet forest.

I began to walk down an empty avenue. All the streets I followed went downhill, as if to keep thrusting me farther toward the heart of this opaque megalopolis. The few cars that passed me looked as if they were fleeing from it at top speed, driving straight ahead. As I walked past him, a tramp stirred in his carapace of cardboard boxes. He put his head out; it was lit by the shop window across the street. He was an African, his eyes heavy with a kind of resigned, calm madness. He spoke. I leaned toward him, but I understood nothing. It was doubtless the language of his country. . . . The cardboard boxes of his shelter were covered in hieroglyphs.

When I crossed the Seine, the sky began to grow pale. For a while I had been walking with a sleepwalker's tread. The joyful fever of convalescence had disappeared. I felt as if I were wading through the still-deep shadows of the houses. My giddiness curved the perspectives inward, rolled them around me. The accumulation of apartment blocks along the quays and on the island looked like a gigantic film set in darkness when the arc lights have been switched off. I could no longer remember why I had left the cemetery.

On the wooden footbridge I looked back several times. I thought I could hear the sound of footsteps behind me. Or the throbbing of the blood in my temples. The echo became more resonant in a winding street that drew me along like a toboggan. I made an about-face. I thought I saw the outline of a woman in a long coat slipping under an archway. I remained standing, without strength, leaning against a wall. The world disintegrated, the wall gave way under my palm, the windows trickled down the pale fronts of the houses. . . .

It was as if by magic that those few words appeared, outlined on a blackened metal plaque. I clung to their message, as a man on the brink of sinking into drunkenness or madness may cling to a maxim that has a banal but flawless logic that saves him from tipping over the edge. . . . The little plaque was fixed a meter from the ground. I read its inscription three or four times:

FLOOD LEVEL. JANUARY 1910

. . . It was not a memory, but life itself. I was not reliving; I was living. Sensations that seemed very humble sensations. The warmth of the wooden handrail of a balcony hanging in the air on a summer's evening. The dry, piquant scents of plants. The distant and melancholy call of a locomotive. The soft rustling of pages on the knees of a woman seated amid flowers. Her gray hair. Her voice . . . And now the rustling and the voice are mingled with the whispering of the long boughs of willows — I was already living on the bank of that stream, lost in the sun-drenched immensity of the steppe. I saw that woman with gray hair, sunk in a clear reverie, slowly walking in the water and looking so young. And these youthful looks transported me onto the deck of a flatcar hurtling across a plain that sparkled with rain and light. The woman facing me smiled, tossing back the wet locks from her brow. Her eyelashes were iridescent in the rays of the setting sun. . . .

FLOOD LEVEL. JANUARY 1910. I heard the misty silence, the lapping of the water when a boat passed. A little girl, her forehead pressed against the windowpane, was looking at the pale mirror of a flooded avenue. I lived that silent morning in a great Parisian apartment early in the century so intensely. . . . And that morning led in sequence to another, with the crunching of gravel in an avenue gilded with autumn foliage. Three women in long black silk dresses, their broad hats trimmed with veils and feathers, were walking away, as if carrying the moment with them, its sunlight and the air of a fleeting era. . . . Yet another morning: Charlotte (I recognized her now) accompanied by a man in the resonant streets of the Neuilly of her childhood. Charlotte, happy in a slightly confused way, is acting as guide. I felt I could distinguish the clarity of the morning light on each paving stone, see the trembling of each leaf, picture this unknown town in the man's gaze and the view of the streets, so familiar to Charlotte's eyes.

What I now understood was that ever since my childhood, Charlotte's Atlantis had enabled me to glimpse the mysterious consonance of eternal moments. Without my knowing it, they had traced the pattern of another life, as it were; invisible, inadmissible, alongside my own. Thus a carpenter who spends his days making chair legs or planing planks does not notice that the lacework of the shavings forms a beautiful ornament on the floor, shining with resin; one day, its clear transparency catches a ray of sunlight breaking through the narrow window piled high with tools, and the next, the blue-tinged reflection of snow.

It was this life that now revealed itself to be essential. Somehow, I did not yet know how, I must let it unfold within me. Through the silent work of memory I must learn the notation of these moments. Learn to preserve their timelessness amid the routine of everyday actions, amid the numbness of banal words. Live, conscious of this timelessness . . .

I returned to the cemetery just before the gate closed. The evening was clear. I sat down on the threshold and began writing in my address book, long since useless:

> My situation beyond the grave is ideal, not only for discovering this essential life but also for recreating it, by recording it in a style that has yet to be invented. Or rather, this style will henceforth be my way of life. I will have no other life than these moments reborn on a page. . . .

For want of paper my manifesto was soon going to peter out. Writing was a very important action for my project. In this high-sounding credo, I declared that only works created on the brink of the grave or indeed beyond the grave would withstand the test of time. I cited the epilepsy of some; asthma and the cork-lined room for others; exile, deeper than any tomb, for yet others. . . . The pompous tone of this profession of faith was soon to disappear. It would be replaced by the pad of rough paper that I purchased the next day with the last of my money, and on whose first page I would write very simply:

Charlotte Lemonnier: Biographical Notes.

Indeed that very morning I left the family vault of the Belvals and the Castelots forever. . . . I had woken up in the middle of the night. An impossible, crazy thought had just crossed my mind, like a tracer bullet. I had to utter it aloud to gauge its extraordinary reality: "What if Charlotte were still alive?"

Stunned, I pictured her coming out onto her little flower-covered balcony, bent over a book. For many years I had received no news from Saranza. So Charlotte could still be living much as before, as she had during my childhood. She would be over eighty now, but in my memory this age did not touch her. For me she always remained the same.

Then the dream flashed into my mind. It was probably its aura that had just woken me. To find Charlotte again, to bring her to France . . .

The unrealistic nature of this project, formulated by a vagrant stretched out on the stone slabs of a family tomb, was so evident that I made no effort to spell it out to myself. For the moment, I decided not to think about the details, to live, and to keep this unreasonable hope at the heart of each day. To live off this hope.

I was unable to get to sleep again that night. Wrapping myself in my coat, I went out. The warmth of the late autumn had given way to a north wind. I remained standing, watching the low clouds, which were gradually becoming infused with a gray pallor. I remembered that one day, in an unsmiling jest, Charlotte had said to me that, after all her journeys across the vastness of Russia, for her to come to France on foot would have had nothing impossible about it. . . .

To begin with, during my long months of poverty and wanderings, my crazy dream was to seem very similar to her sad bravado. I would picture a woman dressed in black entering a little frontier town in the very early hours of a dark winter morning. The hem of her coat would be caked with mud, her big shawl drenched with the cold mist. She would push open the door of a café at the corner of a small sleeping square, would sit down near the window, beside a radiator. The *patronne* would bring her a cup of tea. And looking through the window at the quiet fronts of the half-timbered houses, the woman would murmur softly, "It's France. . . . I have returned to France. After . . . after a whole lifetime."

15

WHEN I LEFT THE BOOKSHOP I walked through the town and began to cross the bridge poised above the sunlit expanse of the Garonne. I recalled that old films had a time-honored trick for skipping over several years in the lives of their heroes in a few seconds. The action would be interrupted, and this legend would appear on a black background with an unashamed frankness that had always appealed to me: "Two years later," or "three years went by." But who would use this outmoded device nowadays?

And yet on entering that empty bookshop in the middle of a heat-stunned provincial town, and on finding my latest book on the shelf, I had just that impression. "Three years went by." The cemetery, the family vault of the Belvals and the Castelots. And now this book in the colorful mosaic of jackets under the sign "New French Novels" . . .

Toward evening I reached the forest of the Landes. I wanted to walk, for two days or perhaps more, sensing that beyond this rolling country covered in pine trees the ocean lay perpetually in wait. Two days, two nights . . . Thanks to the *Notes,* time had acquired an extraordinary density for me. Despite living in Charlotte's past, it seemed to me that I had never experienced the present so intensely! Those landscapes of days gone by threw into a singular relief this patch of sky between the clusters of pine needles; this glade lit by the setting sun like a river of amber. . . .

In the morning, back on the road (a gashed pine trunk, which I had not noticed the previous evening, was weeping its resin — what the local people called its *gemme*), I remembered, for no special reason, those shelves at the back of the bookshop, "Eastern European Literature." My first books were there, sandwiched, and at the risk of inspiring giddy megalomania in me, between those of Lermontov and Nabokov. All this was the fruit of a pure and simple literary hoax on my part. For the novels had been written directly in French and rejected by publishers. I was "some funny little Russian who thought he could write in French." In a gesture of despair I had then invented a translator and submitted the manuscript, presenting it as translated from the Russian. It had been accepted, published, and hailed for the quality of the translation. I told myself, at first bitterly, later with a smile, that my Franco-Russian curse was still upon me. But whereas in childhood I had been obliged to conceal my French graft, now it was my Russianness that failed to find favor.

That evening, settled down for the night, I reread the latest pages of my *Notes*. In the fragment jotted down the previous evening I had written,

> A boy of two has died in the big *izba* facing the apartment block where Charlotte lives. I see the child's father propping up against the handrail on the front steps an oblong box draped with red cloth — a little coffin. Its doll-like dimensions terrify me. I need immediately to find a place under heaven, or on earth, where one could imagine this child still alive. The death of a human being younger than oneself calls the whole universe into question. I rush to Charlotte. She perceives my anguish and says something to me that is astonishing in its simplicity: "Do you remember how we saw a flight of migrating birds in the autumn? They flew over the courtyard, yes, and then they disappeared. That was that, but somewhere in distant lands they are still flying. It is only because our eyesight is too weak that we can't see them. It's the same with people who die. . . ."

As I slept, I thought I could hear the branches making a sound that was more powerful and continuous than usual. As if the wind had not ceased blowing for a single moment. In the morning I discovered that it was the sound of the ocean. In my weariness the previous evening I had stopped, without knowing it, on the frontier where the forest began to merge into the wave-lashed dunes.

I spent the whole morning on that deserted shore, watching the imperceptible rising of the waters. . . . When the tide began to ebb, I resumed my journey. Barefoot on the wet sand I would go down toward the south now. Walking along, I thought about that little bag that from the time of our childhood my sister and I had called "the Pont-Neuf bag" and which contained the little pebbles wrapped in scraps of paper. There was a "Fécamp," a "Verdun," and also a "Biarritz," a name we associated with quartz and not with the town, which was unknown to us. . . . I was going to walk beside the ocean for ten or twelve days and find that town, of which a tiny fragment was lost somewhere in the depths of the Russian steppes.

16

*I*T WAS IN SEPTEMBER, through the intermediary of a certain Alex Bond, that the first news from Saranza reached me. . . .

This "Mr. Bond" was in fact a Russian businessman, a very characteristic representative of the generation of "new Russians" who at that time were beginning to make their presence felt in all the capitals of the West. They butchered their names, American style, thus often identifying themselves without realizing it either with the heroes of spy novels or with extraterrestrial beings from the science fiction stories of the fifties. At the time of our first meeting I had advised Alex Bond, alias Alexei Bondarchenko (meaning "Cooper"), to gallicize his name and present himself as "Alexis Tonnelier," rather than mutilate it as he had done. Without a ghost of a smile, he explained to me the advantages of a short and euphonious name in business. . . . I had the impression I was understanding less and less of the Russia that I now saw via these "Bonds," these "Kondrats," and these "Feds." . . .

He was going to Moscow and, touched by the sentimental aspect of my commission, had agreed to make a detour. Going to Saranza, walking in its streets, meeting Charlotte, now seemed a good deal more strange to me than traveling to another planet. Alex Bond had been there "between two trains," as he put it. And, without an inkling of what Charlotte meant to me, he spoke on the telephone as if this were an exchange of news after the holidays: "No, but what a black hole that Saranza is! Thanks to you, I've discovered darkest Russia, ha ha. All those streets that lead straight out onto the steppe! And the steppe with no end to it. . . . She's very well, your grandmother, don't you worry. Yes, she's still very active. When I arrived she wasn't there. Her neighbor told me she was at a meeting. The tenants in her apartment block have created a support group, or whatever, to save an old *izba* in the courtyard that they want to demolish. A huge building, two centuries old. So your grandmother . . . No, I didn't see her; I was between two trains. I had to be in Moscow that evening come hell or high water. But I left a message. . . . You could go and see her. They let everyone in these days. They say the iron curtain's nothing more than a sieve now, ha ha ha. . . ."

All I had were my refugee papers, plus a travel document that authorized me to visit "all countries except the USSR." The day after my conversation with the "new Russian" I went to the Préfecture de Police to obtain information about the formalities for naturalization. In my mind I was trying to silence the thought that kept creeping back: "What you are embarking on now is an invisible race against the clock. Charlotte is at an age where every year, every month, could be her last."

For that reason I did not want to write or telephone. I had a superstitious fear of compromising my project with a few banal words. I needed to obtain a French passport quickly, go to Saranza, spend several evenings talking with Charlotte, and bring her to Paris. I saw all these actions being accomplished simply, in a flash, as in a dream. Then abruptly this image became blurred, and I found myself once more caught in the glutinous lava that clogged my movements — time.

The dossier I was required to assemble reassured me: no documents impossible to find, no bureaucratic snares. Only my visit to the doctor left me with a painful impression. Yet the examination lasted a mere five minutes and was, when all's said and done, quite superficial: my state of health turned out to be compatible with French nationality. Having listened to my chest, the doctor told me to bend over, keeping my legs quite straight, and touch the ground with my fingers. I complied. It must have been my excessive alacrity that made him uneasy. The doctor seemed embarrassed and stammered,

"Thank you, that's fine," as if he were afraid that in my zeal I might bend over again. Often some trifle in our attitudes is enough to alter the meaning of the most ordinary situations: two men in a small consulting room in a glaring white light; suddenly one of them bends, touches the ground almost at the feet of the other, and remains thus for a moment, awaiting, it seems, the second man's approval.

As I went out into the street I thought of the camps where they used similar physical tests to sort out the prisoners. But this excessively exaggerated comparison still did not explain my unease.

It was the eagerness with which I had fulfilled the command. I came across it again in leafing through the pages of my dossier. I perceived that this desire to convince someone was everywhere present. Even though it was not asked of me in the questionnaires, I had mentioned my distant French origins. Yes, I had mentioned Charlotte, as if I wanted to ward off all objections and dissipate all skepticism in advance. And now I could not rid myself of the feeling that I had in some way betrayed her.

I had to wait several months. I was told there would be a delay until May. And at once those far-off spring days were bathed in a special radiance, standing out from the round of months and forming a universe that lived according to its own rhythm, in its own climate.

For me it was a time of preparations, but above all of long, silent conversations with Charlotte. As I walked along the streets I now had the sensation of observing them through her eyes. Of seeing, as she would have seen, an empty quay where the poplar trees, in a sudden breeze, seemed to be transmitting an urgent, whispered message to one another; of sensing, as she would have done, the resonance of the paving stones in this little old square, within whose provincial tranquility, in the heart of Paris, lay concealed the temptation of a simple happiness, of a life without dazzle.

I understood that throughout the three years of my life in France the slow and discreet progress of my project had never been interrupted. From that vague image of a woman dressed in black passing through a frontier town on foot, my dream had moved on toward a more real vision. I saw myself going to meet my grandmother at the station, and accompanying her to the hotel where she would live during her stay in Paris. Then, once the period of the bleakest poverty was finished, I had begun to picture a more comfortable interior than a hotel room, one where Charlotte would feel more at ease. . . .

Perhaps it was thanks to these dreams that I was able to endure the poverty and humiliation that go with one's first steps in the world in which the book, that most vulnerable organ of our being, becomes merchandise. Merchandise that is hawked, exposed on market stalls, discounted. My dream was an antidote. And the *Notes* — a refuge.

In those few months of waiting, the topography of Paris changed. As on certain maps where the arrondissements are colored differently, the city became filled in my eyes with varied shades that Charlotte's presence gave nuances to. There were streets whose sun-drenched silence, early in the morning, held the echo of her voice. Café terraces where I guessed at her weariness at the end of a walk. A facade, a stained glass window, which under her eyes assumed the light patina of memory.

This daydream topography left a good many white patches on the colored mosaic of the arrondissements. Our outings would quite spontaneously avoid the architectural audacities of recent years. Charlotte's days in Paris would be too brief. We would not have time to come to terms with all those new pyramids, glass towers, and arches by looking at them. Their silhouettes would congeal into a strange, futuristic tomorrow, which would not disturb the eternal present of our excursions.

Nor did I want Charlotte to see the district where I lived. . . . Alex Bond, when he came to meet me, had exclaimed disdainfully, "For goodness sake, we're not in France here. This is Africa!" And he embarked on a harangue, whose content reminded me of the remarks of so many "new Russians." It was all there: the degeneracy of the West and the imminent end of white Europe; the invasion of the new barbarians ("including us Slavs," he had added, to be fair); a new Mahomet "who will torch all their Pompidou Centres"; and a new

Genghis Khan "who will put an end to all their democratic kow-towing." Drawing inspiration from the endless procession of people of color walking past the café terrace where we were sitting, his discourse was a mixture of apocalyptic prophecies and hope for a Europe regenerated by the young blood of the barbarians, promises of a total race war, and faith in universal interbreeding. . . . The subject fascinated him. He must sometimes have felt on the side of the moribund West, for his skin was white and his culture European, and sometimes on the side of the new Huns. "I don't care what you say," he concluded his speech, "the fact remains, there are too many of these wogs!" forgetting that a minute before it was to them that he had been entrusting the salvation of the old continent. . . .

In my dreams our excursions made a detour round this quarter and the intellectual ferment that its reality would give rise to. Not that its population could have shocked Charlotte's sensibility. An émigré par excellence, she had always lived in the midst of an extreme multiplicity of peoples, cultures, and languages. From Siberia to the Ukraine, from the Russian North to the steppe, she had known the whole ethnic diversity of the empire's melting pot. During the war she had encountered them in hospital, facing death in absolute equality; in naked equality, as bodies undergoing surgery.

It was by no means the new population of that old district of Paris that might have upset Charlotte. If I did not want to take her there it was because you could walk along whole streets without hearing a word of French spoken. Some saw the promise of a new world in this exoticism, others, a disaster. But we were not seeking exoticism, whether architectural or human. The change of scene we would experience in our days together I thought would be much more profound.

The Paris that I was preparing to let Charlotte rediscover was an incomplete Paris and even, in some respects, illusory. I remembered Nabokov's memoirs, where he spoke of his grandfather living out his last days; as he lay in bed he believed that what he could perceive through the thick material of the curtain was the brilliance of the southern sun, with attendant clusters of mimosa. He smiled, believing himself to be in Nice, in the spring sunlight. He did not suspect that he was dying in Russia in the depths of winter, and that the sun was a lamp that his daughter had fixed up behind the curtain, to give him that happy illusion. . . .

I knew that Charlotte, while respecting my itineraries, would see everything. The lamp behind the curtain would not deceive her. I could see the quick wink she would give me in front of some indescribable contemporary sculpture. I could hear her comments, full of very subtle humor, the delicacy of which would only serve to emphasize the dull aggressiveness of the work observed. She would also see that district, mine, which I was trying to avoid. . . . She would go there all alone, in my absence, searching for a house in the rue de l'Ermitage where the Great War soldier once lived, the one who had given her that little ferrous splinter that as children we called "Verdun."

I also knew that I should do my very best not to talk about books. And that we would talk about them all the same, a great deal, often till late into the night. For the France that had appeared one day in the middle of the steppes of Saranza owed its birth to books. It was indeed essentially a bookish country, a country composed of words, whose rivers flowed like lines of verse, whose women wept in alexandrines and whose men quarreled in broadsides. That was how we discovered France as children, through its literary life, its verbal substance, shaped into a sonnet and honed by an author. Our family mythology attested that a little volume with a battered cover and a tarnished gilt top traveled with Charlotte on all her journeys. As the last link with France. Or perhaps as the constant possibility of magic. "There is a tune for which I'd gladly part . . ." How many times in the wastes of the Siberian snows had these lines shaped themselves into "a brick-built castle, faced with cornerstones,/With lofty windows, stained in crimson tones"? We confused France with her literature. And true literature was that magic, a word, a verse, a chapter of which transported us into a changeless moment of beauty.

I wanted to tell Charlotte that that kind of literature was dead in France. And that in the multitude of books I had devoured since the start of my reclusive life as a writer, I had looked in vain for one that

I could imagine in her hands in the middle of a Siberian *izba*. Yes, the book open, a little gleam of tears in her eyes . . .

In those imaginary conversations with Charlotte I became an adolescent again. My youthful extremism, long since quenched by the realities of life, was awakened. Once again I sought an absolute, unique work. I dreamed of a book that could remake the world with its beauty. And I heard my grandmother's voice responding to me, understanding and smiling, as in the old days at Saranza on her balcony: "Do you still remember those tiny apartments in Russia that groaned under the weight of books? You know, books under the bed, in the kitchen, in the hall, piled right up to the ceiling? And those unobtainable books that you were lent for one night and which you had to give back at six o'clock sharp in the morning? And yet others, retyped, with six carbons at the same time; they gave you the sixth copy, almost illegible, or 'blind,' as they called it. . . . You see, it's difficult to compare. In Russia the writer was a god. The Last Judgment and the Kingdom of Heaven were expected from him at the same time. Did you ever hear anyone there talk about the price of a book? No, because books had no price! You could go without buying a pair of shoes and freeze your feet in winter, but you bought a book. . . ."

Charlotte's voice broke off, as if to give me to understand that this cult of the book in Russia was only a memory now.

"But the unique book, the definitive book. Judgment and Kingdom at the same time?" exclaimed the adolescent I had once more become.

My feverish whisperings jerked me out of my invented conversation. Ashamed, like someone who has been caught talking to himself, I saw myself for what I was. A man gesticulating in the middle of a little dark room, where a blind window faces onto a brick wall and needs neither curtains nor shutters. A room that can be crossed in three steps, where objects, for lack of space, crowd together, encroach on one another, become entangled: old typewriter, electric stove, chairs, shelves, shower, table, spectral clothes hanging on the walls. And everywhere sheets of paper, bits of manuscripts and books, which give this cluttered interior a kind of highly logical madness. Outside the window the start of a wet winter's night, and — floating up from the maze of ancient houses — an Arabic melody, a mixture of lament and celebration. And the man is dressed in an old light-colored overcoat (it is very cold). On his hands he wears mittens, necessary for typing in the freezing room. He is talking to a woman. He addresses her with that confidence that one does not always have, even for the intimacy of one's own voice. He is questioning her about the unique, definitive work, without fear of seeming naive or ridiculously pathetic. She is about to reply to him. . . .

Before I went to sleep, I had the thought that in coming to France, Charlotte would seek to understand what had happened to that literature from which a few old books represented for her, in Siberia, a miniature French archipelago. I imagined coming into the apartment where she would be living one evening and seeing on the edge of a table or the windowsill a book open, a recent book, which Charlotte was reading in my absence. I would lean over the pages, and my gaze would fall on these lines:

> It was, in fact, the mildest morning of that winter. The sun shone as in the first days of April; the hoarfrost was melting, and the wet grass glistened, as if drenched with dew. . . . I had spent this unique morning reviewing a thousand things, with an ever-increasing melancholy beneath the clouds of winter — I had forgotten the old garden and the cradle of vine, in whose shadow my life had been decided. . . . How to live in the image of this beauty? that is what I should like to learn. The clarity of this country, the transparency, the profundity, and the miracle of this meeting of water, stone, and light — that is the only knowledge, the first morality. This harmony is not illusory. It is real, and faced with it, I feel the necessity of the word. . . .

17

*T*HE BLISSFUL DISAPPEARANCE of routine is something young betrothed couples on the eve of their wedding, or people who have just moved house, must have a sense of. It feels to them as if the few days of celebration or the happy chaos of settling in will last forever, becoming the very stuff of their lives, light and sparkling.

During my last weeks of waiting I lived in a similar intoxication. I left my little room, and rented an apartment I knew I could only afford for four or five months. That was of scant importance to me. From the room where Charlotte would live one could see the blue-gray expanse of roofs reflecting the April sky. . . . I borrowed what I could; I bought furniture, curtains, a carpet, and the household paraphernalia that I had always dispensed with in my previous dwelling. The flat as a whole remained empty; I slept on a mattress. Only the room destined for my grandmother now had a habitable air.

And as the month of May drew closer, so my cheerful recklessness and my spendthrift madness increased. From secondhand shops I began buying small antique objects that might, as I saw it, give a soul to this rather ordinary looking room. At an antique dealer's I found a table lamp. He lit it, to give me a demonstration; I pictured Charlotte's face by the light of its shade. I could not leave without that lamp. I filled the shelves with old leather-backed volumes of illustrated magazines from the turn of the century. Each evening I spread out my trophies on the round table that stood in the middle of this decorated room: half a dozen glasses, an old bellows, a pile of ancient postcards. . . .

In vain I told myself that Charlotte would never want to leave Saranza, and above all Fyodor's grave, for long, and that she would have been as comfortable in a hotel as in this improvised museum: I could no longer stop myself buying and adding finishing touches. For even when initiated into the magic of memory, the art of recreating a lost moment, man remains overwhelmingly attached to the physical fetishes of the past: like that conjurer whom God blessed with the gift of working miracles, but who preferred the nimbleness of his own fingers and his suitcases with false bottoms, which had the advantage of not upsetting his common sense.

And I knew that the real magic would be revealed in the bluish reflection of the roofs, in the aerial fragility of the skyline outside the window that she would open on the day after she arrived, very early in the morning. And in the sound of the first words that she exchanged in French with someone on a street corner. . . .

On one of the last evenings of my waiting I caught myself praying. . . . It was not a formal prayer. I had of course never learned one; I grew up by the skeptical light of an atheism so militant, it was almost religious in its tireless crusade against God. This was more a kind of dilettante and confused plea, whose addressee remained unknown. Catching myself red-handed in this unaccustomed act, I hastened to make a mockery of it. I thought that, given the impiety of my past life, I could have exclaimed, like that sailor in Voltaire's story, "I have trodden on the crucifix four times on four voyages to Japan!" I told myself I was a pagan, an idolater. Nevertheless these jibes did not banish the vague internal murmuring that I had become aware of deep within me. Its intonation had something childish about it. It was as if I were proposing a bargain to my unnamed interlocutor; I would only live another twenty years, well, fifteen years — all right, only ten — provided this meeting, these moments regained, were possible. . . .

I got up, and pushed open the door to the next room. In the half-light of a spring night the room was awake, animated by a subdued expectancy. Even the old fan, though bought only two days ago, looked as if it had lain on the little low table for long years in the nocturnal paleness of the windowpanes.

*   *   *

It was a happy day. One of those lazy, gray days adrift among the days of holiday at the beginning of May. In the morning I nailed a big coat-rack to the wall in the hall. You could hang at least ten garments on it. I did not even ask myself whether we would need it in summer.

Charlotte's window remained open. Now between the silvery surfaces of the roofs one could see, here and there, the light patches of first greenery.

That morning I added another short fragment to my *Notes*. I remembered that one day at Saranza Charlotte had talked to me about her life in Paris after World War I. She told me that the postwar era, which, without anyone having any inkling of this, was turning into the years between the wars, had something deeply false about its atmosphere. A false joy, a too easy forgetfulness. It reminded her strangely of the advertisements she used to read in the wartime newspapers: "Warm yourself without coal!" led to an explanation of how one could use "balls of paper." Or again: "Housewives, do your washing without fire!" And even "Housewives, economize: *pot-au-feu* without fire!" When Charlotte went off to join Albertine in Siberia, she had hoped that when she returned with her to Paris, they would discover prewar France again. . . .

As I noted down these few lines, I told myself that I would soon be able to ask Charlotte so many questions, verify a thousand details, learn for example who the gentleman in the tails was in one of our family photos and why half of this picture had been carefully cut off. And who that woman in a padded jacket was, whose presence among the people of the belle epoque had long ago startled me.

It was when I went out at the end of the afternoon that I found the envelope in my mailbox. Cream in color, it bore the insignia of the Préfecture de Police. Stopping in the middle of the pavement, I took a long time to open it, tearing it clumsily.

The eyes understand more quickly than the brain, especially when there is news the latter does not wish to understand. In that brief moment of indecision the eye tries to disrupt the implacable sequence of words, as if it could change the message before the intellect is prepared to grasp their meaning.

The letters danced before my eyes, riddling me with bursts of words, with bits of sentences. Then heavily, the essential word loomed up, printed in large letters, spaced out, as if to be intoned: UNACCEPTABILITY. And, mingling with the throbbing of the blood in my temples, the explanatory formulas followed it: "Your situation does not correspond to . . . ," "You do not combine, in your case . . ." I remained motionless for at least a quarter of an hour, my eyes glued to the letter. Finally I began to walk straight in front of me, forgetting where I was supposed to be going.

I was not thinking about Charlotte yet. What upset me in these first few moments was the memory of my visit to the doctor: yes, that absurd bending to touch the ground and my eagerness to do so now seemed to me doubly useless and humiliating.

It was only on returning home that I really grasped what was happening to me. I hung up my jacket on the coatrack. Beyond the inner door I saw Charlotte's room. . . . So it was not Time (oh, how wary one must be of capital letters!) that threatened to thwart my project, but the decision of this petty public official, by means of a few sentences on a single typewritten sheet. A man whom I would never know and who only knew me obliquely through the forms I had filled in. It was to him, in fact, that I should have addressed my dilettante prayers. . . .

The next day I lodged an appeal: "an appeal for grace" was the term for it in the letter. Never had I written a letter so falsely personal, so stupidly arrogant and so imploring at the same time.

I no longer noticed the days slipping by. May, June, July. Here was this apartment that I had filled up with old objects and with feelings from times past, this disaffected museum of which I was the useless curator. And the absence of the one I awaited. As for the *Notes,* I had not added a single one since the day of the refusal. I knew that the very nature of this manuscript depended on that meeting, our meeting, which despite everything I still hoped to be possible.

And often during those months I had that recurring dream that woke me in the middle of the night. A woman in a long dark coat entered a little frontier town on a silent winter's morning.

*   *   *

It is an old game. You select an adjective expressing an extreme quality: "abominable," for example. Then you find a synonym for it that, while being very close, expresses the same quality slightly less strongly: "horrible," if you will. Next time there will be the same imperceptible dilution: "awful." And so on, descending each time a tiny amount in the stated quality: "wretched," "intolerable," "disagreeable" . . . To arrive eventually at quite simply "bad" and, going via "mediocre," "average," and "so-so," to begin to climb the scale again with "modest," "satisfactory," "acceptable," "suitable," pleasant," "good." Arriving, a dozen words later, at "excellent," "wonderful," "sublime."

The news I received from Saranza at the beginning of August must have followed a similar modification. For, transmitted first to Alex Bond (he had left Charlotte his telephone number in Moscow), this news and the little package that came with it had been a long time in transit, passing from one person to another. At each transmission its tragic import was reduced, the emotion was eroded. And it was almost on a jovial note that an unknown man told me over the telephone: "Listen, I've been given a little packet for you. It is from . . . I don't know who it was, anyway your relative who has died . . . In Russia. I expect you've heard about it already. Yes, well, she's sent you your testament, eh, what . . ."

He had meant, jokingly, to say "your inheritance." By mistake, thanks in particular to that verbal imprecision that I had often noted in the "new Russians," for whom English was becoming their principal working language, he had used the word "testament."

I spent a long time waiting for him in the foyer of one of the better Paris hotels. The cold emptiness of the mirrors on each side of the armchairs corresponded perfectly to the blank that filled my gaze and my thoughts.

The stranger emerged from the lift, stepping aside for a tall, dazzling blond woman, with a smile that seemed directed at everyone and no one. Another man, very broad shouldered, followed them.

"Val Grig," the stranger introduced himself, shaking me by the hand, and introduced his companions to me, specifying, "My flighty interpreter, my faithful bodyguard."

I knew that I could not avoid the invitation to the bar. Listening to Val Grig would be a way of thanking him for the service rendered. He needed me in order to enjoy to the full the comfort of this hotel, his new status as an "international businessman," and the beauty of his "flighty interpreter." He held forth about his own triumphs as well as the Russian disaster, perhaps not realizing that a hilarious relationship of cause and effect was thus unintentionally established between these two subjects. The interpreter, who had certainly heard these stories many times before, seemed to be asleep with her eyes open. The bodyguard, as if to justify his presence, glared at all the people who came and went. "It would be easier," I suddenly thought, "to explain how I feel to Martians than to these three. . . ."

I opened the package in the Métro train. One of Alex Bond's visiting cards slipped onto the floor. There were a few words of sympathy, excuses (Taiwan, Canada . . .) for not having been able to hand me the package in person. But, above all, the date of Charlotte's death. September 9 of the previous year!

I no longer noticed the sequence of stations, only coming to my senses at the last stop. September of the previous year. . . . Alex Bond had been to Saranza in August a year ago. A few weeks after that I had submitted my application for naturalization. Perhaps at the very moment when Charlotte was dying. And all my initiatives, all my projects, all those months of waiting, had already occurred after her life. Outside her life. Without any possibility of connecting with that life, which was finished . . . The parcel had been kept by the neighbor, and then given to Bond only in the spring. On the brown paper there were a few words written in Charlotte's hand: "Please ensure that this envelope reaches Alexei Bondarchenko, who will be good enough to convey it to my grandson."

I got onto another train at the end of the line. As I opened the envelope I offered myself the sad solace that it was not the decision of the official that had in the end wrecked my project. It was time. Time, endowed with a grinding irony, and which, by means of its tricks and inconsistencies, is forever reminding us of its indifferent power.

All the envelope contained was a score of manuscript pages stapled together. I was expecting to read a farewell letter, so I could not understand this length, knowing how little Charlotte was given to solemn turns of phrase and verbal effusions. Not feeling able to embark on a full reading, I leafed through the first few pages, without anywhere encountering expressions in the manner of "when you read these lines I shall no longer be here," which was just what I was afraid of finding.

In fact, at its start the letter did not seem to be addressed to anyone. Skimming rapidly from one line to another, from one paragraph to the next, I thought I grasped that this was a history quite unconnected with our life at Saranza, or with the imminent end that Charlotte might have hinted at for me. . . .

I left the Métro and, not wanting to go up right away, continued with my absentminded reading, seated on a bench in a park. I now saw that Charlotte's story did not concern us. In her elegant and precise handwriting, she was transcribing a woman's life. Inattentive, I must have skipped over the place where my grandmother explained how they had become acquainted. In any case, that mattered little to me. For the tale of this life was only the fate of one more woman, one of those tragic destinies from Stalin's time, which shocked us when we were young, whose pain had since become dulled. This woman, the daughter of a kulak, had as a child experienced exile in the marshlands of western Siberia. Then after the war, accused of "anti-kolkhoz propaganda," she had ended up in a camp. . . . I perused these pages like those of a book I knew by heart. The camp; the cedar trees that the prisoners cut down, sinking in the snow up to their waists; the daily, banal cruelty of the guards; sickness; death. And the forced love, under the threat of a weapon or of an inhuman workload; and the love bought with a bottle of alcohol. . . . The child that this woman had brought into the world won relief for its mother: such was the law. In this "women's camp" there was a hut, set apart, provided for those births. Then the woman died, crushed by a tractor, a few months after the amnesty, decreed at the time of the thaw. The child was almost two and a half. . . .

The rain drove me from my bench. I hid Charlotte's letter under my jacket. I ran toward *our* house. The interrupted story seemed to me very typical: at the first signs of liberalization, all Russians had begun to bring out the censored past from the deep hiding places of their memory. And they did not understand that history had no need for all these innumerable little Gulags. A single monumental one, recognized as a classic, sufficed. In sending me her testimonies, Charlotte must have succumbed like the others, by the intoxication of glasnost. The touching uselessness of this missive upset me. Once again I had a measure of the disdainful indifference of time. This woman prisoner with her child was hovering on the brink of ultimate oblivion, held back only by these few manuscript pages. And Charlotte herself?

I pushed open the door. A draft stirred the two halves of an open window with a dull crash. I went to my grandmother's room to close it.

I thought about her life. A life that linked such different eras; the start of the century, that almost archaic age, almost as legendary as the reign of Napoleon, and — the end of our century, the end of the millennium. All those revolutions, wars, failed utopias, and successful terrors: she had distilled their essence in the sorrows and joys of her days. And this throbbing body of lived experience would soon sink into oblivion. Like the miniature Gulag of the prisoner and her child.

I stayed at Charlotte's window for a moment. For a number of weeks I had imagined her gaze resting on that view. . . .

That evening, mainly from an access of conscience, I decided to read Charlotte's pages to the end. I went back to the imprisoned woman, the atrocities at the camp, and the child who had brought a few moments of serenity into this hard, defiled world. Charlotte wrote that she had been able to obtain permission to come to the hospital where the woman was dying. . . .

Suddenly the page I was holding in my hand was transformed into a fine sheet of silver. Yes, it dazzled me with a metallic reflection and seemed to emit a cold, thin sound. One line flashed out — like the filament of a lightbulb lacerating one's eyeball. The letter was written in Russian, and it was only at this line that Charlotte switched to French, as if she were no longer sure of her Russian. Or as if French, that French of another era, would allow me a certain detachment from what she was about to tell me: "That woman, who was called Maria Stepanovna Dolina, was your mother. It was she who wanted you to be told nothing for as long as possible. . . ."

A little envelope was stapled to that last page. I opened it. In it was a photo that I recognized without difficulty: a woman in a big *shapka* with the earflaps pulled down, wearing a padded jacket. On a little rectangle of white cloth sewn beside the row of buttons — a number. In her arms a baby swathed in a cocoon of wool . . .

That night I rediscovered in my memory the image that I had always believed to be a kind of prenatal reminiscence, coming to me from my French ancestors, and of which, as a child, I was very proud. I used to see in it a proof of my hereditary Frenchness. It was that autumn day bathed in sun, at the edge of a wood, with an invisible feminine presence, a very pure air, and the gossamer threads rippling across the luminous space. . . . I now understood that the wood was in fact an endless taiga, and that the delightful Indian summer was about to be swallowed up into a Siberian winter that would last nine months. The gossamer threads, silvery and light in my French fantasy, were nothing other than new strands of barbed wire that had not had time to rust. I was out for a walk with my mother in the territory of the "women's camp." . . . It was my first childhood memory.

Two days later I left the apartment. The owner had come round the day before and had agreed on an amicable solution: I left him all the furniture and antique objects I had accumulated over several months. . . .

I slept little. At four o'clock I was already up. I packed my rucksack, planning to leave that very day for my habitual journey on foot. Before departing I glanced one last time into Charlotte's room. By the gray light of morning its silence no longer evoked a museum. No longer did it seem uninhabited. I hesitated for a moment, then I seized an old volume laid on the windowsill and went out.

The streets were empty, misted over with sleep. Scenic views seemed to take shape as I walked toward them.

I thought of the *Notes* I was carrying away in my bag. That evening, or the next day, I told myself, I would add a new fragment that had come to mind that night. It was at Saranza during my last summer at my grandmother's. . . . That day, instead of taking the path that led us across the steppe, Charlotte had turned in among the trees of the copse cluttered with weaponry that the locals called "Stalinka." I had followed her with a wary tread: according to rumor, you could step on a mine in the thickets of the Stalinka. . . . Charlotte had stopped in the middle of a broad clearing and had murmured, "Look!" I had seen three or four identical plants that reached up to our knees. Great indented leaves, tendrils clinging to the slender canes stuck in the ground. Dwarf maples? Young blackcurrant bushes? I did not understand Charlotte's mysterious joy.

"It's a grapevine, a real one," she told me at last.

"Oh. Good . . ."

This revelation did not heighten my curiosity. In my head I could not connect this modest plant with the cult dedicated to wine by my grandmother's homeland. We remained for several minutes in front of Charlotte's secret plantation at the heart of the Stalinka. . . .

Recalling that vine now, I experienced almost unbearable grief and at the same time profound joy. A joy that had at first seemed to me shameful. Charlotte was dead, and on the site of the Stalinka, to judge by Alex Bond's account, they had built a stadium. There could hardly be a more tangible proof of total, final disappearance. But joy carried the day. Its source lay in that moment I had lived at the center of a clearing; in the breeze from the steppes; in the serene silence of this woman standing before four plants, under whose leaves I now detected the young clusters.

As I walked, I looked from time to time at the photo of the woman in a padded jacket. And now I understood what gave her face a distant resemblance to the people in the albums of my adoptive family. It was that slight smile that appeared thanks to Charlotte's magic formula, *"petite pomme"*! Yes, the woman photographed beside the camp fence must have pronounced those enigmatic syllables to herself. . . . I stopped for a moment; I stared at her eyes. Then I said to myself, "I must get used to the idea that this woman, younger than me, is my mother."

I put away the photo, and went on. And when I thought of Charlotte, her presence in these drowsy streets had the reality, discreet and spontaneous, of life itself.

What I still had to find were the words to tell it with.